"You chilled meat," the stickie threatened

"Mebbe," Ryan replied, shuffling his boots in the soft earth to try to establish a good footing.

The creature's musket was swirling around in a maniac circle, hissing like a runaway windmill. The mutie had the advantage of higher ground, and Ryan realized that this wasn't going to be the slick and easy execution that he wanted.

"Yesss!" The mutie hissed out the warning as it suddenly charged its enemy.

The stickie's speed was alarming, and it was all that Ryan could do to get the panga up to parry the blow.

The case-hardened steel rang out against the chipped wooden stock of the Kentucky musket. Ryan's arm was jarred clear to the shoulder by the force of the impact. The butt split lengthwise, exploding into white splinters.

The power of the crushing attack sent the man off balance. The mutie dropped its broken gun and lunged for him, its suckered hands grabbing at his arm and neck.

Instantly there was pain. A ripping sound flooded Ryan's ears, coinciding with a burning sensation in his left wrist.

The one-eyed warrior's skin was being shredded by the stickie's fingers.

**Other titles in the
Deathlands saga:**

JAMES AXLER

DEATH LANDS®
Moon Fate

A GOLD EAGLE BOOK FROM
WORLDWIDE®

TORONTO • NEW YORK • LONDON
AMSTERDAM • PARIS • SYDNEY • HAMBURG
STOCKHOLM • ATHENS • TOKYO • MILAN
MADRID • WARSAW • BUDAPEST • AUCKLAND

This one is for Derek and Margaret for very many
excellent reasons spread over many years.
With my sincere thanks.

Second edition April 1999

ISBN 0-373-62554-5

MOON FATE

Copyright © 1992 by Worldwide Library.

Printed in U.S.A.

What is a biological mutation? It may be a slight imperfection on an earlobe, or an extra toe on each foot, or three eyes or two heads. Whatever form it takes, there is no doubt that it will inevitably lead to some degree of harassment and persecution by those in society who consider themselves to be "normal."

—From *The Outsider Is You,* by C. F. Kane, Xanadu Press, Florida, 1990

Chapter One

The morning was scorching hot, and a light wind carried the sharp scent of sagebrush to the nostrils of Ryan Cawdor and his son, Dean. They stood together, drawing in deep breaths of the New Mexico air.

It hadn't been a bad jump.

Dean had been sick, and Ryan had suffered a small nosebleed. But now they were out of the claustrophobic depths of the ruined redoubt, only a few miles from Jak Lauren's homestead, where they could both have a good hot bath that would wash away the yellow taint of sulfur that clung to them. A near deadly adventure in the cold north had left the pair coated with the stinking stuff.

"We need a good meal—eggs, potatoes and some thick-sliced ham," Ryan said, putting his arm around the boy's shoulders. "And sleep for a day and a half."

"Sure, then…" He paused, shading his eyes as he stared across the plain from the high ground. "What's that, Dad?"

"Dust storm, or—"

"Looks like smoke." Dean sniffed. "Yeah. You

can actually smell it. Burned wood and a kind of scent like charred meat.''

The column of dark smoke rose and curled high above the desert until it vanished.

It came from the direction of Jak and Christina Lauren's home.

Ryan felt his heart shrink into cold marble.

"Come on, Dean," he said quietly. "Best go take a look."

BEHIND THEM in the redoubt's heart, the walls of the silvery armaglass that formed the gateway chamber were beginning to fill with a pallid mist, and the disks in floor and ceiling were starting to glow.

Someone had triggered the mat-trans mechanism and was in the process of making a jump.

Someone.

Something?

Chapter Two

The shadows shortened around them as they picked their way across the scorching desert. Every now and then the monotony of the plateau was broken by a towering saguaro, while the light breeze rustled among the dust-dry mesquite.

The dark pillar of smoke grew thinner and paler, more like a hickory camp fire.

"Could be something caught on the stove," Ryan said.

Dean nodded.

It was close to noon when they drew near to the edge of the ridge. Once they were on the other side they'd be able to see across the wide valley to the Lauren homestead in the distance.

The wind had veered more northerly, whipping up occasional bunches of tumbleweed. A small hawk with a golden beak and a brilliantly crimson breast soared in the sky, wings spread, riding a thermal, eyes scanning the barren land below. The two walking figures had been spotted immediately as they left the redoubt. But they were too large, and their gait was too regular to interest the bird of prey.

Dean paused near the rim, still fifty paces short of being able to see over.

"Not the cooking stove, is it?" he said.

Ryan also stopped, bracing his shoulders to try to ease out some of the stiffness he'd acquired during the past few murderous days up north.

"Mebbee, son. Mebbee not."

The boy's young-old face turned to him. "You think it's trouble."

"I think it could be."

The boy spun on his heel and started to run toward the point where the plateau began to fall away. Ryan shouted after him, warning the boy to keep clear of the skyline. Dean slowed and then crouched, crawling the rest of the way on hands and knees. He stared at the scene a long time, then turned to face his father who was walking steadily toward him.

"Not the cooking stove," he said flatly.

The land was shrouded in a shimmering curtain of haze, with the temperature well above the hundred mark. It was difficult to see clearly when outlines were blurred. But father and son could see well enough to realize that the smoke had its origin on the spread owned by Christina and Jak.

RYAN CARRIED his 9 mm P-226 SIG-Sauer with the built-in baffle silencer, his son had a big Browning Hi-Power tucked into his belt.

But he knew that a couple of blasters weren't likely to prove much use against whatever it was that had attacked the fortified homestead and reduced it to smoldering ashes. Other than Christina and Jak, both well armed, Ryan's traveling companions, J. B. Dix, Krysty Wroth, Mildred Wyeth and Doc Tanner, had been there, with enough firepower between them to hold off a small army.

The pair had more than halved the distance between the bottom of the bluff and the spread, and every step brought a more chilling certainty that evil had walked this way.

"Stop here," Ryan ordered a short time later.

A scant quarter mile remained now, and they were close enough to see the details. Most of the buildings had gone, including the large weatherboard barn. Part of its back still stood, splintered and blackened, the interior awash with brimming smoke. The fences were also down, and there was no trace of the Laurens's livestock. From where they'd stopped, Ryan could see that the vegetable garden was trampled into rutted dirt.

Worst was the house.

Not one brick of the exterior or interior walls stood upon another. Every window was shattered into pieces in the dust. All that remained, like an accusing finger pointing toward the serene, cloudless sky, was the central chimney.

Many months ago Doc had enthralled them with stories of what he called "the war between the States." He claimed that he'd had an uncle, named Washington Tanner, who'd fought on both sides in the great civil conflict, who'd marched from Atlanta to the sea, watched Richmond burn and had ridden with Quantrill and known a famous outlaw, Jesse James. Washington Tanner had told his bright-eyed young nephew, Theo, about the ravaged land of Kansas, how houses were razed and families butchered, and all that a man saw as he cantered across the state, from dawn to dusk, were the tall stone chimneys.

That thought came to Ryan as he stood with his son and looked intently at the total ruin of a friend's dream.

"We going on?" Dean asked.

"I'm going on. You're staying here. Keep watch out for my back. Yell if you see anything moving anyplace. All right?"

The boy nodded solemnly. "Sure, Dad." He hesitated. "You think that Jak, Krysty and..."

"Wait here," Ryan replied, drawing his blaster and moving over the last quarter mile.

THE GRINDING TIREDNESS of the days in and around the sulfur mines up north had taken their toll on him. Once he stumbled over some uneven ground, and once he realized that he'd lost concentration and had been walking mindlessly toward the ruins.

"Fireblast!" He stopped and took several long, slow breaths. He knew it was partly a reaction against the desolation that faced him. The thought of being home, eating well and sleeping and making love with Krysty had filled his mind and kept him going. Now

the earth had shifted beneath his feet and he didn't
know what to do.

The pause gave Ryan a chance to gather himself
and his thoughts.

The voice from behind him was shrill and nervous.
"You okay?"

He waved a hand to the boy and moved on.

Ryan wished he'd been a better tracker. The dirt
all around was clearly trying hard to tell him the story
of what had happened, but he couldn't quite make it
out.

There were wagon tracks, deep furrows made from
iron-rimmed wheels, crossing and crossing again.
They seemed to have come in from the northwest of
the homestead. The footprints had already become
smudged and blurred by the ceaseless desert wind, but
enough remained for him to see that there had been
a large number of strangers around the spread. Adults
and children.

The breeze veered and freshened for a moment,
blowing the smoke toward him, making him avert his
face.

"No spent rounds. No chills."

It didn't make any sense to him.

A lot of strangers had come along a day or so back,
riding in ox wags, and now the farm was destroyed
and everyone had vanished.

He looked back at his son. "Cast around in a big
circle, Dean, then come on in. Look for tracks leaving
the place."

The boy waved a hand and set off purposefully to the east. Ryan realized that Dean must be feeling just as gut weary as he did himself, but he kept on going.

Near the house the signs were more confused, and more helpful.

Ryan bent down, finding crusted patches of sand that had once been pools of fresh-spilled blood. He spotted a broken knife blade and three spent cartridges from a 9 mm blaster. From their placement Ryan guessed that they'd been kicked out of an automatic weapon, like J.B.'s Uzi.

The shattered remnants of some of the low walls of the outbuildings gave him another clue. They were pocked and chipped with fresh bullet holes, the spent lead gleaming like fool's gold against the smoke-dusted adobe.

He stood still, his eye caught by the diminutive figure of Dean plodding around a perimeter a quarter mile away. The ground to the north was far more rocky and wasn't likely to show any tracks.

One thing was certain-sure—nobody was living anywhere near the Lauren spread. Everything was gone.

Inside the ruined house there was nothing but ashes. Ryan sniffed, catching the unmistakable scent of gasoline, which explained why the destruction had been so total. The place had been fired, and all of its contents destroyed. His toe caught on something almost buried in the soft ashes and he kicked at it, finding the springs of one of the beds, fused by the intense heat. There was some glass, melted into a shapeless puddle of dark green.

There was no sign of any food left behind.

With that realization came the awareness that he was very thirsty. Jak had kept some self-seals of beer in a cold box at the back of the kitchen. Ryan walked carefully through to where the rear wall had been, scuffling with his combat boots in the layers of fine ash. He discovered the remains of the store of cans and jars that Christina had built up, all totally ruined by the fire.

The pall of gray that still hung over the farm made him think about the smokehouse out by the big barn. There'd been several hams and some joints of meat, along with dozens of dried strips of fish, dangling from the beams.

Dean had completed his circuit and was now making his way slowly toward his father, constantly turning his head from side to side.

"Anything?"

"Wags coming in and not going out."

Ryan was puzzled. "Wags not gone. Must've done. Not here."

"No. Seen them in that shallow draw back south, all burned out like the house. Just the wheel rims left in the ashes."

It was making less and less sense.

Who burned the wags?

Why?

And where had everyone gone, when there didn't seem to be any graves?

THERE WAS STILL FOOD strung up on some of the scorched beams. Ryan stood looking at it, wondering at yet another piece in this increasingly bizarre puzzle.

Because the meat and the fish had all been smoked, it should have stayed edible for months, even in the heat of the New Mexico summer.

But it was rancid, crawling with tiny yellow thread-worms. They'd bored through the firm, dry hams, so that they now crumbled apart in greasy fragments of rotting flesh.

"So much for eating," Dean commented. "Didn't feel that hungry, anyways. But..."

"The well," Ryan said. "Least we can get ourselves some good cold water."

Saying it made the feeling of thirst much worse. He suddenly started thinking about bathing in the crystal streams that flowed from the high Sierras and bubbled over sun-warmed boulders. There was the heightened awareness of how dry and cracked his lips were, his tongue swollen like old leather.

The well was at the side of the main house, close to the tumbled barn. Ryan led the way, Dean at his heels.

To his relief it didn't seem to have been damaged at all. From the amount of rope showing on the windlass, the bucket was near the bottom. He took hold of the smooth iron handle and began to wind it up.

They could both hear the tinkling sound of drops of water falling from the bucket into the cool depths of the well.

Just before Ryan finished turning the handle, with the top of the bucket in sight, he noticed something tied to the rope above the level of the water.

It was a crumpled, handwritten note from Krysty Wroth.

Chapter Three

The paper was handmade, with a crinkled, deckle edge. Written with a dark blue ink, the lettering was hasty and smudged.

Ryan, lover, if you read this then you're alive and made it back. With Dean, I hope. Had some times of "seeing," but it was so dark, cold and wet I feared for you.

Dean was reading over his father's shoulder, puzzling at some of the less legible parts but sticking with it.

"She's a real doomie, isn't she?"

"No. Doomies are double rare. They see the future. Krysty can't generally do that. She just has these 'feelings' that give clues. But she's right about cold, wet and dark."

The letter continued.

First things first. In Gaia's name, lover, don't drink the water. Not a drop. Even if your life depends on it. You'll have seen the meat in the smokehouse. Never mind what the water looks

like, it's deadly poisoned. Wish had time to tell
all, but we have to leave this place of blood. Job
to do first. If time, will leave further note.

"Where've they gone?" Dean said, falling behind
as Ryan turned over the piece of paper to read the
other side.

"Hasn't said yet."

Remember, don't drink or eat anything until
you're away beyond the gorge to the north.
We've gone there. Follow us soonest, lover.

Krysty

"North?" the boy repeated, hand resting on the
butt of his blaster.

"What she says."

Dean reached and swung the bucket in toward himself, balancing it on the rough stone rim of the old
well. He stared at its limpid contents, shaking his
head, blue eyes turning questioningly toward his father.

"Looks okay, Dad."

"Krysty couldn't have put it more strongly. You
know her and you know she won't—"

"But we could mebbe try it and—"

"For fuck's sake, Dean, cut it out!" He couldn't
hide the anger and the tiredness.

To relieve the moment of tension, he pushed at the
bucket, sending it falling to the well. The windlass

spun fast as the rope uncoiled again, and there was the hollow splash as the bucket struck the surface of the water.

The boy took three clumsy steps backward, nearly tripping over a length of burned wood. "I only thought we…"

Ryan shook his head. "No, no, son. You didn't think. That's the whole point."

"Sorry."

"Never apologize, Dean. It's a sign of weakness."

"We've got to have some water."

"Sure. Krysty says the gorge north. That's about six miles. Five, mebbe."

The boy sighed. "It's so hot."

Ryan looked around. There was a small patch of shade behind the last remaining chunk of the barn wall. Overhead, the sun was blazingly high, turning the gray sand to an oven.

"Rest up until dusk, then go for the gorge. Could catch up with the others by this time tomorrow."

"Truth?"

"Sure."

THE SUN WAS STILL well up over the western hills, but its cruel heat had diminished. Beyond a bank of high cloud they could see the vivid beginnings of a spectacular chem storm. Great streaks of pink and purple lightning were stripping layers off the sky, exploding into star bursts of nameless colors from beyond deep space.

"She say another note?"

"If she could."

"What do you figure happened, Dad?"

"Something bad enough for the bodies to be removed. Yet it looks like Krysty and the others had a few minutes to prepare departure."

"Who was it came in on the wags?"

"Questions, Dean. Too many fireblasted questions. Give it a few hours and we might start finding out some of the answers."

The terrain was rough, and twice they stopped when they heard the lonesome howling of a pack of coyotes. The animal still retained some of its old skulking, cowardly habits from before sky dark, but Ryan had known them to run in hunting packs like timber wolves. They were huge mutie creatures with jaws that could go clean through a man's thighbone.

But the sound was a long way off and faded into the evening stillness.

"Clouds coming," Dean observed as a patch of darkness spread like spilled blood over the eastern horizon.

Ryan looked around in the fading light. "No cover. Just have to take it."

It was a short and brutally savage downpour. Rods of water fell vertically from the lowering sky, stinging Ryan and Dean through their coats. It bounced off the rocks, soaking into the dusty earth. Within minutes the land had absorbed all it could and the rain began to run off, first in thin, hesitant trickles, then gathering momentum and becoming full-blown streams.

Ryan had taken care not to get them caught in a steep-sided canyon where a flash flood could have devastating and murderous consequences. They were wringing wet in seconds, but that was the worst that was going to happen to them.

The storm lasted less than twenty minutes, but it left the desert sodden, foaming torrents coursing down every incline—washing away any signs of tracks that Krysty and the others might have left.

The one bonus was that the downpour had given father and son a chance to quench a little of their thirst. Standing bareheaded, faces up, eyes closed, mouths open, they managed to swallow the liberal bounty, sometimes coughing as it splashed into nostrils.

Dean stood there, water still trickling from his pants and his lank hair, grinning at Ryan, his teeth white in the gloom.

"Feel better," he said.

Ryan nodded. "Yeah."

THEY REACHED THE RIVER that surged through the gorge a couple of hours before midnight. With the passing of the rain the wind had fallen, leaving the night humid and oppressive, the sky heavy and overcast.

"What's that smell?" Dean asked.

Ryan had also noticed it, seeping from somewhere among the maze of jagged boulders in the ravine.

"What do you think?"

"I think it smells like death."

The one-eyed man couldn't agree more. With darkness settling in and the gorge a hiding place for all manner of animal and reptile life, Ryan decided that it was far too dangerous to risk any sort of exploration.

They found a high place where they could sleep, beneath a massive overhang of sandstone lined with the frail silver lace of quartz. One end was blocked with a fall of rock, so that they could be approached up a steep and narrow path from only one direction. The track was covered with tiny pebbles that rattled at even the most careful footstep.

It was as safe as you could get.

"Want to take watch and watch around?" Dean asked in the tone of voice that failed to hide the fact that he hoped his father would say no.

"No."

"Sure?"

"Get some shut-eye and I'll sit up awhile. If I feel any danger I'll wake you later."

"Thanks. Good night, Dad."

"Good night, Dean."

Ryan lay down but didn't sleep for some time, turning over in his mind all of the disparate clues they'd found at the ruined farm. The spent bullets and the use of gasoline; Krysty's explicit warning about the water being contaminated; the total destruction of the buildings and the vanished livestock; the wags of the strangers being burned to ashes.

Though he tried hard, Ryan couldn't construct a scenario that would accommodate all of these facts. It was a puzzle shrouded in a mystery.

Eventually he dozed off into a deep and dreamless sleep.

WHEN THEY WOKE together at dawn the smell was worse—the unmistakable stench of decay and corruption. It was all too easy to track down the pile of rotting corpses.

But it simply made the enigma more bewildering.

Chapter Four

The river had dropped closer to its normal level, running steadily over the gleaming stones into dark swirling pools.

The bodies had been tumbled into an abandoned strip mine that resembled a circular pit about fifty feet deep. Apart from the ghastly smell, Ryan and Dean could have found the charnel house by tracing the column of flies.

They circled like smoke, their resonant buzz resembling a vast and vaguely discontented machine. As Ryan picked his way to the brim of the open cavern, he had to brush them away from his face. They tried to settle on his neck and hands, great bloated insects with bodies of leprous gray white, their prismatic eyes goggling from narrow heads.

Dean pulled up his hood, cursing in a monotone at the flies. He joined his father on the brink and peered down.

"Shit a melon! That's the worst..."

Ryan breathed slow and easy, keeping his mouth slightly open, a trick that the Trader had taught him for places where the stench could be overwhelming.

It was impossible to count the bodies.

"What's that white stuff all over them?" Dean asked.

"Guess it's lime. Quicklime. Something like that. To try and render the corpses down and destroy them quicker."

"So, who put that on?"

"Maybe Krysty and J.B. How should I know that, Dean?"

The boy opened his mouth as though he were going to ask yet another question, but then changed his mind and stared down with a horrified fascination.

It was about as bad as anything Ryan had seen.

There were about twenty. Or it could be only fifteen or it could be thirty. It was such a tangling of arms and legs that it was impossible to tell.

Ryan could make out enough to be sure that Krysty and the others weren't among them. It had to be the strangers, which meant that his friends could well be safe and alive.

Somewhere.

What was ghastly to see was the state of deterioration. It seemed as if the massacre had only taken place a day or so earlier, yet the visible evidence was that they'd been dead for a week.

The layers of rotting blackened flesh were actually moving with a seething life—rippling maggots and long pink worms.

The soft tissues of the bodies had gone first: eyes, lips, earlobes and the genitals. Bellies had swollen and burst from the trapped gas, releasing the wafting smell of bodily corruption.

"There's kids, Dad."

"I see them."

The little corpses were somehow worse to see than the adults.

As far as Ryan could make out under the thick layer of dusty lime, most of the bodies had been wearing plain cotton shirts and pants. Many were barefoot and several of the males had long beards.

"What chilled them?"

Ryan had been wondering that himself. There seemed hardly any evidence of blood. A couple of the corpses had black patches on their chests that might well have been from bullet wounds.

Dean tugged at his father's sleeve. "Want me to go down and take a look?" The boy hissed through his teeth in disgust as more of the flies tried to insinuate themselves between his parted lips.

Ryan hesitated, aware that one of them should do it. It was important to know how these strangers had come to meet their deaths. But the thought of going into that hideous shambles made even him draw back a moment.

The boy sensed that. "I don't mind, Dad."

"I should.... I'll do it."

"I'll go."

Before Ryan could do or say anything, Dean slithered over the edge of the pit and climbed quickly down the steep side. The flies, angered at the disturbance to their luxurious gourmet feeding, rose around him in a humming spiral of beating wings.

"Careful," Ryan called.

The boy reached a steeper part and slipped, managing to stay upright, landing on the top of the pile of bodies with a sickening squelching sound. A cloud of lime rose above him, making him invisible to the watching man.

"Dean?"

The noise of coughing and what seemed like puking reached Ryan's ears. Gradually the white dust settled.

"All right, Dad."

"Be quick and try not to breathe in all that filthy shit."

"Yeah."

He was a small, ghostly figure, stooping among the spilled guts and crumbling, slippery flesh, heaving at an arm here, lifting a skull with strands of yellowing hair pasted to it.

Ryan looked away, brushing more flies from his face. The patch over his missing left eye seemed to fascinate the insects, and several were making concerted efforts to get behind it.

"Want me to check them all?"

It looked as if it were going to be a beautiful southwest morning. Ryan tore himself away from the sun-brushed mountains to the north.

"No. Not unless... What did you find?"

"Most shot."

"Yeah?"

"Back of head. Single bullet."

"The kids?"

"Three I can see the same. Kids got exit wounds...blown away most their faces. Men and women most just got the entrance hole."

"Come back up!" Ryan shouted.

"Sure?"

"Yes. You done well, son. Want a hand?"

"No. I'm okay."

He scrambled up on hands and knees, kicking out when he found that his boots were smeared with maggots and that one of the long, snakelike worms was trying to crawl up his right leg.

"Let's get away from here and freshen up," Ryan suggested.

THE TRAUMATIC EFFECT of rummaging among the stinking bodies caught up with the boy shortly after he'd stripped off and had a dip in one of the dark green pools.

He'd plunged in eagerly, whooping at the biting cold of the meltwater. He leaped up and waved his arms, dark hair plastered over his face, shaking himself like an exuberant puppy.

Ryan had also taken the chance to wash himself from top to toe, making sure that his weapons were dry and ready to hand on a sun-warmed boulder.

He'd gotten out first, stretching luxuriantly by his blaster and panga to dry himself. Dean had stayed in longer, constantly ducking himself and scrubbing at his skin with sparkling handfuls of icy water.

As the boy was getting out, his skinny body shivering, he suddenly stopped, knee-deep, hands going to his face, shoulders trembling.

"You all right?" Ryan stood.

"No, not...not really." His voice was barely audible above the rumbling sound of the white water rushing through the deep gorge.

"Sit here." Ryan took him by the arm and helped him from the pool.

"Be triple fine when—not that I'm scared or nothing like..."

"Hell, I know that, Dean. I'm just pleased you went down and not me. I couldn't honestly face doing that."

The pale mask turned up. "Honest?"

"Honest. You did real good there. Finding out how they died's important."

"Why?" His voice broke, but he continued as Ryan draped a coat over his back. "Thanks, Dad. Why do you think they got chilled that way?"

"Like an execution? I'm beginning to get a sort of feeling. Like there was a fight. The strangers tried something on. Failed. Then Krysty and the others must've found something out. Something real double bad. Had to do something about it. Bullet through the back of the head each."

Ryan was feeling the cold and he quickly got

dressed, more comfortable with the weight of the blaster at his hip.

Dean recovered, pulling on his own clothes, buckling on the big Browning.

Before they moved on, the boy climbed higher up the sides of the gorge, reaching a jagged pinnacle of rock and balancing on it, shading his eyes as he scanned the horizon.

"See anything?" Ryan called.

The boy didn't reply. He was still staring back toward the remains of the Lauren homestead.

"Dean! You hear me?"

"Come up here a minute. Thought…"

Ryan picked his way up the cliff to join his son. The rock was broken and fragmented by frost and rain. His boots slipped in a patch of mica and he banged his knee.

"Fireblast!"

"You want a hand?"

Ryan grinned at the eager note in the boy's voice. "I'll make it. Don't need a wheelie yet." He pulled himself onto the top. "Now. What did you drag the old man up here for?"

"Over there." The lad pointed back down the hillside, toward the open expanse of desert.

"What was it?"

Dean shook his head. "Lots of ridges and arroyos down there. Thought… No, guess I was mistaken. Must've been the sun off a bit of broken glass or something like that."

Ryan stared out, but the sun was high enough to cause a shimmering haze across the gray landscape. He could see nothing moving.

"Something shining?"

"Yeah. Polished metal. Just as I got up here and I thought it was something moving."

"A wag?"

"Not so big."

"Animal?"

Dean sighed. "Can't tell, Dad. It was only there for a moment. But it looked about as big as me. And the sun came off it. I don't know."

They stood together for several seconds, but the land seemed lifeless.

"Back down?" Dean asked.

"Sure."

As THEY WALKED through the shady depths of the gorge, heading north, Ryan spotted the message, scratched on the barren rock with the point of a knife: R LOOK FORK PINON K.

"From Krysty? For you. What's it..."

Ryan had already spotted the piñon, only a few paces away, its trunk forking about eight feet from the ground.

The wad of paper, several pages thick, had been protected from the weather in a small bag of oiled cloth.

If you've got this you're following on, lover. Have a bit of time to write you and explain. This is what happened....

Chapter Five

They'd seen the dust trail rising into the sky for some time before they could actually make out the details of the wag train.

Jak and Christina had their defenses prepared against the unexpected arrival of any strangers, particularly when it was a relatively large number of strangers. In the covered ox wags it was impossible to tell just how many people were hidden and what kind of weaponry they might have.

J.B. walked out to meet the train, Jak following him to give cover. Both men were heavily armed. The rest watched from the house, with the heavy ironbound shutters ready to slam across. The fire was doused and Christina had enlisted Doc, Krysty and Mildred to carry in buckets of fresh water from the well.

Three wags, each hauled by a spavined pair of oxen, looked as though they were near the limits of exhaustion.

J.B. held up a hand when the first wag was about fifty yards from him, a quarter mile off from the homestead. The Uzi was in his hands. His new toy, the Smith & Wesson M-4000 12-gauge repeating scattergun, was across his shoulders. Its lethal load of seven fléchette rounds was snug in the mag, one more in the chamber. Each round held twenty of the tiny, inch-long arrows.

"Stop right there."

A cadaverous man held the reins of the first wag. His eyes were sunken so far into his unshaved skull that it looked like they were set on coming out the back. Livid sores streaked his cheeks, and his nose was running. He wiped it on the black sleeve of his coat.

"We're pilgrims on the road, brother, having a hard time of it."

"How many?"

"Eight men, six women and four little ones."

When I heard him speak, his voice reminded me of melted butter oozing over a steel file. But they didn't seem a threat, and J.B. waved them in. They said all they wanted was some water for themselves and for their stock. Christina offered them the fixings for a good rich stew, and they accepted.

JAK INSISTED that they keep the house on an armed alert, what he called a Condition Orange.

A couple of the men wore battered rebuilt blasters on their hips, poor, low-caliber weapons that looked like they'd do more harm to their owners than to any enemies.

They also had a half-dozen smoothbore muskets

that they stacked neatly together by the side of the fire they'd built at the back of the corral.

The thing that struck Krysty and the others was the frail state of the strangers' health. They seemed listless, sometimes stumbling. The children didn't play or run around, simply sitting mute and still where grown-ups had put them. Several of them also looked to be in some kind of pain, occasionally touching themselves tenderly in the armpit. Or in the groin.

Mildred told their leader that she was a doctor and offered to examine them, but he refused.

"The will of the Almighty shouldn't be gainsaid, sister, though I thank you for your charity. Truly is it said that man pays his price to live with himself, on the terms that the Lord wills for him."

It had come late that evening.

The cooking fire had died down to smoldering embers. The remains of the stew had congealed in the caldron. Doc Tanner had noticed that few of the strangers seemed to have any kind of an appetite.

Christina and Jak had gone to bed early.

Mildred and J.B. were sitting quietly together, rocking gently on the swing seat on the porch.

Krysty had been standing close to the well, looking out across the empty space of the desert, when Doc went to join her.

"Might I offer you a penny for your thoughts, dear lady?"

"Not worth a penny, Doc."

"Could it be that you are pondering the fate of a

certain man who is somewhat deficient in the number
of eyes? Item—one Ryan Cawdor, no doubt safe and
sound in another place.''

''Think so, Doc? I can't tell. Have some bad, dark
feelings about him.''

''He'll be fine, Krysty. Always was and always will
be. Would you care to accompany an old man on a
stroll before retiring for the night?''

She dropped him a full curtsy. ''I'm honored, Doc.
Truly.''

He was doing his best to take my mind off wor-
rying over you, lover. Pointed to a flaring light,
way out in space. Probably some sort of ancient
nuke rubbish falling back. Didn't notice that the
strangers were all grouped together in the
shadow of one of the wags. Their leader came
sliding out toward us with two of the other men.
Don't know if I caught the glint of moonlight on
steel, or if it was just I finally got to ''see'' the
danger. But...

''LOOK OUT, Doc!''
Her voice was shrill, like a razor over glass, loud
enough to make the old man stagger back so that the
knife thrust missed opening up his belly, loud enough
to bring J.B. and Mildred off the porch and loud
enough to tear Jak and Christina apart in their bed
with the antique Amish quilt.

''Red-haired bitch!''

The leader of the wag train raged at Krysty, hand going to the blaster in its holster.

Despite his shock, Doc had reacted with unusual speed, for once drawing the mighty Le Mat from his hip without even a fumble, cocking and firing in a single, fluid movement.

The .63-caliber shotgun round was useless at anything much over thirty feet. The Armorer used to tease Doc that he'd do better to throw the heavy blaster at any potential enemy.

But this time the range was less than six feet and Doc's aim was true.

The shot didn't have time to spread, and it ripped out the center of the man's throat, slashing through his windpipe and tearing the cervical vertebrae of the upper spine into shards of splintered bone. The impact was so devastating that it almost removed the man's head from his body.

Blood fountained into the night sky, pattering in the dry sand. For a macabre moment the corpse stayed upright, even taking a half step away from the smoking cannon in Doc's fist.

Krysty, not fearing any threat, had stupidly left her Smith & Wesson .38 on the small table at the side of her bed.

Seeing that she was unarmed, a second of the travelers rushed toward her with a slender skinning-knife, held low to gut her.

Instead of retreating, Krysty stepped in, propelling

herself into a ferociously high leap, kicking out with her right foot and aiming for the man's face.

The stubby heel of her dark blue leather Western boot smashed home, hitting on the upper lip and then into the base of the attacker's hooked nose.

Teeth cracked and snapped off at gum level, and Krysty felt cartilage pulping under her boot. She landed with an acrobat's easy grace, seeing the man falling back, hands to his wrecked face, blood pouring between his fingers.

She heard a burst of fire from the Uzi, and someone screamed.

The sneak attack by the wag train of travelers was doomed to failure, even before it got properly started.

One of the women stopped a bullet from Jak Lauren's satin-finish Magnum, which kicked her backward over the low stone wall around the well. Legs flailing, she toppled out of sight.

A musket boomed, a great cloud of black powder smoke giving away the position of the shootist. J.B. immediately blasted half a clip at him, seeing him go spinning away from the rear of the wag.

The strangers had scattered all over the spread, some of them trying to hide in the barn, a couple of older women making for the smokehouse.

Within less than five minutes the homesteaders had the situation back under their control, though it took another quarter of an hour to round up all the survivors.

We sat them all down in a huddled group. Oh, lover, they did look a sorry bunch. Two men were chilled. One by J.B. and one by Doc. And we still hadn't got the woman out of the well. Christina had shone a lantern down and said she was a floater. We figured she could wait. Odd thing was none of them seemed to care a grain of sand about what had happened. One of the kids was lying down, breathing fast and odd, crying that the lumps was killing him. So Mildred said she'd have a look.

THE BLACK WOMAN TOOK one of the older children into the house, picking her way between the splashes of clotting blood.

J.B. stayed on guard with Doc and Jak, though the strangers were so apathetic that it hardly seemed worth the effort.

Krysty and Christina stood in the parlor and watched the examination.

The boy looked to be about twelve, shivering uncontrollably.

"Take off the shirt," Mildred said.

"Fuck you, bitch."

Without the slightest change of expression she slapped him across the face. The slap rang out in the quiet house, her fingers leaving a bright pattern on the pale skin.

"Take off the shirt," she repeated, "and take the pants off, too."

Sniveling, the boy obeyed her, tugging off the ragged cotton shirt, dropping it by his bare feet. More slowly, reluctantly, he unbuttoned his pants and let them fall to the scrubbed pine boards. His ribs showed through like a picket fence, and he cupped his hands over his genitals.

"I want you to lift up your arms and stand with your legs apart," Mildred ordered, stooping to stare closely at him. She turned to Krysty and Christina. "You two better go outside."

"What?" Krysty said. "Think I haven't seen..."

Mildred turned, her brown eyes narrowed. "Just do it. Please."

There was a snap of anger in the voice and something else that Krysty couldn't quite identify. But she obeyed, walking into the cooling night with Christina.

"Don't you fucking touch me, bitch."

"Stand still and keep quiet. Just answer my questions."

He was deathly white, heart visibly pounding, respiration rapid. His skin was glittering with a ghost of sweat.

"How long you been like this?"

"We all got it."

She repeated the question. "How long, son? When did it start?"

"Dawn day before today."

She lifted an oil lamp off the table and stooped to look at the shadowed place beneath the boy's lifted arms.

There were great lumps there, like full-grown to-
matoes, but black and shining, with a mirrored ma-
levolence. Mildred drew in a slow breath.

"Any idea how you all got ill?" Her voice was
soft and gentle.

"Came on a camp. Lot of dead. Rotted right
to...kind of like thick brown water. There was food.
That smelled bad and tasted... Look, I got to go shit."

In the lad's groin Mildred saw the same signs of
the virulent disease. But if the boy was telling the
truth and it had reached this terminal stage in less
than forty-eight hours...

"You all have it?"

"Yeah. All. Lost five dead last night. Look, I got
to go."

"Outside! Far from the house as you can get, before you—oh, Jesus Christ, kid!"

It was too late. The boy shit everywhere. Like
watery gruel, with kind of grains of rice in it and
thick specks of black. And some blood. Then he
threw up.

Got to go on now. J.B. says he thinks there
might be muties around. Anyway, lover, you
probably guessed what was wrong and what we
had to do.

"What?" Dean asked.

"Plague," his father replied.

Chapter Six

Doc Tanner turned to face the woman, his rheumy eyes protruding like boiled gooseberries.

"Plague?"

"Right." It was an effort for her to keep her voice from cracking.

"Black death?"

"If that's what you want to call it."

"Bubonic plague, Mildred. Are you positive in your diagnosis?"

"Doc, why don't you go and take a flying fuck at a rolling doughnut? The boy's got big black lumps under his arms. More in his groin. Glands like patent leather baseballs. Sweating. Raging dysentery. Rapid pulse and respiration. What the fuck more do you want, you gibbering old cretin?"

Jak was still watching over their cowed prisoners, but the others were all standing around Mildred, all staggered by the venom of her outburst.

Doc was quickest off the mark. "I can only apologize, my dear Dr. Wyeth. I was foolish to speak in the way that I did, and you were quite right to reproach me for it."

Mildred sighed, patting him on the wrist. "No, I'm

the one who should be saying sorry, Doc. Just that it tore my heart to see that child like that. He's only a couple of hours from the last train to the coast. I mean from death.''

Krysty sighed. ''It's that bad?''

Mildred looked at her. ''No, Krysty. It's not *that* bad. It's much, much worse. Boy says he got the way he is since last morning. Even the most virulent bubonic plague would never run its full course in that short a time. No way.''

''Think it's a rogue virus?'' the Armorer asked, keeping one eye toward the huddled group from the wag train.

Mildred took a deep breath, as though she were readying herself for a plunge into freezing water. ''It's worse. Not my speciality this kind of disease. But it must be massively contagious, mainly through food and water. But also carried in the air. Like spores that settle on everything.''

Christina ran a hand through her shoulder-length hair. ''I'm beginning to hear spaces between the words, Mildred. And I don't like what I'm hearing in those gaps.''

''It's simple. There's blood, shit and spit all over the farm. In the house. The well. The smokehouse. I think there's a small but real...fatally real risk of contamination.''

''What do we do?'' J.B. asked.

''We move. Now. Within the hour. Take no food or water. All tainted.''

"But what about our home? What are we going to do with the homestead?" Christina looked stricken.

Mildred was nearly in tears. "I might be bloody wrong, Christina. Might be, but I don't think I am. Only one way. Fire."

"Burn the house?"

"Everything. The barn and the outbuildings. Let the stock all go and hope to round them up again later. Can't take them with us. Too slow."

"Where are we going?" Doc asked.

"Into the hills. North. Should be the fire'll destroy the disease and we can come back in a week or so. No quicker."

J.B. cleared his throat. "One thing," he said quietly.

"What?" Mildred looked at him.

"Those people. What are we going to do with all of them?"

EVERYONE WAS BUSY. The dead woman was hauled from the deep well and placed in the bed of a wag, along with the bodies of the two shot men.

Krysty scribbled a note and fixed it to the rope, just above the well's iron bucket.

The animals and fowl were all released into the surrounding desert.

Jak and Christina insisted on pouring the gasoline around their home, the woman weeping as she limped around with the cans. Jak was totally silent, as though he were in shock.

Mildred made everyone wear heavy work gloves and masks of linen, soaked in lye.

The oxen were harnessed to lead the wags away, some distance from the homestead where the rigs and the bodies would be burned to ashes. Doc took charge of that part of the mission, telling the others he'd wait for them where the land started to rise toward the steep rocks of the gorge.

One reason for his early departure was linked to the question of what was to be done with the handful of survivors from the diseased wag train.

The discussion had been, of necessity, brief and heated.

Doc had been simply for leaving them where they were, though Mildred had insisted that they all faced nothing more than a miserable and agonizing passing within a few hours.

Christina had been for sending them away at gunpoint.

Jak had spit on the ground. "They chilled home. Chill them."

J.B. had agreed with the view of the albino teenager. "Trader used to say that a choice between a dead enemy and a live enemy wasn't any sort of choice at all."

Krysty had looked at the circle of faces. "Two say let them live, even if it's only for a while, then a dreadful passing. Two say take them all out now. Quick and clean." She looked at Mildred. "You're a doctor. What do you say?"

"Six men, five women and four little children," Mildred said quietly, sorrowfully. "Suffering little children."

"What are you saying?" J.B. asked.

Mildred shook her head. "I go with taking away the suffering."

The Armorer squeezed her hand. "Fine. I'll do it."

"No," Jak argued. "Me."

"You gotta light the fires with me."

He looked at his wife. "Some things can't ride around," he said.

In the end the argument was resolved.

J.B. HAD STOOD GUARD with the Uzi, gesturing for the travelers, one by one, to go around the corner of the broken wall toward the main barn. Though it was obvious what was happening to them, out of sight of the group, nobody made an effort to run or to fight.

Or even to protest.

Mildred held her ZKR 551, the Czech target pistol made at the Zbrojovka Works in Brno. The 6-shot revolver was now chambered to take a standard Smith & Wesson .38-caliber full-metal-jacket round.

At her own request, she shot the children first, all of them frail and fretful from the bubonic plague, moaning in pain. Her hand was steady as if she were back home in Lincoln, Nebraska, carrying out delicate microsurgery, following her old speciality of cryogenics.

"Don't be frightened," she said, turning her head

away in order to avoid getting splashed by blood and brains.

After the children came the women, most kneeling as dutifully as children at their first communion. Their eyes were blanked out by the sickness, and Mildred shot them one by one.

After three of the men, she stopped to reload the blaster for a second time, biting her lip as she fought back the tears.

Next came the oldest of the party, a tall man in a plaid shirt, a length of homespun rope holding up his pants. One of the grotesque boils had burst beneath his right arm, and a mixture of pus and blood soaked the material down to his waist.

He nodded at her, managing a cocky grin at the blaster, like it was an old friend.

"Best this way."

Mildred hesitated. "You reckon?"

"Sure. We done things and been places that the Lord Almighty never meant. I figure you just stock up treasure in heaven." He knelt in front of her, bringing his hands up in prayer. "Yeah, gold in heaven and shit in hades. Pull the trigger, lady."

So, there it is, lover. Took us awhile to dig the grave. But now it's done. Now we're moving north again, into the higher country. Catch up with us, lover, as quick as you can. Want to see the boy again. And I want to feel your...

Ryan stopped reading, finding that he was closer to blushing than he'd been since the age of five.

"That's all she says, Dean."

He looked down and found that his son, stone exhausted, had fallen asleep.

Ryan smiled. "Sure, boy. Guess I'll take a little of the same. Then, when we both feel like it, we'll be pretty up and walking good to get together with the others again. 'Specially Krysty."

Chapter Seven

Ryan shot a startled buck rabbit a little after dawn the next morning, knocking it over with a single round from his blaster. He ran after it as it kicked and flailed in the dry grass, and finished it off with a sharp blow to its nape.

"We could take it with us and cook and eat it later," he said, grinning at the expression on his son's face. "Or we could mebbe do it now. Seems like this is a real good place. What do you think?"

"Yeah."

"Carried by a majority of two."

IT WAS AN idyllic setting. They had moved along the trail that wound upward from the spray-filled ravine. It headed roughly northward and was the only track that the others could feasibly have taken. It was lined with a variety of pines, some with needles that were light gray green, some deep blue purple, which stood on either side of the narrow, rutted pathway, their scent filling the morning.

Their campsite—a clearing about eighty feet across, with a fringe of ripening thimbleberries at its borders—was just a little higher, alongside a place where the river opened up into a deep, mirrored pool. There was a fallen live oak at the edge, its roots rotted and dry.

While Ryan took out his flensing knife to skin and gut the rabbit, Dean went scavenging in the surrounding woods for some small sticks and larger branches for the fire.

"Lay it with some of the tinder from under the pines," Ryan instructed. "Get a handful of the dried needles and first lay them on some—"

"Dad."

"What?"

"My mother didn't raise no kids who couldn't lay a fire."

"Sorry."

"Never apologize. It's a sign of weakness, Dad. That one of the Trader's sayings?"

"Yeah. Trader had hundreds of sayings. One for every occasion. Longer you knew the old bastard, the more you realized that some of his sayings would directly contradict others."

"Sometime, I'd really like to hear lots more about the Trader."

"Get the fire going. Rabbit's near ready. And set up the framework to carry a skewer."

"Sure. You reckon the Trader's really gone right back to the spring?"

"Dead?"

"Yeah. You reckon?"

"Year or so ago I'd have laid any odds you wanted

he was sleeping the big sleep. Now, there's whispers and rumors. Takes a mighty sharp arrow to pierce through the dust of those rumors, Dean. Here.'' He tossed him flint and steel.

"You saw him last?"

"No, that was… Fireblast! What was his name? It was—"

"Not J.B.?"

"No. Abe. That was him. Abe was last guy to see Trader. He's dead now, I guess. Skinny guy with a mustache and long hair. Used to get kidded about his hair. He saw Trader take a last walk into the forest. No, he's dead all right."

A curling tendril of light smoke rose from the carefully constructed little fire that the boy had started.

He handed Dean the rabbit, ready for cooking. The water in the pool was surprisingly deep, and Ryan watched dragonflies darting just over the placid surface.

The morning was quiet, with only the wind sighing through the branches of the trees. The crackling of the fire began to override it, and the smell of roasting meat drifted to the one-eyed warrior's nostrils. It was good to relax in safety, though in Deathlands, you could never just lie down and close your eyes. Krysty's mention that there might be muties in the mountains made Ryan extra cautious.

But nothing could spoil the moment.

Dean lay down by the cooking rabbit, occasionally turning the makeshift spit.

Ryan rested against the fallen live oak, hands clasped behind the back of his head, staring up through the moving branches at the clear blue sky. Occasionally birds flew by, darting so fast that there was no time to recognize them, though their shrill piping washed around the forest.

"Think we're close to Krysty and the others?" Dean asked.

"Been wondering about that myself. Can't tell how far behind them we are. I figure it can't be more than twenty-four hours or so. We just keep going, and we'll find them camped someplace. Then everything'll be just fine."

"Wish you'd shot two rabbits, Dad."

"Why?"

"Then I could eat this one all on my own and you could have the other one."

Ryan laughed. "I prefer it where I eat this one and you get the one that we haven't shot yet."

The wood burned bright and true, sending its column of smoke vanishing above them. It was light enough that Ryan didn't worry about it being spotted by anyone, particularly after it had been dissipated through the branches. Occasionally a globule of fat from the cooking meat would crackle in the flames with a burst of sharp sound.

"Soon be done."

"Good. We can drink water from the pool there. Looks clean enough."

Ryan stretched out, feeling the growing heat of the

sun soaking into his strained and abused muscles. It had been hard going for the past week or so. Despite the bad news of the homestead having to be burned against the disease, it would be good to spend a month or so helping Jak and Christina rebuild it.

"Be good," he whispered to himself.

Dean waved a hand, mouth open, pointing to the fringe of the clearing, close by the pool. Ryan looked and saw a small deer, standing stock-still, almost invisible among the dancing shadows. Its delicate feet were hidden in the long grass, the narrow head focusing on the two intruders.

The boy mimed drawing a blaster, aiming it and squeezing a trigger, then rubbing his stomach with a comical expression of hunger fully satisfied. Ryan shook his head.

There was a time to kill.

The mountains were teeming with game, and when they next wanted to eat it would only take a few minutes to shoot something for the pot. To wantonly butcher the young deer would have been to defile the beauty of the quiet place.

With a cold shock, Ryan was suddenly aware that the clearing had become even quieter.

The piping of the birds that had been swooping overhead, etching their silhouettes against the azure sky, had stopped.

The whole forest had fallen quiet. There had been cicadas clicking rhythmically in the brush. Now there was a silence that was broken only by the faint sounds of the cooking fire.

Dean had caught it as well, eyes turning nervously toward his father.

Ryan drew the SIG-Sauer, touching it to his lips in a warning gesture to the boy.

The deer had been drinking from the pool, long neck arched. Now it had stopped, head lifted, brown eyes open wide.

Ryan started to stand, when his eye caught the flicker of movement.

There, in a pool of spilled sunlight at the edge of the clearing, death stood poised and waiting.

Chapter Eight

Ryan's mind flashed back to the redoubt that he'd visited only a few days ago, to the row of machines that he'd seen in a dim, dusty hall: Five humanoid robots, standing patiently, legs slightly bent at the knees, arms dangling at their sides. They were no more than five feet tall, built mainly from rods of chromed steel. They still gleamed in the overhead lights, untarnished by the passing of long, solitary years.

Their heads were polished domes, with small crystals set in place of eyes. They were dull and lifeless. Below them was the android equivalent of a mouth, a metallic slit, half-open, with the hint of teeth within. Was there a sharpness there? It wasn't possible to tell.

Their necks were tubular, articulated, like the small scales on the the throat of a serpent. Their chests were armored, broad, containing all the comp controls. Each arm was slightly longer than a human's would be, in proportion to its height, giving the robots the appearance of an orangutan, slouching toward eternity.

One arm ended in three digits. Two were like pincers, with honed edges. The third was a clubbing hammer. The other arm terminated in four sharp blades, their points winking like needles.

The droids' legs were a little shorter than those of a man, ending in flexible platforms, each tipped with shorter versions of the finger knives.

They were the ugliest creations that Ryan had ever encountered.

"Wouldn't like to meet you guys in a dead-end street at midnight," he had said.

Ryan was about to turn away, but a fallen notice captured his attention.

Part of his concentration was focused on the quintet of stunted robots, and he ignored the red line and the warning painted on the floor. He stepped across it and bent to pick up the large card.

Far away one of five dark panels on a control console became illuminated with a single word: Activate.

The card was creased, corners dog-eared and bent. The writing was covered in dust and Ryan wiped it clear with his sleeve, his forehead wrinkling as he followed the faded printing.

It was headed with a single line in maroon capital letters: SEC HUNTERS.

Underneath there was an explanation, as though the five creatures had been exhibits in some sort of military museum.

Developed in the nineties using latest cybernetic technology, the sec hunters are the most sophisticated devices known to man and are years ahead of any comparable machinery from the Eastern Bloc. They "sniff out" the genetic body pattern of their prey. Once locked on to that one individual they will follow and destroy, even though it takes them to the ends of the known world. Nothing short of total destruction will divert them from their lethal purpose.

On that distant console, another block of screens had lighted under the heading of Genetic Recording.

THREE OF THE ANDROIDS had already been destroyed, narrowly thwarted in their lethal pursuit of the human life-form known as Ryan Cawdor. All of the information about his genetic makeup was irremovably programmed into the core of their linked, gestalt, computer souls.

A fourth robot had malfunctioned, though Ryan had no way of knowing that.

Now, the last of the sec hunters had pursued him, following by the merest luck, via the Last Destination button on the mat-trans gateway, emerging some distance behind Ryan and the boy into the blistering heat of New Mexico.

Like a wasp in summer, it now had no possibility of returning. It would slay Ryan Cawdor, then its own death would follow only a second or so after his life ceased.

That was how it would be.

Chapter Nine

The techno-creature that stood among the thimble-berry bushes bore little relationship to the polished exhibit that Ryan had first encountered in the forgotten depths of the far northern redoubt.

One of the red eyes glowed like a ruby fire, but the other was flat dead. Its mouth was open, and something moved quickly within it, from side to side, like a razor.

It took a hesitant step toward them, its head turning slowly from side to side, as though it were checking out the boy and the motionless deer. Ryan noticed that it seemed a little unsteady, and he could hear the loud whining of gears that weren't quite meshing properly.

The once-glittering carapace of hardened, chromed steel was now dented and smeared with dirt. One arm was making strange, twitching motions, the pincers continually snapping open and shut.

Ryan noticed that this android had a number stamped into its right shoulder. A neat, geometric number five. In the nightmare battles against the previous three techno-assassins, there had never been time to spot something like that. Now, in bright sunlight, it was very clear.

If this was the fifth of the five, then somewhere along the line something must have happened to one of the others. It must have malfunctioned before it even reached him, perhaps in the black, airless tunnels of the old mining shafts.

There was a tiny consolation in knowing that this must be the last of them.

If Ryan could defeat this one, then at least he wouldn't have to keep glancing over his shoulder for yet another programmed butcher.

"If," Ryan said.

Dean had stood, drawing the big Browning, glancing across at his father, waiting to be told how they were going to play this one.

The deer still hadn't moved, seeming hypnotized by the appearance of the metal android.

"Bullets won't stop it, unless we hit something vital," Ryan said.

Now that it had reached the climax of its pursuit, the droid seemed lethargic. There was the clearing between them, then the large, deep pool. The trees were thick around the edges of the open space, and Ryan wasn't sure that he and Dean could outrun the lethal creature. And in his heart he didn't honestly think he wanted to do that.

"Come on, you dumb fuck," he snarled. "Let's end this right here." Ryan smiled grimly at the futility of talking to a heartless collection of wires and circuits.

"Why don't we run different ways?" Dean hissed. "Can't get us both."

"It'll take one of us. Best try to chill it together."

It was still moving, lifting the left foot up then setting down. The servomotors hummed, and the right foot repeated the action. Slowly.

Its arms were spreading like grotesque wings, telescoping outward to cover any attempt to break past it. The hammer suddenly whirred around at fantastical speed, and Ryan readied himself to duck, in case it propelled it at him.

But the motion stopped as unexpectedly as it had started.

"Could swim for it, Dad."

"You're full of ideas, son. Told you. Want to finish it here and now."

"But, Dad—"

"Concentrate, Dean. Watch for the moment and then grab it."

Ryan took two slow steps to one side, planting his feet like an expert in martial arts, keeping his balance on the shifting carpet of pine needles. The android's head jerked toward him, and it altered its direction.

"Go the other way, Dean," he said. "Want to see what it does."

At the boy's movement, the head twitched back to follow him, but it kept on its inexorable progress toward its programmed prey.

A ceaseless whine came from deep inside the metal shell. Ryan had a flash of hope that its terminal malfunction might happen now. There would be a flash of sparks and grinding of gears, and it would fall over only inches from him.

But he had lived long enough to be certain that things like that only happened in books.

He backed away, toward the fringe of the lake, his eye never leaving the killer droid as it moved after him.

"Why not blast it, Dad?"

"No need to whisper. It can hear you, but it sure can't understand what you say. It's armored. Have to be a fluke if you hit anything real vital. By then it's on you."

The grating sound grew louder, and the droid clicked into a murderous overdrive. Both arms started to revolve in opposite directions. The hammer whirred and the cutting shears clicked and clacked. The needle blades in the toes went in and out so fast that the movement was only a glittering blur.

"Out the way!" Ryan yelled, balancing on the balls of his feet like a knife fighter, the gun probing at the air in front of his hand.

Dean ran a few steps farther to his left, then stopped, crouching and leveling his own blaster, bracing his wrist as J.B. had shown him.

It was like facing a madman, a crazed lunatic with triple speed and high-tech weapons.

For a moment the hunter droid waited, like a fighting bull, pawing the ground before the last charge. Then it began its rush.

Ryan opened fire, pumping ten of the fifteen rounds in the clip at the middle leg joints, seeing sparks fly and hearing the bullets scream off into the trees. Dean also opened fire, more slowly, having to reaim after each heavy kicking explosion of the Browning.

One of his shots came within a finger's width of taking out the robot's only functioning eye.

As Ryan powered himself toward the water, the young deer, terrified out of its skull, broke for safety.

With one eye gone, and propelling itself over the treacherous ground at an unsafe speed, the droid was distracted by the flash of speed from the panicked animal.

Hardly pausing, it swung the clubbing hammerhead at the deer, catching it a glancing blow across the side of the neck. The force was enough to knock the animal to the dirt in a tangle of kicking hooves. The droid swooped down on it, battering at the helpless creature as though it were its target.

It was almost as though it had a human killing urge, like a berserker.

Ryan thought it was probable that the first strike had butchered the fragile animal, breaking its neck. But the sec hunter was demented in its blind fury, kicking, cutting and hitting the mangled corpse, all at the same time. None of the bullets seemed to have had the least effect on its lethal power. The slaughter was happening less than a yard from the edge of the small lake, and Dean's suggestion about getting away by swimming suddenly came to Ryan.

"The water," he said.

It was the best shot they had.

He dodged around the droid, wading into the pool, feeling the cold shock as it rose above his combat boots to his knees, making his movements slow and fettered. He paused when it was halfway up his thighs, keeping the SIG-Sauer leveled.

"Hey!" Ryan shouted. The robot took no notice, preoccupied with mangling the corpse. "Come on, shit for brains! Get over here." He snapped off three more rounds, leaving himself with only a couple of bullets.

This time the droid stopped, its head moving with an infinite slowness, the metal greasy with slick blood. Its single red eye looked at the one-eyed man for long seconds.

"Be careful, Dad!" Dean called.

The hunting robot turned to focus on the boy, taking a hesitant step toward him. Blood was dripping from the steel hammerhead, and a length of muscle tissue was trapped between the pincers.

Ryan fired off the last two shots, bringing its attention back to him as the 9 mm rounds hit it in the chest.

The metal was pitted and scored from the amount of lead poured into it, but the droid's efficiency wasn't impaired. It took two steps that brought it right to the edge of the dark water, where it stopped.

"Come on, you piece of rusting shit," Ryan taunted. "Here I am!"

"Dad," Dean said quietly.

"Things go wrong, head north for the others. This bastard won't follow you."

"But I—"

"Just this once do like I say, Dean. Please."

One foot touched the surface of the pool, then drew back. The robot's head turned, and the comp controls buzzed angrily.

Ryan holstered the empty blaster and waved his hands in the air, shouting at the droid to keep it coming at him. He backed away a little deeper, nearly falling as his foot slipped on a slimed, rotting log, buried in the mud.

The robot seemed to be assimilating a jumble of input information, its red eye blinking off and on, its arms trembling at its sides. Then it made its decision and took two bold steps into the lake, to its armored knees.

Ryan was now waist-deep, drawing the heavy panga in his right hand and hefting it, though he knew it would be like waving a piece of straw at a charging stickie.

"Come on," he urged, beckoning it deeper, closer.

The water had risen to what would have been the android's groin.

And there it stopped.

Ryan took an instant chance. Instead of moving farther away, toward the possible safety of the lake's center, he chose to go forward, closing the gap between himself and the hunter-killer robot.

Holding out the long panga, he growled, ''Lost your balls, have you?''

The droid extended its arms and swung them both toward him, but it was just too far away. Ryan waved the steel blade, bringing the creature a cautious half step toward him.

He needed to have it at least chest-deep for there to be a chance of the water soaking through into its main control unit.

A small part of his brain wondered if the original inventors had taken the precaution of sealing the comp unit and making it waterproof.

If they had, then Ryan could look forward to about ten seconds more of life.

Judging it to perfection, he offered the panga again, bringing the robot another foot closer. Now the dark lake was lapping at the bottom of the droid's round, fluted chest unit.

The sec hunter was making a strange chittering sound, as though a flock of tiny metallic birds were fluttering inside its controls.

It stopped, head fixed toward its prey, arms retracted and froze, both pointing in Ryan's direction. For twenty, thirty seconds, nothing happened.

Ryan watched it, hawklike, waiting for the next move in the murderous game.

A minute. Two minutes.

''Think it's fucked, Dad?''

"No. Eye's lit. Can hear it still whirring away in its guts."

But the droid wouldn't move deeper.

"Fireblast!" Ryan yelled, the anger that was always present suddenly breaking out.

He dived beneath the surface of the dark pool, kicking hard with his legs as he drove straight at the waiting robot.

His groping hand felt the rigid struts of the leg supports, and he grabbed at them, swinging and pushing himself off the bottom of the pool.

The droid responded quickly, pumping its arms below the frothing spray. Ryan felt a savage blow on his right shoulder, but he hung on. The steel of the panga clashed against the robot's other arm, blocking the slicing cutters.

It was stumbling, struggling to keep its balance, the free leg shuffling, the other pulling against Ryan's grip.

With a titanic effort, Ryan managed to get the leg out of the mud. He braced himself and heaved, lifting the heavy android, tipping it.

The droid smashed another blow into the small of Ryan's back with its hammer hand, but it was done.

The breath exploded from Ryan as he surged out of the chill water, seeing the sec hunter disappearing, only its arms remaining above the pool.

There was a bright flame beneath the surface, like flaring phosphorus. Ryan let go and splashed his way quickly to the shore, looking back over his shoulder, nearly falling into the bloody bones of the mangled deer.

The android was going into appalling convulsions, as if it were suffering a high-tech fit. Sparks showered from its open mouth, and a trickle of molten metal burst through the dead eye.

Its right arm bent backward at an impossible angle and snapped off, the jagged stump revolving like a sickle harvester.

It fell again, and rose for a second time, mud and water streaming from its surface.

Dean moved to stand by his father, the Browning dangling, forgotten, from his hand.

The red eye blinked, and the android started to move toward Ryan on dancing, jerking legs. But the lines were going inexorably down, and it fell a third time, rising more slowly. Then the eye went dark.

Its good arm rose above its head in what looked almost like a macabre salute. Then it vanished forever beneath the dark waters. The pool became placid once more.

Chapter Ten

The rabbit was burned, though they managed to break open the charred outer surface and pick off some dried meat that wasn't too scorched. Dean scuffed at the shattered remains of the young deer, but the flesh was spoiled with hundreds of fragments of splintered bones, all tainted with the pulped and ruptured intestines.

"Soon get us something else to eat," Ryan promised, sitting stripped off by the fire, drying himself and his clothes.

His shoulder and back showed two deep bruises, purplish black, red around the edges, where the sec hunter had come close to chilling him.

But he'd bathed them in the cold lake, taking great care to pick a section a good distance away from where the android had gone down for the third and final time.

Now the warmth of the sun and the heat of the fire were drawing out the pain and tenderness.

"We going on soon, Dad?"

"Hell, why not?"

AFTER THE HORRIFIC early morning, the rest of the day unwound with a serene, untroubled beauty. They followed the river endlessly northward, along a valley with sides that grew ever more steep.

Birds flew around them, dipping the tips of their beaks into the fast-running water. Their wings and breasts shone with a dazzling range of iridescent greens, reds and golds.

Across the far side of the valley Ryan spotted a dozen or more curve-horned goats, picking their way along a high, invisible trail.

The sun was just past its zenith and they were taking a brief rest. The cliffs had closed right in on either side, the water flowing with muted thunder over shelves of glistening boulders.

"Look," Dean said, pointing at a steep drop of eight or ten feet, the river tumbling like a solid curtain of dark green.

"Fish. Salmon? Trout? Not very good on names of things I'm going to eat."

"Can I go and try to catch us one?"

Ryan nodded lazily. "Sure. They look good and big. But watch you don't go in off the top there. Be double slippery."

He watched the sight that had attracted his son's eyes—flashes of bright silver scales, gleaming like rainbows among the rushing falls. The river seemed to be teeming with fish, all of them battling their way upstream, presumably propelled by some atavistic spawning urge.

The boy scrambled down the side of the ravine,

picking his way with a surefooted ease. His father lay back in the warm sunshine, feeling a paternal pride in his son's skill and courage.

It was a good moment in a Deathlands afternoon.

Dean showed his extraordinary speed and hand-eye coordination by using his small turquoise-hilted knife to catch a large fish. He waited patiently, lying flat on his stomach, his head and chest overhanging the waterfall.

Again and again there was the dazzling display as the fish made their leaps, and Dean lay and stared, working out where most of them were going, where the current was a little weaker than in other places, where the shelf was less high.

When he struck, it was so quick that Ryan almost missed it.

A breath of steel flickered in the golden sunlight, and Dean had a fish struggling on his blade. He heaved it upward and clubbed its head on the rock in front of him. Holding it up, tail flapping in its death throes, he beamed up at his father.

FOR THE SECOND TIME in seven hours, a column of thin smoke wound its way between the high walls of rock, vanishing almost instantly as it broke free into the windy heights above.

The cleaned fish, which was neither trout nor salmon, was cooking merrily on the spit. Ryan's guess had put it at about a seven-pounder, plenty for a decent meal for both of them. Enough would remain to sustain them on their northward journey.

"Think they're far away now?" Dean asked, patiently honing his knife on a flat stone.

"Don't know. Never quite work out what happens to time when we make a jump. Occasionally it seems like we come out at about the same time of day, month and year as when we went in. Then, there's other jumps when things feel sort of different."

"But when you came after me..."

"Who knows? Didn't keep a real careful count, did you? No? Nor me. But it looked like we came back around a day or so after the massacre at the homestead back there."

"Rocks like this don't carry much of a trail, do they?"

"No."

"Will Krysty feel us getting closer to her?"

"Mebbe."

"Why hasn't she left us another message to tell us we're on the right track?"

"She warned about stickies in the region. Could be on account of them."

"Stickies can't read, Dad!"

"You don't know that."

"But they don't."

"Could do."

"Couldn't."

"Turn the fish again, Dean."

RYAN PICKED at his teeth with one of the long, flexible rib bones of the big fish. In the end, he and the boy had easily managed to eat it all. With nothing left over.

"That was *soooo* good," he said.

"What was the best meal you ever had?" Dean asked him, trying to smother a belch.

"Difficult."

"Bet you had some triple-rare banquets. That the proper word? Banquets?"

"Right word. Yeah, I guess I have. Remember when Trader had done a big favor for a baron up in the Cascades. Him, me and the Armorer got an invite. Best of everything."

"Tell me."

"Gold plates and silver forks."

"Wow!"

"Didn't make the food taste any better, though. Crystal goblets. Some wines he said were about a hundred and fifty years old."

"What were they like?"

Ryan grinned. "Tell you the truth…they were terrific. And we had some sort of fish and cheese to start. Said it was lobster from way north and some special kind of goat's cheese. It was okay, but it stank like a gaudy…" He changed his mind about the image he was about to use to the ten-year-old.

"What kind of meat?"

"There was some crab cooked in brandy, then a sort of white fish, poached with herbs. Wild boar in a ginger and honey sauce. That was real good. With glazed potatoes and greens. Ice cream of all sorts of fruit flavors finished off the meal. The banquet.''

"And that was the best meal you ever had? Sounds real mouth-filling.''

"No. That was a memorable meal all right. But not the best I ever had.''

"What was?''

"Kick out the fire before we go, and I'll tell you about it.''

The afternoon was wearing on, the sun beginning to sink slowly toward the west. They were out on a rocky platform, above the steep falls, with the thunderous sound of the tumbling water as a permanent backdrop.

Dean stood and started to push around the smoldering ashes, knocking them over the edge into the racing water. The last trickle of smoke died away to nothing.

"Tell me, then.''

"Best meal ever? I was sixteen, mebbee seventeen. Got taken by a sec patrol, halfway along the Big Miss. Picked me off a sinking boat along with seven dead men and a woman priest. Took me back. Baron was a runt-assed bastard with no nose. Tried to...you know, use me. Told him I'd chill him. Threw me in a cell that filled with muddy water and shit twice a day up to a few inches from the ceiling. Got bread thrown in, but it was always covered in the filth. Came close to starving.''

"How long?"

"In there? Lost count. I remember throttling a rat and eating it raw, but it made me puke. I reckon around ten days. Each time he came and asked me to suck his cock, and I refused."

"What happened? And how's this tie up with a great meal?"

"Patience." Ryan grinned. "Guard came in on about the eleventh day. I took his knife and gutted him, then went and found the baron in his room, jolted to the eyes. Woke him. Cut his throat open."

Ryan had first severed the man's genitals and jammed them into his gaping mouth. But he chose not to mention this to his son.

"Yeah!" the boy whooped.

"There was a bowl of water at the side of his bed. Don't forget I was this naked skeleton, covered in layers of stinking ooze. I washed my hands in this bowl. Remember it had a blue-and-white picture of a little bridge and a kind of temple on it. I wiped my hands on the sheets of the bed."

He thought he'd heard the sound of cautious movement. But he looked around, and he and Dean were still alone.

"Go on."

"By the bowl was a porcelain plate. Real thin and delicate. On it was a single peach. Fresh and ripe, and juicy and tender. I ate it. And *that* was the best damned meal I ever had in my entire life!"

From a few paces behind him, Krysty Wroth laughed. "Last time I heard you tell that story, lover, it was a pigeon, not a rat. And an orange, not a peach."

MOON FATE   75

Just a few paces behind him, Krysty Wroth
finished. "Dark night. I hoped you'd tell him. Any, Jovai.
It was no prison. Not a jack. And no damage, just a
prick."

Chapter Eleven

"Awake?"

"No. I'm fast asleep."

"Can't stand the pace?"

Ryan rolled on his side, seeing Krysty propped up
on one elbow, her tumbling fiery hair seeming almost
black in the stark moonlight. The blanket had slipped
down, uncovering her breasts, shadowed and splendid. She was smiling at him.

"Twice is enough for starters," he responded.

"I call that big talk for a one-eyed old man. Been
too long without you to be satisfied with a couple of
quickies."

"Quickies!"

She touched her finger to his lips. "Shh. You'll
wake the others. Don't want them all to know about
your incessant demands on my body."

Ryan ran his hand through her hair, seeing the
dancing sparks of pure fire burning in the still, warm
air. They were lying a little distance from the others,
at the center of a grove of tall sycamores whose
branches stirred softly.

"I think I can feel another of those incessant demands creeping up on me," he said.

Her hand moved under the blankets, across the flat, muscular planes of his stomach, lower into the curling tendrils of wiry hair. She cupped him in the palm of her hand, squeezing, sighing as he stirred into hard life again.

"I can feel it as well, lover. Let's do something about it."

She eased him onto his back, straddling him, gripping his body with her powerful thighs, guiding him with her fingers, gasping with pleasure as he thrusted into her. Krysty lowered her head toward him, her hair falling into place like a sentient veil.

"So good to have you back safe with me, lover," she whispered.

"Good to be back."

"I love you, Ryan."

"Yeah. Love you, too."

KRYSTY HAD SEEN the thin column of pale smoke, following it back south for a couple of miles, eventually finding father and son relaxing after the meal of fresh-caught fish.

The camp was a little distance from the river, on the banks of a narrow, fast-running stream. There'd been an earth slide some months ago that had brought down twenty or thirty trees in a tangle of splintered timber, which meant a plentiful supply of firewood of all sizes.

There was plenty of game in the forested hills, and already they'd smoked and dried a brace of goat, as well as three small deer. And there was ample fish in a shaded pool a quarter mile upstream.

Some of the stock had found its way along the same trail. J.B. and Mildred had gone to stay in a box canyon about four miles east, in order to tend them.

When Krysty led Ryan and Dean back into the camp, Doc was shaving with the honed blade of a knife, using a second knife as a mirror. He nearly cut himself as he spun around, and he rushed to embrace both of them. Jak and Christina were playing pinochle on a red-edged horse blanket.

Considering the cruel blow that fate had dealt them with the arrival of the infected travelers, and the subsequent destruction of their home, both were in surprisingly good spirits.

Most of the first couple of hours was taken up with mutual telling of stories, filling in the gaps left in Krysty's notes and recounting what had happened in and around the sulfur mines during the rescue of Dean from the talons of Gregori Zimyanin.

While Ryan was telling them about the last battle, with occasional interruptions from his son, Doc kept punching his left hand into his right palm, exclaiming, "Oh, marvelous! Yes, that's where the corn is cut, my friends! Not to be gainsaid, Ryan! Oh, the rogue and peasant slave!"

The sun was sinking out of sight, and Ryan agreed that it would be foolish to risk getting caught by nightfall halfway to the canyon where the Armorer and Mildred were camped.

AFTER THEIR THIRD ROUND of lovemaking, Ryan lay with his arm resting across Krysty's shoulder.

"Might get up and have a drink of that spring water in a minute," he said. "Warm night."

"Been hotter. It's cooler up where Mildred and J.B. are settled."

"Things still okay between them?"

Krysty nodded. "Sure are. Better than okay. Seems to be a real solid relationship going on between those two."

"Think they want to settle down together someplace?"

"Doesn't everybody, lover?"

There was a long stillness between them. Ryan didn't move, and eventually Krysty's hand found his and clasped it firmly.

"Seeing Jak and Christina together..." she began, allowing the sentence to trail into the quiet darkness around them.

"I know."

"Good places around here. Plenty of land for the taking."

"Sure. Clean water. Climate's great. No nuke hot spots."

Krysty sighed. "But there's always something around the next corner, Ryan. Something to keep moving on for. Dragons to be slaughtered and innocent maidens to be rescued."

He let go of her hand. "Don't get that."

"Never mind, lover. Most times I push it way back.

Then it comes creeping forward again, like a sore place you can't stop yourself from picking at.''

Ryan deliberately changed the subject, taking it to safer grounds.

''Any sign of stickies?''

''Rather talk about muties than us settling down, eh, lover? Stickies? Jak reckons they're around in these hills.''

''What proof?''

''Some old miners' shacks burned out.''

Ryan wiped sweat from his forehead and sat up. ''Got to get some water.'' He looked around the clearing. ''These shacks…''

''Yeah?''

''Couldn't they have been fired a hundred years ago? Or any time in between?''

''Jak says not. Very recent. Even before we arrived here he'd been finding tracks of stickies. Says there could be as many as fifty up in the high country to the east and north.''

Ryan stood, stretching. He pushed his hands onto his hips and arched his back to try to ease an old stiffness from the middle vertebrae. A pinched disk had been Mildred's diagnosis, sometimes squeezing a nerve and putting a muscle into spasm on the right side of his spine.

''You mean up where J.B. and Mildred are staying?''

He saw the blur of movement as Krysty nodded her answer. ''But Jak doesn't seem to think that they'd be much of a threat to J.B., not with all of his experience.''

''I guess not. But fifty's a shit lot of stickies to have hiding someplace around you. Sneaky bastards. Might be a better idea if we all kept in the same camp.''

He walked and knelt by the stream, cupping his hands and drinking a copious draft from the cold stream. The more he thought about it, the less happy he was at the idea of the Armorer being alone in an isolated box canyon, even with Mildred's sharp-shooting to help him.

The good thing about stickies was that they generally didn't function well in groups. They were too uncontrollable and triple crazy for that. But fifty of them...

THE NEXT MORNING brought another wonderfully bright and sunny day. In the early hours, just before the hesitant light of the false dawn, Ryan had woken to hear the distant rumbling of a chem storm, the southern horizon a dazzling display of pink and purple spears of lightning. But it was moving toward the far west and faded away within the hour.

Dean and Doc cooked breakfast, heating some venison in a small iron caldron, while eggs spit and chattered in a shallow skillet. Krysty saw Ryan looking questioningly at the eggs.

''Mildred said eggs were safe, long as they'd already been laid before the stickies arrived. We got quite a few sealed jars of preserve and jellies. And some bottled plums and apples."

Christina came limping across from the stream, carrying a bucket of water in her right hand, leaning over to balance it. Ryan was about to leap up and help her with it when he caught the warning in Jak's ruby eyes, and he sat again.

"Going to meet with J.B. and Mildred today?" she asked, recovering her breath, wiping her hands on her checked cotton skirt.

"Yeah. Dean best stay here and stock up on his strength."

"Oh, Dad, you—"

"Dean!"

"All right, Dad."

"I'll come along," Krysty said.

Ryan nodded. "Be good."

Jak cleared his throat and everyone turned to look at him, but he glanced ostentatiously toward the stream and didn't speak.

Christina laughed. "Course you can."

"Sure?" His white face was bright with anticipation, then clouded. "Ryan? Mind if..."

"Glad to have you along, Jak. You know that. Doc?"

"At your service, my dear fellow. What can I do for you?"

"You can stay here with Christina and the boy. All right?"

The old man shook his head. "Oh, calamity! And

I was so looking forward to clambering four miles across a landscape not unlike the devil's hindquarters, in scorching heat. Now I'll just have to remain here with this whining brat and this ineffably boring housewife, here in the shade, stretched out, snoozing gently by a bubbling brook. You ask much of your friends, Ryan Cawdor.''

"BE BACK BEFORE DUSK. Keep a good look out for any sign of stickies.''

Ryan had his bolt-action Steyr SSG-70 rifle, complete with laser image enhancer and Starlite night scope. His P-226 was at his hip.

Jak wore his Magnum on his hip and hefted an old M-16 carbine on his shoulder.

Krysty simply carried her snub-nosed Smith & Wesson 640, the double-action model that held five .38-caliber rounds.

Jak led the way from the camp, his long hair, bleached whiter than wind-washed ivory, blowing in a freshening breeze.

It was a truly beautiful morning. The kind of day when every muscle in your body felt relaxed for the sheer pleasure of being alive.

Chapter Twelve

"Feel something, lover."

They all stopped at Krysty's words.

They'd covered about two miles, crossing a hog-back ridge as a shortcut toward the box canyon where J.B. and Mildred were tending the stock. The only sign of life had been a yellow-flecked lizard, warming itself on a sunbaked spike of orange rock.

"What?" Ryan's right hand fell to rest casually on the butt of the SIG-Sauer.

She shrugged, pushing an errant strand of hair off her forehead. "Just something. It's like if you've got a wag that you drive every day. Comes the time you can sort of feel that something isn't running quite like you know it usually does. But you can't quite put your finger on what it is that's wrong. You know the feeling I mean?"

Jak answered. "Sure. Stickies, mebbe?"

"Gaia! I don't know, Jak. But it could be. Doesn't seem like a good feeling."

Ryan sniffed. "Let's move to orange and all take some extra care."

He went out to point, with Krysty walking about

ten paces behind him. Jak was a farther twenty steps behind her.

All of them had their blasters ready.

The trail was steep and narrow, overhung with the long trailing branches of dense spruce. Every now and again the trees would clear, and it would become possible to see way down to the left toward the valley bottom.

"Canyon forks off another mile or so along here. You can get to it by going down along the stream, but this is quicker."

They stood together, the air around them filled with the wonderful resinous scent of the pines. They could faintly hear the whispering sound of the small river as it busied itself among the moss-covered boulders.

Jak's vision in bright sunlight was notoriously poor, but in less good light, like among the shadowing trees, he could see better than any of them.

"There," he said, finger pointing downward like an arrow of divine vengeance.

Ryan and Krysty looked where the albino teenager was indicating, and both immediately spotted the flicker of darkness in the dappled patchwork below. Even from that height, they could immediately read bad news.

The pair of figures were moving in a stooped, loping trot, heads down like wolves following a trail.

"Stickies," Ryan breathed.

The muties were about a hundred feet below them,

the noise of the stream drowning out any sound from the trio above.

"Both got blasters," Krysty said, her voice revealing her disbelief.

Stickies never used firearms. No, that wasn't quite true. Ryan could think of a handful of skirmishes with the distinctive creatures where blasters had appeared. But they were exceedingly rare and never used with anything approaching skill.

"Look like smoothbores."

Jak nodded. "Homemades or patch-ups. Long blasters for stickies."

Again, that was strange.

The elongated barrels of what looked from a distance like Kentucky muskets, using crude black powder, were specialized hunting weapons.

The stickies vanished around the far edge of a granite bluff that protruded from the hillside on the opposite flank of the valley.

"They're heading for canyon." Jak whistled softly between his teeth. The breeze was tugging at the mane of snow-white hair that tumbled across his shoulders. "Be on top J.B. and Mildred real soon."

"Think they're deliberately hunting them? Know they're there?" Krysty looked around at Ryan. "What do we do, lover?"

"Go after and chill them."

There wasn't any other answer. Not when you were dealing with stickies.

Jak led the way.

It was his home terrain, and he knew it inch by inch. The only problem was that the teenager was so light on his feet that he was leaving Ryan and Krysty behind him.

Repeatedly stopping and turning, looking behind him along the winding path, his face betrayed his impatience.

"Quicker," he snapped. "They got faster trail. There first."

"Anyplace we can see them from above? We've got two long guns."

Jak hesitated at Ryan's query. "This track drops steep soon. Unless they stop won't get clear shot. Nowhere."

"Fireblast!" Ryan stood still, leaning a hand against the cool bole of an alder, closing his eye as he tried to consider all of the options.

"Depends on what the stickies are after," Krysty said.

"Cattle. Chilling J.B. and Mildred. Scouting. Mebbe all three."

"Right, Jak. Mebbe all three. Way they were running was creepy. Kind of hunting, but knowing where they were going."

"Talk's costing," Jak said, his crimson eyes glowing in the half dark under a big, overhanging spruce.

"Place where the stickies are going to reach the end of the box canyon."

"Yeah?"

"No way we can overlook it if we stay up high here?"

The albino considered the question for a long moment. "No," he said finally. "Mean picking way in trees. Too slow. Still wouldn't get clean shot. Have to chase hard."

"Right," Ryan said. "Then, let's do it."

THE TRAILS JOINED about a quarter mile farther on. The last hundred yards had been steep, with slippery, loose rocks. Krysty nearly lost her footing, only just saving herself by a teetering dance on the edge of the path.

In any kind of pursuit, Ryan was always conscious of the danger that the prey might have somehow turned and be the hunter instead of the hunted.

Down near the stream the path was damp and muddy, showing the unmistakable prints of a pair of stickies, moving fast and low.

A thread of water from a bank of glistening emerald moss was still oozing into the center of one of the impressions, showing Ryan that their targets weren't far ahead of them.

He stooped and picked a fallen sycamore leaf from the footprint.

"Can't be more than three, four minutes ahead of us," he told his companions. "Looks like they've slowed up some."

"Let me after them?" Jak's right hand brushed

against the back of his camouflage jacket and reappeared holding one of his taped throwing knives.

"Could be more of them. Stickies go around in tens and twenties. Not just in pairs."

"So we follow them?" Krysty asked.

Ryan nodded.

THE TRAIL SQUEEZED between green-soaked walls of rock. The little river chuckled away to the right, oblivious to the lethal hunt that was taking place on its pretty banks.

"They drive stock along here?" Krysty asked very quietly.

Jak sniffed, wiping his nose on his sleeve. "Sure. Narrow track's best. No place else to go."

Ryan had been conscious of the machine-gun tapping of a woodpecker somewhere a quarter mile or so ahead of them. Had to be close to the entrance to the box canyon.

It had suddenly stopped.

"Listen," he said, holding up his hand.

"What?" Krysty had her double-action Smith & Wesson .38 already drawn.

"Bird."

"Don't hear it. In fact, I can't hear any birds at all." She looked at Ryan. "Course. What a stupe I am. Means the muties are near in front of us."

Ryan beckoned Jak closer, dropping his voice. "Whereabouts would J.B. and Mildred be? They camped this end of the canyon?"

"No. Under back wall. Pool there. Rock house built old ones."

"Old ones?"

The boy looked puzzled. "Christina calls that. Old ones. Back before...before dark nights. Long, long before."

Krysty tapped Ryan on the arm. "Guess he means ancient Indian ruins. Anasazi I think they were called. Lots of their places are scattered all around the Southwest here."

"When did they live in these parts? Same time as Doc Tanner?"

Krysty smiled. "We're talking seriously old, lover. Thousand years and more."

"Oh. And they got some of these old houses in the canyon?"

Jak looked around as though he'd heard something. "Yeah. Under cliff."

Ryan finally reached his decision. "We'll take the stickies out. In case there's more of them close by we'll try it quiet."

JAK BENT AND STARED at the track beneath an overhanging wall of quartz-flecked granite.

"Only marks are stickies," he whispered. "Means not come here before. Scouting."

Since the ravening muties generally traveled in groups of a dozen or more, this almost certainly meant that there would be others close by. It also brought an uncomfortable prickling at Ryan's nape.

"Feel anything?" Ryan asked.

Krysty shook her head. "Been my time of the month. Always messes up the seeing."

She almost said something else, but she knew that Ryan hated it if he thought she was just blind guessing. For about a quarter of an hour now she'd had a blurred feeling of danger. But it was so vague and unfocused that she couldn't be certain. It might easily involve the pair of stickies ahead of them.

Or it might not.

The trees thinned out as the entrance to the box canyon grew nearer. The track became a little wider and climbed for about a hundred feet. Jak was still out in front and he suddenly stopped dead, holding up a warning hand.

With his jacket of melded browns, greens and grays, the teenager almost vanished into the dappled pools of shadow and sunlight under the sweeping branches.

"There," he mouthed as Ryan and Krysty joined him.

Ryan followed the white, pointing finger. "Let's take them," he whispered.

Chapter Thirteen

A wide, open space sloped up ahead of them—loose, sandy soil, with scattered pebbles and a few large rocks. It was obvious that the ridge offered a good viewpoint down into the canyon where Jak and Christina's stock was being kept. And where J.B. and Mildred were currently camping.

From where Ryan stood with Krysty and Jak, they could see nothing beyond the rise—but they could see the two stickies lying on the soft dirt, side by side, legs splayed, each with a long musket clamped firmly to its shoulder.

It didn't take a giant leap of imagination to guess what the weapons were sighted on.

Jak was quickest.

The throwing knife whirred through the warm air and buried itself with a precise accuracy exactly where the skull joined the spine. The honed point drove into the spinal column and instantly shut down all lines of communication.

The stickie gave a hiccuping grunt and dropped the smoothbore blaster from nerveless fingers. Its toes began to kick at the sand as though they were trying to propel the breathing corpse over the brink of the ridge.

Ryan had dropped his rifle and had the SIG-Sauer half drawn, prepared to use the silenced blaster. But Jak's speed of reflex was even faster than he remembered, and the boy already had a second blade winging its way toward the other stickie.

The sudden gasp from its comrade, and the musket falling into the dirt, had alerted the surviving mutie. It started to bring the gun around.

Jak hadn't anticipated such a fast reaction from the thing, and the knife clipped the creature's right shoulder, cutting its pale blue shirt but doing no serious harm.

"Mine," Ryan called, steadying his right wrist with his left hand, dropping by long, long habit into the traditional shootist's crouch, side-on, to present a smaller target to his enemy.

He had a tiny shard of broken time to take in the appearance of the stickie.

Most of the mutated creatures that infested the darker parts of Deathlands wore, at best, rags. This stickie was dressed in a neat, clean shirt and pants, with a black slouch hat. Its feet were bare. Ryan saw the crazed anger in the mutie's face that he'd witnessed many times before. Wide eyes protruded like a frog's, and its mouth opened in a snarl of hatred.

"You fuckhead piece of shit," it raged with surprising clarity.

The mutie was rising to its feet as Ryan opened

fire, squeezing off three rapid rounds. The P-226's integral silencer coughed discreetly.

The other stickie was still thrashing around, moaning like an old man with a fishbone jammed in his gullet. One of its legs shot out, kicking the crouching mutie hard on the thigh and sending it tumbling helplessly sideways.

It was enough to make Ryan's triple burst miss. The range was barely forty feet, but all three of the 9 mm bullets kicked up a small fountain of dirt.

"Fireblast!" He saw from the corner of his eye that Krysty was about to open fire at the mutie with her own snub-nosed Smith & Wesson. "No noise!"

Ryan was moving sideways, about to take out the stickie. But having only one eye gave him limited peripheral vision and he never saw Jak Lauren, sliding toward him through the loose scree, fumbling for the third of his concealed knives.

They bumped hard into each other. The boy dropped the weighted blade in the loose dirt and Ryan inadvertently squeezed the trigger on the blaster, sending a wasted round into the trees to his left.

The stickie, pale, raw lips peeling back in a triumphant smile, leveled the musket at the one-eyed man and pulled the trigger. Ryan winced, hearing the dry snap of a misfiring percussion cap.

"Shit," the stickie said in a strangely moderate voice.

"Mine." Ryan placed the blaster carefully by his feet and drew the polished steel blade of the eighteen-inch panga that he always wore sheathed on his other hip.

The hilt of the heavy machete fitted into his palm like a dream of childhood.

The stickie came down the slope toward him, gripping the useless firearm by the end of the barrel, swinging it onto its shoulder like a club.

Ryan glanced back at the albino. ''Use my blaster if I get in trouble.''

''Sure. Don't go close.''

Part of Ryan's mind was intrigued by the fact that the stickie was coming at him so hesitantly. All his experience of the breed had been that they were triple-crazy fighters, rushing at any enemy with a screaming, blind hatred. Caution was out of the question.

''You chilled meat,'' it threatened.

''Mebbe,'' Ryan replied, shuffling his boots in the soft earth to try to establish a good footing.

''Maggot food.''

''Sure. And you're two hundred pounds of dog shit in a fifty-pound sack.''

The musket was swirling around in a maniacal circle, hissing like a runaway windmill. The mutie had the advantage of the higher ground, and Ryan realized that this wasn't going to be the slick and easy execution that he wanted.

''Yesss!'' The mutie hissed out the warning as it suddenly charged.

The mutie's speed was alarming. Ryan barely had time to get the panga up to parry the blow.

The case-hardened steel rang out against the chipped wooden stock of the Kentucky musket. Ryan's arm was jarred clear to the shoulder by the force of the impact. The butt split lengthwise, exploding into white splinters.

The power of the crushing attack sent Ryan off balance. The mutie dropped its broken gun and lunged, its suckered hands grabbing at Ryan's arm and neck.

At such close contact, the long panga was useless and Ryan dropped it, concentrating on trying to hold off the grappling hands. He'd seen plenty of the horrific injuries caused by stickies. Their palms and fingers had tiny mouthlike suckers, almost like those on the arms of an octopus, but with an inhuman strength. They would grip on to smooth surfaces, like the armored flanks of war wags, enabling the stickies to climb effortlessly up the sides of speeding vehicles.

It was when it came to sucking contact with human flesh that the power of the stickies was so truly appalling.

A montage of hideous memories came shrieking into Ryan's mind.

A girl from a gaudy house near the Pecos River went outside to use the outhouse and was caught by a lurking stickie, who had ripped the skin from the length of her right arm, like peeling off an antique, elegant glove. Then the mutie had gripped her by the side of the throat and tugged away the deeper flesh, tearing the throbbing artery open.

One of the rear gunners from War Wag Two, who'd been a close friend of Abe, had been ambushed during a night camp in the Cascades. He'd stabbed his assailant and come staggering back into the circle of light from the crackling fire, screaming as if he were a doomed soul and holding his hands out in front of him like a blinded man.

A blinded man.

The devilish suckers had plucked both eyes from their sockets like boiled eggs from China cups, leaving raw pits that welled blood.

The Trader had spit out the stub of a cigar, grabbed his battered Armalite and shot the man twice through the chest, showing him a brutal mercy.

Worst had been a crèche in a first-floor room of a baron's fortress, in a ramshackle ville that had been perched halfway up a hillside on the western flank of the Green Mountains. When the sentry had checked in at ten o'clock there'd been a dozen babies sleeping peacefully.

When he looked in again an hour later there was a bloody shambles that had driven him stark mad on the spot.

Ryan had heard the noise and been one of the first into the vaulted chamber. The guard was a middle-aged man with grizzled hair, and he was sitting in a lake of crimson in the center of the room, paddling his fingers in the cooling blood, giggling secretly to himself.

The soft skin of the little babies had been particularly attractive to those stickies.

Ryan remembered all of that, and more, in the jagged nanosecond before he and the mutie rolled in the dusty earth.

Instantly there was pain, and a ripped-calico sound flooded his ears, coinciding with a burning sensation on his left wrist.

Ryan realized that the noise was his skin being shredded by the stickie's fingers. He tried to ram his knee into his opponent's groin, but the creature clamped its thighs together, stopping him.

With a great effort Ryan succeeded in wrenching his left arm away, throwing several short, stabbing punches into the mutie's midriff, solid, thudding blows that brought gasps of pain. The stickie wriggled a little away from him, giving Ryan a moment to gather breath.

The thing's face was close, its open mouth snapping toward Ryan's cheek. The fetid sour-sweet stench of rotten meat made Ryan gag. The stickie strained to reach him and for a moment the tip of its reptilian tongue brushed against Ryan's skin, almost making him yell out in revulsion.

In a violent reflex Ryan slammed his forehead into the stickie's face and felt the satisfying crunch of broken bone and pulverized cartilage. Blood gushed from its smashed nose, into his own mouth, hot, salty and with a slight undertaste of fish.

The Oregon kiss was enough to make his opponent wrench away, moaning in pain, hands up to its face.

"Broke it, fucker."

Ryan was aware of Jak and Krysty dancing anxiously around the fringes of the fight, both holding blasters, waiting for a chance to take out the stickie. But both were aware of Ryan's warning about keeping the noise down in case of other muties.

A small, thin-bladed knife was in a sheath at the small of Ryan's back, a reserve weapon that he rarely needed to use.

But he needed it now, and it slipped into his hand like a gift from an old friend.

As the stickie rolled away, bare feet digging in the sandy dirt for a purchase, Ryan went after it on hands and knees.

His single eye burned with a ferocious blood lust, and every part of his being was concentrated on killing the stickie. There was nothing on earth that would turn Ryan Cawdor aside from his purpose once his heart was set on death.

The mutie saw that in his face and tried to escape, blood streaking its mouth and chin, bubbling over its lips.

It flailed helplessly away from him, holding out both hands in a kind of supplication.

The knife darted in and out.

Each coldly struck blow severed tendons in both wrists, so that the stickie's suckered fingers curled helplessly in on the palms.

"No," it panted.

"Yes," Ryan snarled through teeth clenched so hard that they seemed on the edge of splintering.

The mutie made a last effort, trying for the top of the rise.

But Ryan was on it, the wickedly slim flensing knife slicing through the tendons behind both knees.

Now the crippled stickie was wriggling helplessly, thrashing like a gaffed salmon, mouth open and pink froth bubbling from its lips. A gasping, mewing noise seeped from deep within it.

Now the final chilling was easy.

Ryan stood, conscious of pain from his left arm, blood dripping from the tips of his fingers. He flexed the hand, making sure there was no major damage done.

The stickie half turned, so that the protruding eyes, watering with agony, drilled into Ryan's face. Beyond the awareness of defeat and imminent death, there was something more, something that Ryan couldn't identify but seemed, bizarrely, like a kind of triumph.

"Do it."

Ryan stooped and drew the ice-sharp edge of the tempered blade across the mutie's throat, cutting deep, slow and even. One hand locked into the raggedy hair to hold the head still, letting it fall into the dirt.

Wiping the dulled steel on the shirt to clean it off, he straightened.

"Now what?" Krysty asked.

"Go see J.B. and Mildred. Warn them that there's company in the hills."

Jak handed him the pistol and he holstered it, then picked up the panga and cleaned off the dirt on his pant leg.

The two bodies were lying still, the spilled blood already attracting a buzzing horde of speckled flies.

Ryan slung the rifle across his shoulder and looked around the clearing. The surrounding forest was quiet as a tomb.

"Let's go see the others," he said, leading the way to the top of the rise where he could look into the hidden deeps of the box canyon.

The day was fresh and clear, and he took in a long breath of the bright air as he reached the crest.

From below, there was no clue that such a large valley lay beyond. It widened out, and he could just see the glint of water through the scattered trees. And there were the dark rectangles of old buildings with shadowed windows.

A few horses grazed contentedly in a makeshift corral, and he could see a dozen or more cattle on a gently sloping meadow.

"There they are," he said.

J.B. was barely a hundred yards away from him, lying on his back, bare to the waist, his fedora covering his eyes. His chest was rising and falling with a steady regularity.

Mildred was nearer the far end of the canyon, walking away from them toward the ruined buildings of the Anasazi.

"Good job got before muties," Jak commented.

"Yeah." Even allowing for the fact that stickies couldn't normally shoot worth shit, with the long-barrel muskets they could probably have picked off the sleeping figure of the Armorer.

Krysty smiled. "Looks a true rustic idyll down there, doesn't it, lover?"

Ryan grinned. "Yeah. Son of a bitch'll be real surprised when we tell him how close he came to buying the farm."

The three friends stood close together, staring down into the canyon. Not one of them turned to look back along the trail.

Which turned out to be a triple-bad mistake.

Chapter Fourteen

"Don't turn around."

The voice was pleasant enough, a thin, rather reedy tenor.

Ryan's right hand moved toward the holster on his hip.

The voice spoke again. "Got eight blasters aimed at you, people. Range is only a dozen paces. You can all get to be dead real quick. Hand away from the handgun, mister."

Nobody moved. The only sound, apart from the light breeze that was making the top branches of the pines sway gently, was the thin patter of blood from Ryan's injured left arm.

"Now, you best drop all the weapons you have in the dirt behind you. I see a big cannon with the snow-haired kid."

"Don't call me 'kid,'" Jak said, not making any effort to obey the command to drop his Magnum.

"Call you what I like, kid. Put down the .357, you little dipshit."

There was a sudden crack of anger and command in the voice.

"Do it," Ryan said.

He unslung his rifle and laid it behind him without turning, then unholstered the SIG-Sauer and put it beside the bolt-action Steyr.

"Now the firehead."

Krysty dropped her .38 beside the other blasters.

It had briefly crossed Ryan's mind that whoever was there might be bluffing about the number of guns he had at his call. But you didn't survive in Deathlands by making wrong guesses in that kind of situation. The man would be a real stupe if he was bluffing. The voice didn't sound like it belonged to a real stupe.

But it didn't sound like any stickie Ryan Cawdor had ever encountered.

"Seems from the look of my brothers' bodies that you got some blades around. Let's see them down. Going to be stripped bare naked in a while, so no point trying to be clever. Just another way of getting to be dead. Drop your knives."

Ryan let the eighteen-inch panga thunk into the ground behind him. Jak allowed one of his throwing knives to fall from his fingers.

The voice laughed. "Stickies are stupes. That what you figure? Mebbe, mebbe not. But I tell you something... This one isn't stupe. Men like you won't just carry one throwing blade and one butcher's ax between you. You got a count of five to empty the pockets of the other knives, then I put a round through the lady's knee." He paused. "For starters."

If they were going to be strip-searched, then there

wasn't much point in trying to conceal any of their weapons.

"Do it, Jak." Ryan pulled out his own thin-bladed knife and watched more of the taped throwing blades appear by magic and join the armory behind them.

"Real good." The edge of tension was gone from the voice.

Ryan looked across the open ground toward the ancient Pueblo ruins. Mildred still walked away from them, and J.B. was still fast asleep.

If any of the group that now held them prisoner were to walk toward the top of the slope, then both the Armorer and Mildred would be seen and quickly butchered.

Ryan glanced over his shoulder. "Can we turn around now?"

"Sure. And come on down. Look like targets in a shooting gallery perched up there. What the hell is up there, anyways?"

"Just a sight more trees. Trail goes along the little stream then looks like it fades away into nothing."

"What I figured. Come on down, people."

They all turned and stepped over the blasters and knives, stopping in a line about ten feet from their captors.

There was a circle of seven stickies, all holding muskets. The eighth was obviously their leader, the one who'd been doing all the talking.

The others looked like the usual run of stickies—

boggling eyes and lank hair, with the suckers visible on palms and fingers, bare feet.

The leader was something else. He stood way over six feet, topping Ryan's six-two by about eight inches, and was so skinny that he looked like he would have to run around in a rainstorm to get himself wet. He wore a white shirt and an elegant brocade vest, with dark blue jeans. A golden medallion hung around his lean neck.

He was holding an Uzi machine pistol, identical to the one that was lying on the cropped turf at J.B.'s side.

The stickie's hair was long and luxuriantly blond, so thick and curling that Ryan immediately suspected that the mutie was wearing a wig.

His eyes didn't protrude as much as normal stickies, and they were almost almond-shaped. He was smiling, showing that he had no teeth at all between the fleshy lips.

"Name's Charlie."

"This is Krysty, Jak and I'm—"

The smile vanished like the last smear of sunlight off a mountaintop.

"You. Man with the patch who rode shotgun with the Trader. Ryan Cawdor! Never forget a name or a face. You and me'll have some talking."

Ryan remembered.

Chapter Fifteen

The time would be about right. Charlie looked to be in his early twenties, and Ryan's memory put the happening about ten or eleven years ago.

It had been up near the Darks, near some ragged-ass ville, centered on an old church with a dome of weathered green copper. Name of the place had vanished, but the incident and the stickie brat with curly yellow hair came flooding back from the past.

Abe had been involved, tall, skinny Abe, with the lugubrious sense of humor and the drooping mustache, hair that he generally used to wear tied back in a ponytail. He'd done mostly jobs around War Wag One. Started off as helper to Loz and the rest of the cooks, then graduated to rear gunner.

And it had been the time of...

"Gert Wolfram," Charlie, said, face as bleak as iced marble. "And the one called himself the Magus, Warlock, Sorcerer. Names not even worth the trouble of forgetting."

Names and men that Ryan himself would never be able to forget.

The Magus. That was most common of his three names.

Sometime in the past he'd suffered an appalling injury. Half of his face was missing, the spaces filled with aluminum and flesh-colored plastic. His eyes were hidden behind steel shells.

His reputation was linked with stickies.

He'd go out into the bleak wildernesses where the muties congregated and bring them back alive, then sell them to the traveling freak master, Gert Wolfram, three hundred and fifty pounds of cherubic evil. He was ringmaster in his own macabre circus that toured the filthy frontier villes where the writ of decency never ran.

The stickies were an integral part of Wolfram's tented horror show. They'd be prodded into fighting against each other, or against bears or cougars or mangy wolves. Wolfram would also arrange cheap displays of erratic pyrotechnics whose explosions and multicolored flaring fires would drive the drugged stickies into a frenzy.

People loved it.

Ryan was trying to remember what had happened to the Magus and to Gert Wolfram when Charlie, the stickies' leader, interrupted his train of thought.

"You recall me, don't you, Cawdor?"

Ryan stood still, left arm lifted across his chest to try to check the bleeding. "Yeah. I recollect the time our paths crossed."

"Our...paths...crossed." The tall mutie nodded. "Way a blood-eyed norm like you would think about it, Cawdor. Bet you a hatful of jack you don't recollect the butchered innocents."

"I remember we came across one of the hunting parties of the Magus. Chilled them. They had a group of…" He hesitated.

"Stickies is the word you're struggling to avoid, Cawdor."

"Yeah. A group of stickies. Trader was ready to set them free."

Charlie's narrow smile vanished. "A 'group,' Cawdor! It was a family. You think stickies don't have fucking families!" Controlling his anger, he dropped Krysty a mocking half bow. "Forgive my language, Firehead, but that was a family. It was my whole family. My father, my mother, three older brothers. Two aunts and five uncles. And me. I was nine summers and eight winters old, Cawdor."

The valley had been dark, steep-sided. The war wags had camped a half mile away, near a still lake where fish jumped. The heavily armed guards of the Magus lay where they'd been shot, the blood still trickling into the leaf mold.

And the stickies huddled together as Abe had struck off their chains.

"We'd have let you go," Ryan said.

"But you didn't."

"No."

Charlie looked around at his silent group of followers. "No, they didn't let us go. They chilled everyone. Except for the little yellow-haired boy. They left him there, surrounded by corpses, his leg and arm broken.''

Ryan bit his lip. He could remember the scene, remember why the massacre had happened. But he figured there wasn't much point in trying to explain to this unusual stickie how it had been. Charlie obviously had his own embittered, impressed memory and nothing would change that.

''Why did you and Trader do that, Cawdor?''

''One of your women had a knife. Several of you backed her when she cut Abe. Started a chilling fight. We lost two good men there.''

''And all I lost was twelve of my family. *All* my family, Cawdor.''

He remembered the rattle of firearms, the screams and then the silence, broken only by the gasps of the dying and the moans of the wounded.

And a little boy crying.

''You didn't give us any choice, Charlie. No fireblasted choice at all.''

''We'll see. Talk more when we get back to our camp. You say there's nothing over the ridge?'' The question was asked with an absence of real interest, as though he were thinking about something else.

''Nothing.''

''Then we'll go. But first we'll check out you don't have any hideaways. If you have, then you're all dead meat. Now and here.''

Ryan was finding it hard to come to terms with what was going on.

Stickies were triple stupes.

Everyone knew that.

Vengeful and murderous, with about as much sense of organization as a confederation of decapitated roosters.

Now this one, Charlie, seemed to be a whole lot brighter than the average citizen of Deathlands, and he ran a tight patrol with a facade of quasilegal organization.

It didn't make any sort of sense.

Ryan started, slowly and reluctantly, to peel off his clothes.

"See one of them did you harm, Cawdor." Charlie pointed at the bleeding wound with the stubby muzzle of the Uzi.

"Tore some skin. Way stickies do, Charlie. You know that."

There was a snarl of anger from two or three of the watchful group, but the tall figure silenced them with a look. "You talk big now, Cawdor. Won't last too long."

They'd moved some little distance from the slope that hid the box canyon from view, but Ryan still had a cold dread that Mildred or J.B. would come strolling into view and get blasted into rags of eternity.

"Quicker with the stripping. All three of you, quicker."

Ryan's eye caught Jak's glance.

The albino was stooped, fiddling with the laces of his combat boots. He'd somehow managed to sidle himself over to the edge of the group, only four or five quick steps away from the dark fringe of the surrounding forest.

The boy made sure Ryan was watching him, then moved his right thumb a half inch toward the trees and repeated the movement.

Ryan nodded his head very slightly.

That was all it took.

He looked up at Krysty, seeing that she'd also caught the infinitely subtle exchange.

She immediately pulled off her shirt, revealing a white cotton bra with half cups that seemed to barely contain her splendid breasts. Her nipples were pressing at the taut material like summer cherries.

Ryan knew that there wasn't a hope in hades of all three of them making it. Charlie held the Uzi steady on his own belt buckle. Only one had a chance, and that had to be the local boy.

Jak.

"All the way," one of the stickies grunted.

Krysty reached behind her, making the bra even tighter, then loosened the catch, dropping the wisp of cotton to her feet.

She stooped to pull off the dark blue Western boots with the silver falcons and slipped in the dirt. She fell flat on her back, crying out in shock, her firm breasts filling everyone's eyes.

Ryan was ready for it, but even he didn't spot the moment that Jak Lauren made his move. One second the slim figure was standing there among them, then he wasn't.

But there hadn't seemed to be any intervening stage of movement.

Charlie saw it first. He spun and held down the trigger of the machine pistol, the stream of high velocity lead missing Krysty's tumbled figure by eighteen inches.

"Get him!"

In his patchwork jacket, the slim teenager was mercury in motion, darting between the close-packed trees, disappearing.

Ryan stood very still, knowing that the anger of the stickies' leader might easily mean instant, summary execution for Krysty and himself.

Four of the patrol lumbered into the shadowed darkness, one firing his musket with a dull, flat sound.

"They won't get him, will they?" Charlie reached into his pocket and calmly reloaded the Uzi.

"I doubt it."

The stickie sniffed. "Well, now he'll go and hunt up some friends and come back here to try to rescue you. We'll be long gone. Shame he did that. Won't make it easier for you two."

"That's the way it goes," Krysty said, sitting in the dirt, not making any effort to cover herself.

"Tell you the truth, it makes it harder for me. These others—" he gestured to the watching circle of stickies, and the shamefaced quartet that was picking its way back through the trees "—depend on me beating norms. Proving I'm better. The snowhead fucked that up for me.''

"I'm real sorry," Ryan said, wondering how far the noise of the shooting would have carried.

"Strip off now. Let's have that over. Then we get moving.''

A moment later Ryan didn't make any resistance to the search for hidden weapons, closing off his surging anger.

Krysty also shut down a part of her mind, so that the probing, clawed fingers and the suckered hands were only a dull sensation. The sniggering and the intrusion into the secret places of her body passed.

As all things did.

Chapter Sixteen

Fire any blaster within a mile of a sleeping John Barrymore Dix, and he'll not only wake up, but he'll be jerked from the land of warm sand with the certain identification of the make and type of the weapon, with a close guess at its caliber.

Which was why he had come to instantly alert consciousness, but in a state of some considerable confusion.

"Nine-millimeter Uzi," his infallible mind told him, a message that was passed on to his lips. But his hand had already picked up his own blaster and was holding it ready.

A nine-millimeter Uzi.

"Who?"

On his feet, crouched, his memory analyzed the sounds he'd heard—a burst of rapid fire, ripping through the stillness, but a little muffled. At least a quarter mile away.

"Farther?"

Behind him, Mildred was by the ancient ruins where they were camped. She'd heard the noise of the shooting and had spun around.

Across the high-walled canyon the cattle and other

stock had stopped eating and lifted their heads with a mild curiosity.

Mildred was about to call out to J.B. when she realized that might not be the best thing to do.

Now the Armorer was on the move, holding the blaster at the hip, stooped over as if he were afraid of catching his hat on low branches. When he saw her he waved an urgent hand, motioning for the woman to get inside, under cover.

In the distance they both heard the flat sound of another gun being fired.

Even Mildred was experienced enough to recognize the distinctive noise of a black powder musket being discharged. She drew her revolver.

J.B. was closing fast. He glanced behind as he ran, but the ridge that closed the box canyon from the rest of the forest was still deserted. And there was no other way that anyone could come at them.

"Got you covered, John!" Mildred shouted, the target pistol already cocked.

J.B. was out of breath when he dived in through the narrow doorway, into the coolness of the building. He sat breathing hard, took off his spectacles and wiped them slowly.

"Still nobody?" he asked.

"Not a sight and not a sound," she replied. "Think it could be Jak or Christina?"

"No. That was an Uzi. Certain-sure. Whatever it is, won't be real good news. I can promise you that, Mildred."

"We stay here?"

J.B. managed a smile for her. "No place else I'd rather be."

Time passed.

The stock had resumed its grazing, and birds had come back to the canyon.

Mildred and J.B. had eaten a snatched meal of potato salad and jerked beef, with water from the spring at the side of the ruins.

It was about two hours after the burst of automatic fire that J.B. spotted someone moving, a slight figure, darting elusively among the trees.

"It's Jak," he said.

It took less than five minutes to hear the whole story, another two minutes to decide that Mildred should go back at her best speed to warn the others while J.B. and Jak started to try to pick up the trail of the stickies and their prisoners.

Chapter Seventeen

One of the things that life in Deathlands had taught Ryan Cawdor was to always try to look for the positive factors in any situation.

He and Krysty had been allowed to get dressed again, but their hands had been tied behind their backs with a brutal efficiency.

The best thing to weigh in the balance was the fact that they were both still alive and relatively uninjured.

The blood from the torn skin on Ryan's left arm had been seeping to such an extent that Charlie had eventually had to order a stop and have it bandaged with a strip of material torn from a shirt.

The pair wasn't entirely without a weapon. Ryan had casually draped his white silk scarf around his neck as he finished dressing, and none of the stickies had made a move to take it away from him.

No one had noticed that both ends were weighted, making it into a lethally effective garotte.

As Ryan and Krysty stumbled on, the barrels of the muskets jabbing them in the small of the back, Ryan tried hard to tick off some more positive factors about their position.

Jak was alive, and he'd quickly get news of their

predicament to J.B. and Mildred. The Armorer would send Mildred down the trail to Christina, Doc and Dean and bring them back at double time.

And J.B. and Jak would be coming after them.

After that Ryan ran out of good things to think about.

STICKIES WERE NOTORIOUS for having great physical stamina, and this group was no exception. They pushed westward, up a snaking trail that crossed over a bare crest of sunbaked rock, pausing briefly by a stream that dashed itself down a wall of undercut stone, falling in a rainbow spray.

Ryan and Krysty stood below it, faces upturned, drinking the icy water. Both took care not to take in too much.

During the late afternoon they stopped again, by a rotting wooden bridge with rusted supports.

"Sit over there," Charlie ordered. "You get some jerky."

"Much farther?" Ryan asked.

The mutie's toothless mouth stretched into a smile. "That's for us to know and you to find out, Cawdor."

He wandered off and sat with his men, joining them in a detailed investigation of the weapons that they'd captured. Ryan's pistol caused most interest to the group.

Charlie turned with the blaster in his hand. "What can you tell us about *my* new blaster, Cawdor?"

"What do you want to know?"

"Everything."

Ryan shook his head to disturb the horde of tiny flies that were buzzing around his face.

"Model P-226, 9 mm SIG-Sauer."

"Fifteen rounds?"

"Push button mag release. Baffle silencer's built-in, but it's getting past its best now. It weighs a touch over twenty-five and a half ounces. Overall length's a little under eight inches. Barrel close on four and a half inches long. Anything else you want to know about it?"

The stickie laughed. "You know your blaster, Cawdor. Heard word of you over the years. You kept rising to the surface like a dead fish. All over Deathlands. I knew our paths would cross one day. Knew it. And I was right."

Ryan didn't reply, and Charlie turned back to his men.

Krysty leaned close to him. "If I used the power I could easily break the cords."

"Then what?"

"Free you."

He looked at her. "Both be dead. Have to wait, lover. If they leave us tonight...or at their camp. Mebbe risk it then. But you know that using the power leaves you drained for hours."

"You might make it."

"Forget it."

There was a long silence between them. One of the stickies brought a handful of the dried meat and dropped it in the dirt, giggling as they had to roll on their stomachs to gnaw at it.

After he'd rejoined the others, Krysty spoke quietly, mumbling through a mouthful of beef.

"Jak and J.B. must be after us."

"Difficult."

"What?"

"Difficult to track us. This skinny bastard is good. Taken us a quarter mile or more over bare rock. Won't leave much of a trail. Crossed the same stream three or four times. Walked along through the water for a ways. I figure that they'll have a triple-hard time trying to follow us. And they'll be real slow, having to keep backtracking and checking all the time. No way they'll move as fast as us."

"But they'll find us in the end."

"Course they will."

The pause was so minimal that an outsider wouldn't have noticed it. But Krysty did.

"Try again, lover. Fails to convince."

"Fireblast! Odds are they'll find us, but it could be way too late."

Charlie and the stickies were standing, ready to move on again.

MILDRED POURED a pitcher of water over her head, dropping to hands and knees, exhausted by the run back to the main camp.

Dean was already pacing nervously around, eager

to start off in pursuit of the stickies that had taken his father.

Christina had merely nodded as the black woman panted out her story, sitting and waiting patiently until she'd finished.

"Knew this would happen," she said. Her voice was flat, bitterness coming dry and hard from every word. "Soon as Ryan Cawdor came back here. Things were good until then."

Doc had been leaning silently against the trunk of a sun-warmed spruce, shaking his head at the gravity of the news. But at Christina's anger he stood, stamping the ferrule of his lion-headed cane in the dirt.

"Forgive me, my dear, but I fear that your concern has made you less than fair."

"What?"

"I concede that your life with the young man has been one that has paralleled Shangri-la itself. But you can hardly blame Ryan for the misfortunes that have struck in the past couple of weeks."

"Oh, yeah? Wrong, Doc. I *can* blame him. Just watch me."

"These stickies did not come to New Mexico to hunt down Ryan, did they?"

She looked down at the ground, moving the surgical boot she wore against a tiny yellow-and-white flower. "Things were good with Jak and me until he came again."

"And they'll be good again," Mildred said. "Course they will."

"Ryan Cawdor," Christina grated. "Jak thinks he's like something between an angel of death and a substitute father. The best thing the Good Lord made since he invented the chambered revolver."

Dean was shuffling his feet anxiously. "Dad does good," he said.

"Sure. Count the men he's chilled good. Women he's widowed good. Little ones that he's orphaned real good. Houses burned good."

Doc pointed the sword stick at Christina. "Allow me to remind you of the somewhat selective nature of your little speech, Miss Ballinger. Or, Mrs. Lauren. Cast your mind back to your life with your sweet-natured father and your fine brothers."

"All right, Doc, all right." Her face showed her remembered pain.

"Ryan chilled them good. Liberated you good. Risked his life good. And in the time I've had the honor of knowing him, he has done a very great deal that is undeniably good."

Christina hauled herself to her feet and nodded, lifting her eyes to meet Doc's. "You're right and I'm not. But I'm pregnant and you're not. And my husband might come back dead."

"We'll all go together, my dear," Doc said, his voice now gentle.

"Sure. Yeah, sure."

EVEN AFTER THE BETTER PART of a day with them, Ryan still found it hard to reconcile himself to the idea of there being intelligent, capable, organized stickies.

The sun was setting, and they'd covered about fifteen miles over tough terrain. And Charlie had constantly been taking precautions to ensure that any pursuit would be slow and laborious. Again and again they would detour to walk over exposed granite, avoiding the softer paths.

Each time they came to water they would deliberately try to pick their way along the center, sometimes altering the direction they were moving in to ensure that anyone trailing them would waste a lot of time.

Once Ryan pretended to stumble, hoping to leave some clue for Jak and J.B.

Charlie took him by the arm, gripping him by the elbow, suckered fingers digging in with frightening power.

"Try that again, Cawdor, and I'll use my hands on the woman's breasts. Think she'd look as good without any nipples?"

Ryan didn't try it again.

Chapter Eighteen

They passed a large open space, with light gravel partly covered with thimbleberry bushes and sagebrush. Beyond it the trail meandered past a row of burned-out buildings so totally destroyed that it was impossible to even guess at what they might have been.

Beyond that was another, much more substantial ruin, the windows missing, dark marks of smeared carbon showing that it had also been ravaged long ago by a ferocious fire.

"It was a place called a Visitor Center," Charlie explained.

"Seen them in the old wilderness parks," Ryan replied.

The last dying daggers of crimson sunlight bounced across from the high sandstone cliffs opposite, reflecting from the dangling golden medallions on the hairless chest of the leader of the stickies.

Krysty had moved a few steps away from Ryan, shepherded by the guards, leaving him alone with the skeletally tall mutie.

"What's going down?" Ryan asked quietly.

"How's that?"

"What happens now?"

"We go to the houses."

"Then?"

"Meet the rest of the community."

"Come on."

"What?"

"Fireblast! You know what I'm talking about, Charlie."

"There'll be eats for all."

Ryan felt the pulse of anger beating at his temples, and the long scar that seamed his face began to throb.

"When do we get chilled?"

"Ah. Get your drift now, Cawdor. Good question. Real good."

The toothless mouth was stretched in a beaming, God-bless-you smile, the protruding eyes half-closed in delight. The stickie's whole body was tense, like someone straining toward a distant orgasm.

Only at that moment did Ryan realize the total hatred the mutie felt for him.

"Krysty doesn't have anything to do with the cards lying between you and me, Charlie." He knew how barren and futile the words were, even before they left his mouth, and knew what the response would be.

"She's your woman, Cawdor. Walks in your shadow. Sleeps in your bed. Fucks you. Eats with you. Her life is your life, Cawdor, and her death will be your cold death."

Ryan took in a slow, deep breath, fighting down the blood rage. "Yeah. I understand."

Charlie patted him on the shoulder. "But first you get to eat and meet some other...visitors, I guess they are."

"Why not chill us right off?"

"Like I said, they—" he gestured toward the armed men that ringed Krysty "—back me, long as I chill norms. More norms I chill, more they think I'm close to a god. If I come up with good way of doing the chilling, then they like it even more. You'll go out with a big bang, Cawdor. That I promise you. Real big bang."

DURING HIS ODYSSEY through Deathlands, Ryan had visited any number of villes and camps, from the richest to the poorest. He'd also seen stickie settlements.

They were filthy and squalid, with oily fires and open middens. Huts leaked raw sewage, with rotting food in stinking heaps. Lousy mongrels fought over scraps, and naked children tormented those weaker than themselves.

Charlie's small empire wasn't anything like that.

There was a winding trail down from the ruined buildings, the lush vegetation on either side cropped back. In the steepest parts it became a sequence of crumbling steps.

Ahead of them they could see a towering cliff, looming over the ravine. The farther they descended, the darker it became.

Charlie pointed toward the wall of orange rock,

smeared with chemical stains of black and gray. "You know that this remained hidden for hundreds and hundreds of years. Local Indians were fearful of it. Bad place. Wasn't found until the middle part of the 1900s. Cowboys were chasing lost cattle. One fell over the edge and broke his neck. Others came down and found this."

He waved the Uzi as they reached a wider curve in the track, gesturing toward the amazing sight below them.

It was like a town, almost buried under a gigantic overhang, a hundred feet or so from the base of the cliff.

At first glance, there seemed to be a limitless number of little dwellings. But a second, slower look showed that there were about forty of them. Many were linked together, some in ruins.

There were plenty of cooking fires burning as well as dozens of oil lamps, hanging in the gloom like golden eyes.

"How many you got in this place?" Krysty asked, hardly able to believe the organization of what she was seeing.

"Last count there were ninety able men and forty-four women. Eighteen little ones." There was a note of bitterness in his voice. "Stickies aren't great at breeding, Firehead. Chromosome chains are faulty. Some young doctor told us that. Just before we filled his ass with black powder and blew his cock over the mountain."

Now the commune had seen them.

Ryan had checked on security, spotting silhouettes on the cliff top, against the pale yellow sky. And he was certain there'd been other sentries in among the trees.

There was whooping and cheers. Someone stirred up the largest of the fires so that a great fountain of bright sparks went whirling into the evening sky. The sight produced even louder yells from the crowd of stickies.

"Still like flames," Ryan said.

"Bred into us in the bone," Charlie replied. "Explosions, lights and flames. Not even I can stop that."

RYAN AND KRYSTY had their ropes cut, but they were replaced with old steel handcuffs that clicked shut, keeping their wrists bound in front of them.

"Got them from a traveling gaudy wagon we took a month ago," Charlie told them proudly. "Twenty sets of cuffs. Portable gallows. Leg stretchers. Plenty of high boots with spurs. Whips of all shapes and sizes. Stuff I never seen the like of. Couldn't figure what it was for. By then the gaudy sluts were all chilled, so I couldn't ask them."

Older women stickies brought them food in wooden dishes. The suckered fingers released their hold on the platters with a strange, moist sound, like a roomful of little children all kissing their hands at once.

The meal was a thick stew of what tasted a lot like

rabbit. But the meat had been ripped and crushed apart so that flesh, gristle and bones were all a mangled gruel.

There were sweet potatoes with it and refried beans, livened with some ferocious silver-green jalapeños. Thick pottery mugs of water washed down the spiced, mediocre food.

"Finished?" Charlie asked, breaking the silence that had lasted through most of the meal. "Good. Then I think it's time that you met your fellow guests. Come on."

"What about his arm?"

The swollen eyes turned slowly to her. "What's that, Firehead?"

"The name's Krysty Wroth. All right?"

He faked a yawn, tongue protruding, showing that it also had a tiny ring of suckers on its upper surface. "Not all right. What do you want?"

"His arm. Needs washing and someone to look at it for him."

"I'll look at it." He grabbed Ryan's left arm, making the one-eyed man wince in pain. "I'm looking at it. Got a bandage. So what?"

Krysty's green eyes drilled into him. "So you get someone to take off the cloth and check the wound underneath."

"Too much trouble. Time he gets gangrene he'll be dead meat."

For a single, scary moment, Ryan thought that Krysty was going to lose all her self-control and use the power of the Earth Mother to break the thick steel links of the cuffs. Then he knew that she would have ripped the stickie's chest open and torn out his beating, pulsing heart.

And no force on earth could have stopped her from doing it, though it would have meant both of their deaths.

"No," he said, as quiet as the whisper of the midnight wind through the ivy on a fallen tomb.

She turned to him, ignoring Charlie with his machine pistol and the ring of stickie guards. "No," she agreed.

The lean figure, with his grotesque mop of yellow hair, advanced to stand right by her, face lowered to glare into her eyes.

But Krysty didn't even flinch, even when his anger showered her with sticky beads of spittle.

"You fuck little bitch! You were threatening me with your..." He stammered as words failed him completely.

"What did I threaten you with? I got cuffs on my wrists. You got twenty or thirty armed men close by. How come you're scared of *me*?"

"Me scared of *you!*" The laugh was hollow and unconvincing. "I'm more scared of something I find stuck to the bottom of my feet after I've been walking in the woods."

Krysty grinned delightedly, sensing his weakness and his fear of her. "All talk's cheap. But triple-stupe stickie talk's cheapest of all."

His left hand flashed out like a cornered rattler, gripping the woman by the jaw, fingers clamping onto both cheeks.

Ryan took a half step forward, ready to try to kick the stickie in the balls. But the barrel of a musket was rammed into his stomach, taking his breath.

Krysty was moaning in a frail, frightened voice. Charlie's hand was squeezing harder, puckering her face, making the bones of her jaw creak under the dreadful pressure.

Ryan watched helplessly as a thin trickle of blood began to seep between the spread fingers. He was tempted to threaten the stickies' leader, but he knew how empty and helpless it would sound. Better to stay quiet.

"Don't...don't...don't...don't...." Charlie was almost chanting the word, more blood oozing over Krysty's neck, down onto her shirt. The tendons in his wrist were as tight as rods of ivory, quivering with the effort of hurting the woman.

"You chill her right now, and you best chill me too," Ryan said, winning the fight to keep his voice steady.

"Norms like you—" the tension in his arm eased as he began to relax his grip "—make me fucking want to puke. But this time...you go the long walk when I want you to, not before."

The suckers peeled away, each removing a thin sliver of skin from Krysty's cheeks, leaving them dappled with tiny circles of scarlet. Her long fiery hair curled forward over her face as though trying to conceal the bitter wounds.

She sniffed and spit in the dirt, missing the curling nails of Charlie's bare feet by a couple of inches.

"Want to take the cuffs off me and try it again?" she asked loudly.

IT WAS FULL DARK and the night was growing colder. Far above them Ryan heard the swishing sound of wings and stared upward into the blackness.

"Bats," Charlie said, recovered a little from his eyeballing with Krysty.

Around them, the camp was readying itself to settle down. A small boy scampered by, casting a frightened glance toward Ryan, who noticed that the child had a hideously deformed face, with his nose missing and the mouth twisted through ninety degrees.

"Keep our guests in what the Navaho, round these parts, call kivas," Charlie said.

There were a number of the circular pits, mostly ten feet across, topped with heavy iron bars. A solitary stickie squatted by each one, cradling a musket.

"Put them together in this one," Charlie ordered. Another of his men was holding a flaming torch, so that the prisoners in the pit could see the faces on the two newcomers.

"Holy shit on a sugar shaker! It's Ryan!"

Chapter Nineteen

There was no time to even catch a glimpse of the speaker. A hand was laid between Ryan's shoulder blades and he was shoved down into the kiva. Someone tried to break his fall, then Krysty was pushed on top of him. He opened his mouth and found it filled with the toe of her boot.

There was a metallic slamming sound as the heavy grille was dropped in on top of them, then the sound of feet moving away.

The light disappeared.

"Fireblast!" Ryan pushed Krysty's foot away from his face and felt hands helping him to get upright, lowering him gently to the slightly uneven floor of the deep pit.

"Stand still till you get used to the size of it," someone advised him.

"Them stickie pricks goin' to choke us to death with more fuckers," a third voice whined.

"Everyone keep still." The first, hoarse voice spoke again, with a snap to it.

A tiny, distant bell rang in one of the back rooms of Ryan's memory.

"I know you," he said.

"Yeah."

"Way back when."

A laugh. "You could say that."

"Trader?"

"Gettin' warm, old friend. You and me knew stickies, Ryan." The voice was so diminished that it barely rose above a strained whisper.

"Abe," he said. Not a question anymore. This time it was a simple statement.

"Yeah. Abe."

"We been talking about you a lot of times over the months."

The whining voice came riding in over the top, like a malfunctioning saw cutting across a sheet of plate glass.

"You guys shut the fuck up and let's all sit down again. Not that it's easy with even more jammed into the hole."

A woman spoke. "Why don't you shut your mouth and give your ass a rest, Harold."

There was a muttered chorus of approval.

"He's got a point, Helga," Abe said. "Everyone sit down slow and careful. Ryan, you and your woman—sorry, don't recollect her name—come this side of the kiva so's we can talk quiet."

"Name's Krysty Wroth, Abe. Real good to see you again."

"You was nearly last thing I ever seen. It was you holding me in the Darks."

RYAN HAD MOVED to stand where Krysty cradled Abe in her arms. The arrow, with its barbed tip, still stuck through his throat at a grotesque angle, blood trickling from both sides. The shaft was made of some sort of aluminum compound. It was streaked crimson. The feathers were the same kind that they'd seen on the warning totems.

Henn had looked up. "Bad, Ryan. Bad."

Abe had fought for breath, fingers moving convulsively on Krysty's sleeve, her bright red hair framing his pale face. His eyes had flickered, seeking Ryan, finding him.

"Doesn't hurt…" His voice was muffled with the blood that was now seeping through his lips. "But a blasted arrow, for nuke's sake. Be funny if…" He'd coughed, a great gout of arterial scarlet.

And they'd left him.

That was the way. If Abe had been an inch or so nearer death, or if the attacking Indians had been a little closer, then Ryan would have put a bullet through the wounded man's skull.

But there was always a chance.

Even for someone who had the Grim Reaper's scythe laid across his neck.

And Abe had pulled through.

THERE WAS shuffling and scuffling until everyone was sitting again.

"How many in here, Abe?" Ryan asked.

"You make numbers nine and ten," Harold replied.

"You ever say anything without sounding like you're about to burst into tears?" Ryan asked.

"Yeah. Fuck you!"

"Better." There was a ripple of nervous laughter before the dark pit settled into stillness.

"Abe?"

"Ryan, you're going to try to shoot off at the mouth about leaving me to die up in the Darks. Please don't."

"You know how it was."

The chuckle turned itself into a deep-throated coughing fit. "'Course. Do the same for you, someday. Live by the Trader's rules and you damned often finished up getting chilled by the same rules. You did what you had to. I hid up. Managed to push the arrow clear through my neck. Never pull it through with a barbed hunting tip to it. Bled some. Slept some. Here I am. You can hear it hasn't done much for my throat, though."

"You never were one of the Lord's chosen singers, Abe," Ryan said, grinning in the darkness. Despite the intense danger of their position in the heart of the stickies' camp, his heart was lifted by meeting again with the tall mustached man.

"Where did Charlie catch you?"

Ryan dropped his voice. "You didn't recognize him, Abe?"

"No. Why? Kind of odd for a stickie, but I never seen him before."

"You have."

"Truly?"

"He knew me. Lucky that he didn't recognize you as well."

"Don't recall. Stickie that walks and talks like a norm is something special. Thought I'd have remembered him."

"Little kid with straw hair. Party we rescued from Gert Wolfram's gang not far from Fishmouth's bar in the Darks."

There was something in the darkness that might have been a chuckle. "That was little Charlie, was it? If I'd known I'd have slit the bastard's neck from ear to ear."

"Guard coming," the woman hissed.

The circular kiva fell silent.

There were feet slapping bare on the stones above them and the sensation of someone standing there, listening closely.

Abe's face was near to Ryan's, his mustache tickling his ear. "Hope the sucker-fingered bastard doesn't piss on us again. Did it last night."

But the feet went away again.

Harold whispered into the velvet blackness. "Can we all get some rest now?"

Nobody argued.

IT WAS COLD in the underground cell, which was hewn from the bare sandstone, but the press of bodies checked the temperature from dropping too low.

As the others slipped into sleep, Ryan stayed awake, trying to marshal his thoughts, trying to make plans to cover any contingency. The way it looked was that Charlie would keep his word and use their execution as an example of his own power over norms. And with the force he seemed to have at his disposal, it would be difficult to do too much about it.

If things came down to the wire, then Ryan would at least try to take the leader of the stickies with him. Even if it meant tearing his carotid artery open with his teeth.

He'd been in many tight spots in his life and he was still alive.

But he recalled something the Trader had said to him as they'd lain under a towering sycamore not long before the sick old man had done his disappearing act. The familiar black stogie had been sending coils of smoke wreathing up into the evening air.

The Trader had used it to gesture to the sylvan calm around them. "Been a good day," he'd said. "Odd when you think that we're all bound to die sometime."

Ryan finally closed his eye and entered the darkness with the pessimistic thought that this might, at last, be the time for him and Krysty.

Chapter Twenty

Ryan's wounded left arm was still tender. Krysty peeled off the makeshift bandage, trying to see how it looked in the gloom of the kiva.

"Seems to be healing."

He flexed his fingers, tightening the muscles of the forearm. "Stiff."

She lowered her head, sniffing to try to catch any taint of infection. "I think it's clean, lover." She wrapped the bandage around it again.

The small, circular scabs on Krysty's face from Charlie's attention were already almost vanished. She healed faster than anyone Ryan had ever come across.

Now there was enough light to see their fellow captives.

Abe was the oldest there, looking much as he had when they last saw him. There was a scar the size of a nickel on one side of his neck, and a larger cicatrix on the other side of where the Indian arrow had been pushed all the way through. He still had a droopy mustache and wore his graying hair tied back in a long ponytail.

He seemed a little skinnier than Ryan remembered him.

"Introduce you to the others," he said, coughing hoarsely.

There was Harold. He was chubby, in his late twenties and had a pair of battered spectacles hanging from a cord around his neck. He'd been a traveling seller of candies and had been caught by a patrol of the stickies a week earlier.

"Should be some sort of baron's sec men around here to rescue us," he complained.

Ryan sighed at the man's stupidity. "No baron," he said. "No sec patrols. No rescue."

"Been telling him that for days, but the stupe clings to his fancies," Helga said.

"Stupe yourself!"

Helga was around forty, with salt-and-pepper hair that was scraped back off her face and tied in a tight knot. She had the freckled, hard complexion of someone who spent most of her life outdoors.

She'd run a spread about eighty miles to the west and had actually met Christina and Jak Lauren a couple of times.

There were five other prisoners.

Danny, who had worked as ramrod on Helga's sheep farm, was in his early thirties, tall and lean. He'd broken his left ankle trying to escape from the stickies' attack, and was suffering constant pain from it.

Bob Leonard was a prematurely bald man of twenty-five, who'd been trapping beaver in the high country to the northwest. He'd been attacked by a grizzly when he was fifteen and bore dreadful facial scars, including damage to his mouth that made his speech difficult to understand.

His wife, Dorina, looked no more than twelve years old, yet she claimed she'd lost three children to a cholera outbreak up in Silver City. The stickies had already raped her.

"Sixty-seven times," she said in her little voice. "I keep score so's I don't forget."

Her brother, Red Folsom, was sometimes called Bitter Creek Folsom. He'd been a part of the team of trappers and hunters that had stumbled into a ranging patrol of stickies. He was a bluff, strongly built man with chestnut hair and had a finger missing from his left hand.

"Lost it in one of my own beaver traps," he explained with a quiet laugh.

The rest of their group had been butchered in the initial attack by the muties.

The last of the stickies' prisoners was a traveling preacher, the Very Reverend Joe-Bob Jarman. He was six feet three inches tall, with white hair that touched his shoulders, and wore a heavy suit of black material.

"All a part of the rich and mysterious pattern of the Lord Jesus," he'd said as Abe introduced him to Ryan and Krysty.

"How do you figure that?" Ryan asked.

"I am a flask being tested in the white heat of the furnace of wickedness. These stickies are my own personal temptation. Find if my faith comes up to the mark.''

''And does it?''

''Of course, Brother Cawdor.'' Ryan knew from previous experience that one of the sure signs of the religious crazies that festered in parts of Deathlands was that they always called you ''Brother.''

''And I shall meet their every challenge,'' he added.

''They're going to kill you, Reverend,'' Krysty said. ''Chill us all.''

A patronizing smile touched the tall man's face. ''You will fall, Sister Krysty, but on the third day I shall rise again and I will sit upon the right hand of the Lord of Hosts.''

''Wish I could be there to see it, Reverend,'' Ryan replied.

AROUND THEM they could hear the familiar sounds of a large camp waking up.

Ryan sat close to Krysty, his feet sticking out toward the center of the cramped kiva. If Charlie collected any more prisoners it would be unbearably crowded.

He looked around at their eight fellow captives, trying to weigh them up, ready for the moment when concerted action *might* save some of their lives. He had no idea of how, when or where that moment might come. Or whether it would come at all.

But he had to be ready.

In case.

Abe would do real well. Couldn't look for anyone much better to stand at your shoulder when the full-metal jackets started flying.

There were two or three other good possibilities for when the shit hit the fan.

Bitter Creek Folsom was a man who seemed like he could look after himself in any tight corner. Same with his younger colleague, Bob Leonard, though the man's problems with speech could prove difficult.

If it wasn't for his broken ankle, Danny would also have taken right and center in any combat line. But he could barely stand.

The preacher didn't figure in Ryan's plan. He'd never met one worth a flying fart when steel flashed and blood spurted.

Little Dorina Leonard looked like a spitball could put her on her back, but Ryan reserved judgment on her. He had vivid memories of small-boned women with killer's eyes.

Helga had the up-and-walking-good look of a woman used to handling trouble in any size or shape, a useful person if you wanted a horse gelded or a baby birthed or a renegade gut shot.

Then there was Harold Lord from Castle Rock, way out east, a soft boy who looked like he'd mess himself if anyone raised a blaster anywhere near him.

J.B. used to say that you could pick out the fighters, give them marks from twenty and add them up. Then you had an idea of how you might line up against the opposition.

On that basis Ryan would give himself nineteen and Krysty eighteen. Abe was at least a sixteen. Red Folsom and his partner would rate about thirteens each. Give Helga the same. Joe-Bob Jarman didn't get to first base to score. Danny might have been a twelve, but his ankle dropped him to a fat zero. Dorina could score anywhere between a one and a ten. Call her a five. No way of guesstimating that. Ryan generously gave Harold a two.

"What are you doing, lover?"

"Trying to work out what our combat total would be."

"J.B.'s magic formula?"

"Yeah."

"What do we add up to?"

"I'm trying to work that out."

"Didn't J.B. say that if you divided the total by the number of people in your group, it had to average at least ten?"

"Yeah. At least! To have any chance."

"Ten of us. Got to reach a total of one hundred, then."

Ryan was never that great at mental arithmetic, and his lips moved silently as he battled with the simple addition.

"You say we needed a hundred?" he asked quietly.

"Right."

"Fireblast! We got ninety-nine."

One thing he hadn't bothered to take into account was that none of them had a weapon of any sort.

Charlie's forces numbered several times theirs, and they were all armed.

They could hear the patter of bare feet above them. Ryan grinned at Krysty, his teeth white in the gloomy half-light.

"Never cared about numbers, myself," he said.

The voice of the stickie guard was loud and harsh. "Get out, norm scum!"

Krysty squeezed Ryan's hand. "Nor me, lover. Nor me."

Chapter Twenty-One

They clambered out, blinking in the bright morning sunlight. Abe and Bob helped Danny, who cursed between gritted teeth as his broken ankle jarred against the stone top of the pit.

Helga looked beyond the ring of guards to where Charlie was standing, hands on hips, watching his prisoners.

"Why don't you let us splint it for him, you triple-mutie son of a whoreson bastard?"

She hardly raised her voice, but the cut of her words lashed across the camp.

Ryan felt his stomach muscles knot up in tension, waiting for the single word from the leader of the large mutie gang that would inevitably trigger the bloody massacre.

But Charlie stood still and calm for a moment, half-smiling, head on one side. The light breeze tugged at the mop of bright ochre hair, ruffling it like Kansas wheat.

His voice was controlled, quieting the murmur of anger that was coming up from the watching, listening stickies.

"You hear her, my friends? Hear the words of the

norm? Proud and arrogant in her certainty and her divine rightness. You have all seen the way we are treated by norms. Your fathers and their fathers, back unto many generations.''

''Amen,'' said the Very Reverend Joe-Bob Jarman, at Ryan's elbow, confirming his belief that the man was an utter fool.

Charlie ignored the interruption. ''Since we have all been together, have we had to put up with this norm shit?''

''No!'' was loudly shouted from dozens of voices all around the camp.

Charlie nodded, repeating the word. ''No. And this woman—'' his suckered finger pointed at Helga ''—will learn that. I promise you we shall all see her crawling and weeping. Before the sun has set and risen three times, every one of those norms will have died to amuse us.'' Charlie raised his voice high above the shouts and cheers. ''We shall then have the brightest fires and the loudest explosions to celebrate their deaths. This I promise you!''

Now every stickie, young and old, was yelping and ululating, banging sticks and spoons on pots and pans. One of them fired off a musket, the puff of black powder smoke rising serenely into the air, drifting up the face of the overhanging cliff.

So, it looked like three days was to be their projected life span. At least it gave Ryan something to work on.

THEY WERE FED in a circle around a spluttering fire of pine branches that sparked and crackled. They were manacled in pairs. Ryan's left hand to Danny's right. Krysty's right to the preacher's left. And so on.

Ryan admired Charlie's cunning. The stickies' leader also had their ankles chained, but in different pairs. So Ryan's right ankle was joined to Helga's left. That way the entire group was linked, one to another and any attempt to escape would have been utter, helpless chaos.

The food was based on old Apache dishes, with beans and peppers mixed with spiced meats. Ryan felt hungry and asked for a second helping. The stickie woman serving him looked across at Charlie, who nodded agreement to the request.

She ladled out a great dollop of the thick, rich stew. Her back was to Charlie, her muscular body hiding what she was doing from anyone else. The woman clumsily spilled a little of the mixture down the front of Ryan's trousers, offering him a thick-lipped half smile of almost apology.

She reached with her fingers and brushed at the dark smear, rubbing harder, the delicate suckers tugging at his pants. To his horror, Ryan found that the movement and the pressure was beginning to rouse him, despite his will.

"Thanks," he said. "Leave it."

"Might do it proper for you, later, norm," she whispered, her breath foul and bitter in his face. The lank hair brushing against his cheek as she straightened to serve the rest of the prisoners. Her handwoven dress hung open, revealing her heavy breasts, the dark nipples ringed with porcine bristles.

His erection diminished as quickly as it had grown, leaving him feeling slightly sick.

The only scant consolation was that nobody else had seen what had taken place.

CHARLIE WAS CONTENT that his captives should be seen all day, setting them in the open in a long row, still chained together. He made no effort to try to force them to do any sort of work, nor were they ill-treated, which was yet another difference from any stickies that Ryan had ever known.

Normally extreme cruelty was all that awaited anyone or anything unlucky enough to fall into their ripping hands.

Deathlands was sprinkled with all kinds of muties, some of them kind and friendly. Some, like stickies, were irredeemably brutal and vicious, always taking their greatest pleasure in the pain and anguish of others.

But there was little evidence of that in the camp at the old mesa settlement.

Around the midpart of the morning, one of the younger muties threw a stone, sly and underhand, at Danny's broken ankle, narrowly missing and striking Harold Lord on the shin. The blow made him whoop with pain, and he tried to hop on one leg, nearly bringing everyone down on top of him.

But Charlie had seen what the teenager had done and beckoned him over.

The toothless mouth stretched into a smile, which never even came close to the swollen eyes.

"Saw you," Charlie said.

The young stickie's lips were so gross that they flapped together as he tried to speak. It was impossible to tell what he was trying to say, but his whole cringing body language made it obvious the youth was terrified of his leader's anger.

"Hold out your right hand." There was a moment of hesitation. Charlie's tongue darted out, the myriad tiny suckers opening and closing with a weird rippling motion. "Do it."

Everyone around had stopped whatever they were doing, watching the menacing little tableau. Charlie, the Uzi slung casually across his shoulder, towered over the hunched figure of the boy.

"Hope he chills the shit-eating little prick," Harold hissed. "That stone really hurt my leg. Take him out, Charlie."

"You keep your mouth shut, or I'll break your neck," Ryan warned in a whisper.

"Why do—"

"If he doesn't break it, I will," Helga threatened. Harold shut up.

"Put out your hand, Shem." Charlie's thin tenor voice was still calm and gentle.

"No."

"Yes."

Very slowly, as though it were being drawn out by some distant but immeasurably powerful magnet, the young stickie pushed out his arm, hand clenched.

"Good. Now put your hand over the muzzle of the blaster."

The Uzi was down at his hip, the stubby barrel pointing toward the darkening sky. Charlie's finger was on the trigger.

"No." The word was breathed out through a stream of tears.

"Yes, Shem. Yes. Just to teach a small lesson to you and everyone."

There was a soft rumble of thunder, sounding as though it came from the distant south. But the high walls of the valley that surrounded the campsites made it difficult to tell, as any noise echoed and bounced off the red cliffs.

The bright start to the morning had disappeared, and the sky was a dark, leaden gray streaked with high pinkish-purple clouds.

The stickie closed his palm over the muzzle of the machine pistol, his eyes squeezed tight shut. His mouth hung open, and spittle dribbled down onto his chest.

"Do what I say. No less than that and no more than that!"

Charlie's voice cracked as the warning was shouted to all his followers.

There was a silence, broken only by the high piping

sound of a lone bird, circling far above the isolated canyon.

The triple burst from the Uzi was peculiarly muffled.

One of the women, watching from a few paces away, lifted her hand and slowly wiped a smear of blood from her face.

Charlie reached and ripped a length off the boy's shirt, using it to clean the crimson spray and ragged shreds of flesh off the blaster.

The stickie teenager passed out, dropping like a sack of discarded clothes at his leader's bare feet. The right hand all but disappeared, a stream of blood flowing steadily from it into the orange dirt around him.

Helga clapped her hands, the chains tinkling as she moved. "Well done, Charlie! Must make you real proud to be a prince among woodcutters."

He made her a half bow and stalked away.

As NOON APPROACHED, the sky turned from a lead color to that of spilled ink. The lighter clouds had been swallowed into the oppressive blackness. The cooking fires seemed to blaze with a tenfold brightness in the deep gloom.

At first the rain fell in a gentle drizzle, laying the dust, beginning to trickle across the overhang above the prisoners.

In less than ten minutes it had turned to a steady, teeming downpour.

"Going to last awhile," Krysty commented, raising her voice above the sound of the rain.

"Making tracking us real difficult," Ryan replied. "Real difficult."

Chapter Twenty-Two

"Make the tracking real difficult."

J.B. was huddled inside a dark green slicker, the collar turned up in a futile effort to stop the ceaseless rain from trickling down into the small of his back.

Jak hunched his shoulders. His long hair, glowing like a magnesium flare in the gloom, was plastered to his long, narrow skull. His eyes glowed like coals of fire, and his delicate fingers toyed with the hilt of one of the throwing knives that hadn't been turned over to the stickies.

"Can't be far from them."

"Distance, my dear young man, is a totally relative concept." Doc Tanner sneezed and scuffed at the mud around his cracked knee boots with the ferrule of his silver-headed cane. "One can be a scant yard away and yet miss by an entire universe. Or a full thousand miles off and yet still be able to reach out and grasp your target."

Christina gave the old man a look that would have frozen boiling soup on the stove. "I never met anyone, Doc, that talked more damned horsefeathers than you do."

"My dear madam, I must…"

He turned and met her eyes, and his voice faded away like rainwater down a storm drain.

"Doc, we're here in this endless rain. Cold and wet. Two men, two women, a boy and an old, old fool, going after we don't even properly know what. But it took away Ryan Cawdor, who is about the scariest person I ever met. Him and Krysty sliced from the air. We've lost their trail."

J.B. interrupted her. "We agreed we had to go after them."

She pointed a finger at him, as though it were a lightning rod. "Fuck that, John Dix. Fuck you, too. Fuck all of you to hell and back."

Jak had fallen silent, sheathing his knife. "Couldn't not go," he muttered.

"Sure. Couldn't not go! Couldn't leave an old friend. Drag your pregnant wife up mountains in the rain, facing a shitty death in the dirt. You can do that, Jak Lauren, can't you?"

THE RAIN PERSISTED all through the afternoon, turning hollows into puddles, puddles into pools, the beds of dry creeks into streams, streams into frothing torrents of muddy water that tore at the roots of trees and filled with plants and the corpses of small, helpless creatures.

Jak managed to calm his wife, hugging her close as they all cowered in a makeshift shelter of broken branches. Mildred dozed off, head against Dean's shoulder. The boy had hardly spoken since hearing the news of his father's disappearance, and seemed to be slipping away into a dark world of his own. His face remained blank, eyes like stone.

J.B. had gone out before evening completely closed off the day's light and scouted along the trail they'd been trying to follow, which was leading them deep into a maze of arroyos and ravines.

But the weather had defeated him.

The rain battered down in a solid wall. J.B. remembered one of the Trader's stories. He'd never really believed it, but now it suddenly seemed to be entirely possible.

Jimmy McCluskey had been a top gunner on War Wag Two. Everyone suspected him of having a mainline jolt habit, but he was always too clever to get caught at it. Then he started showing the symptoms of one of the horrific diseases that still clung to a malevolent life in dark corners of Deathlands. This one was known as "trips."

According to the Trader's version of McCluskey's ending, the man had realized that all that remained of his life would be short, brutish and painful.

It had been raining like it was now.

The way it was told, McCluskey had gone out alone at night and stood in the open, head back, face turned to the dark heavens, mouth gaping wide, hands down at his sides.

And drowned.

As J.B. picked his way through the dripping, dank wilderness, he thought about the story. At times it almost seemed like the air around him was too supersaturated with water for a man to be able to breathe.

When he got back, he woke Mildred.

"Anything?" she asked, rubbing her eyes on her wet sleeve.

"No. Any tracks there might have been are long gone now."

"So?"

"Sleep. Wake up and it'll have stopped raining. And we go on deeper. Until we find them."

Mildred smiled at him. "Then we rescue them and go home safe and live happily ever after."

"Yeah. Something like that."

Chapter Twenty-Three

The atmosphere in the stickies' camp was thoroughly miserable. Although nobody actually came and told the prisoners, they saw the corpse of the young man that Charlie had maimed being carried away in a crude litter, uncovered rain pattering down into his staring eyes.

"Guess he must have bled to death," Red Folsom said.

"Got what you wanted," Helga taunted, nudging Harold.

But the fat young man ignored her.

The day dragged on in a strange, desultory sort of way. There was a ceaseless rain, skirling around the canyon, making it hard to see more than fifty yards in any direction. It was coming off the cliff above the ancient dwellings in a solid sheet of dull silver, pouring down into the river that was widening among the trees.

Charlie kept away from them. Food was brought in what was probably the middle of the day. It was the same sort of hot, spiced stew.

"Get used to it, Ryan," Abe said with a cackling laugh.

"This all there is? Well, I guess I've eaten a lot less and a whole lot worse."

Red grinned mirthlessly. "Sure. The finest stew in the finest stickie camp in all Deathlands."

Helga wiped her metal dish clean with a hunk of corn bread. "This place serves beans well done, beans medium rare, beans over-easy, beans on the side, bean salad, chicken-fried beans and refried beans. I leave anything out?"

"Yeah," Danny said, lying awkwardly on his right side to take any pressure off his broken ankle. "You forgot something, Helga."

"What?"

"Just plain beans."

RYAN TRIED TO TALK to the other captives, weighing them up, trying to figure how they might react when the firing pin came down.

Danny, despite his pain, was more than ready to do what he could.

"Trouble is, Ryan, it's little I can do."

There was no doubt about Helga. Just put a sawed-off in her hands and a box of 12-gauge shells, and she'd take out an army of stickies.

"Heard trouble was around," she said, "but I didn't figure it for stickies. Neighbor to the west, away from Jak and Christina's spread, lost cattle and a couple of his men to a sickness. Wondered if there was lepers traveling through."

"Lepers! Fireblast, I haven't heard of them since I was in my teens. Thought they'd died off."

Helga shook her head, brushing away an importunate blowfly. "Nope. We get all sorts of crazies." She poked the Very Reverend Joe-Bob Jarman with her toe. "That right, isn't it, preacher man? Some real crazies."

He turned away from her, presenting his back in its tight broadcloth suit.

Helga grinned at Ryan, making a jerk-off movement with her right hand.

He grinned right back at her.

The preacher and Harold were no-hopers in any plan, not even of any potential use as a diversion. He wondered if chilling them would be a good or a bad move, then decided to let that lie awhile. They had at least two more days, according to Charlie.

Dorina Leonard slept most of the time, occasionally muttering under her breath in what sounded to Ryan like some sort of a Mex dialect. If it came to placing a narrow-bladed dagger in a man's groin while he was dreaming, then he guessed the waiflike woman would be a prime choice.

But she was so physically tiny and frail that her value in a knockdown drag-out fight was going to be a touch limited. And it didn't look as though she had the stamina to travel any distance cross-country if they made a break.

Red and his brother were prime candidates to enlist in any escape plan.

But when he managed to have a few private moments with each of the trappers, he found he hadn't been entirely right.

Bob Leonard shook his scarred head at Ryan's overture.

"Nope. Couldn't leave me wife. Dorina'd like die if I was to get went. Lost our little 'uns. She was wed before."

"How old is she?" Ryan couldn't believe that this woman-child was more than sixteen, tops.

"Near twenty, she figures, Ryan." His mutilated mouth tried for a smile and didn't miss it by much. "Don't look it, does her?"

"No."

"She wed. Lawman up in Kansas. July Randall. He was took by a breed in a knife fight. Blindsided him in the dark."

"No more children?"

"Sure did. One was dead-birthed. Other was four and the breed cut off its head."

Ryan whistled soundlessly between his teeth. "That does beat all, Bob. And I understand about Dorina. Not wanting to try anything without her."

One eye squinted at him, from under the furrowed mass of tumbled scar tissue. "Thanks, Ryan. Good on you."

There was also an unexpected problem with Red Folsom.

As soon as Ryan started to talk, very casually, about what their hopes might be of escaping, the tough redhead grabbed him by the arm, jerking on the links of the cuffs that joined him to Harold.

"Hey, why do…" The complaint was stillborn as his neighbor glared at him.

"Get away from me, Harold. Far as you can."

"Why pick on me, Red?"

"Because you're the best there is, fat boy."

The one-time candy seller shuffled away, until his chained arm was out straight, nearly four feet along the ledge from Folsom.

"Trust him far as I can piss into a hurricane, Ryan. Get me?"

"Sure. Think he'd betray us to Charlie?"

"Do barons screw virgins?"

"If he did, Charle'd chill him just the same. Wouldn't make any difference."

Folsom grinned. "You know it. I know it. But does Harold know it?"

Ryan nodded. He'd already picked Lord as one of the two possible traitors. The Very Reverend Joe-Bob Jarman was the other.

"What is it you don't want him to hear?" he asked the big man.

"We know that the strawhead stickie bastard got plans to send us off to buy the farm with a big bright bang. Couple of days. Got his men watching us." Folsom made the word "men" sound like something he'd picked up on his front fender.

"So? Sooner we get a plan worked out, the better it is."

Folsom shook his head. "Sorry, Ryan. Not much of a man for other folk's plans. Just take you a good long look at the others. You might be fine, and your woman seems like she'd swim most rivers and climb most mountains. But Danny's lost. Abe's old, and his breath's not good. Helga might not go without Danny. My partner won't move unless Dorina goes too. Minister and fat boy are out. Never was good at numbering. But it seems to me that if you take nine away from ten you get one. Comes down to me."

Ryan wasn't surprised. Nor could he honestly pick many holes in Folsom's thinking. A man alone would often have the edge on a group.

"Sorry to hear that," he said finally, staring out across the rain-swept camp.

"Way it is." Flat and final.

"Sure. Figured we might get our blasters back and do some damage. That way we might—only *might*—have a chance of getting the others sprung."

Folsom spit. The white globule landed in the slippery mud and immediately vanished in the pitted, orange slime.

"Hear what you say, Ryan."

"You got yourself a plan?"

Folsom laughed. "I've known Bob Leonard there for around seven years. Spent some hard winters and harder times with him. I haven't told *him* what I intend, Ryan."

And that was just about the end of the conversation between them.

CHARLIE PADDED OVER near late afternoon, the Uzi kept dry under a long slicker. He was bareheaded, the water flattening his hair to his scalp.

"Had a good day, pilgrims?" he asked cheerily.

Helga gave him the finger. "Stick it in your ass, freak."

"I'm going to think of something special in the way of lonely, humiliating, agonizing deaths, lady," Charlie said, smiling, his tongue darting out to lick his lips.

Most of the cooking fires had been extinguished by the torrential rain, but several of the Anasazi dwellings now had the scent of cooking drifting from their openings.

"Going to be a hard night." Charlie laughed. "Those kivas are all around three feet deep in water. You norms come on like gods. See how you are at floating off to sleep!"

He walked away, shoulders shaking with merriment at his own joke.

Danny shifted, trying to get more comfortable. "Still aren't real used to a fucking stickie with a sense of humor," he said.

BY THE TIME THE LIGHT began to fade the gloom of late afternoon to the darkness of early evening, everyone was utterly miserable.

Though the massive cliff gave them shelter from the direct force of the rain, the wind had blown it into a fine, drizzling spray, which had seeped through to every corner of the camp.

A thin veil of water lay on top of the stew, cooling it. The wrist cuffs were taken off for them to eat, with a ring of guards watching carefully.

"Them muskets can't be too reliable in weather like this," Folsom said to Ryan. "Flash in the pan they will, even if they tried to keep their powder dry."

Ryan wasn't about to risk his life on that possibility.

Once the huddled meal was over, the ankle cuffs were also removed and the stickies started to shepherd them away from the shelter, along the raised walkway, toward the row of kivas. Ryan and Folsom helped Danny along, supported between them.

They stopped near the entrance to the partly flooded kiva, while Krysty led the rest down inside.

Folsom looked across at Ryan. "So long," he whispered.

And made his break.

Chapter Twenty-Four

He didn't even make twenty steps.

Folsom let go of Danny's arm, allowing Ryan to take his full weight. The injured man screamed in pain and toppled sideways, dragging Ryan down into the mud with him.

As he fell, the one-eyed man squinted through the spray, watching the pathetic failure of Folsom's escape attempt. In dry weather, he might just have had a chance, as stickies were far from the most agile creatures and ran about as well as pigs climb trees.

He had the advantage of surprise, as the sodden guards were already, mentally, back in the warmth of their own homes. And Danny's yell, combined with the two men collapsing into the mud, threw the stickies off balance.

Folsom jumped down off the walkway, punching one of the patrol in the groin, managing to snatch a knife from his belt as the stickie folded over.

He was only thirty yards from the narrow bridge over the stream—now a river—that raged down the valley. Beyond that was good cover provided by the trees and the sheets of rain.

It wasn't a bad try.

An unlucky try.

Two of the muskets fired, the sound flat in the teeming open space. Another misfired, with a sullen click.

Folsom was dodging, his plaid shirt darkened with the rain, feet kicking up gouts of red-orange spray around him.

The ground was rippled from centuries of feet pounding across it. In dry weather you were hardly conscious of how uneven it was. In wet weather it simply appeared like a smooth lake of featureless mud. But in places the mud was a half-inch deep.

In other places, a yard away, it might be nine inches deep.

Folsom found one of the pockets where the clammy ooze came halfway up his calf. It trapped his boot, wrenching his ankle, while his other foot skidded away, out of control.

He crashed down on his side, trying to take the impact with his right hand. But Folsom was lost. His elbow struck first, with a sickening crack of bone. The large knife, his only weapon, went spinning from nerveless fingers, skittering through the slick mud, over the brink of the central drop and into the brown water of the river.

By the time he got onto his hands and knees, shaking his head like a bullock under the poleax, it was all over.

"Fireblast," Ryan swore quietly, reaching to help

Danny to his feet again. Harold came to his assistance. Krysty also did her best to aid the fallen man.

The others were watching, faces stricken at the disaster.

One of the guards kicked Folsom in the ribs, a dull, vicious blow that rolled him onto his back, one hand covering his eyes against the teeming rain. The rest of the stickies clustered around him, their muskets hefted by the long muzzles, ready to beat the man to death.

Ryan glanced around, wondering with a flash of intuition whether this might be a good moment to try his own break. But Krysty was caught, half-in the flooded pit, trying to support the injured Danny. There was no way she could get out fast.

The moment passed.

Charlie appeared and shouted a warning to his men not to injure Folsom, warning them in the same breath to keep a better eye on the other nine captives.

The men drew back reluctantly from the prostrate figure.

"Get him up and imprison him away from the other norms!"

"Leave him alone!" Helga called, but the lack of hope in her voice rode over every word. She knew. They all knew.

THE RAIN EASED an hour or so later and finally stopped around eight o'clock that same night.

By nine the skies had cleared, and the air tasted fresh, green and very cold.

The fires were lighted again, heaps of dry wood piled on until the darkness seemed to be filled with cascades of crackling sparks.

The first hour or so in the kiva had been difficult and dangerous.

The water was draining very slowly, even after the heaviest of the torrent had ceased. It took three of them to keep Danny's head high enough to save him from drowning, which meant that all of the others were cramped into chillingly cold and uncomfortable corners.

It was the Very Reverend Joe-Bob Jarman who complained most.

"I'm the tallest, so I should be in the center," he said, trying to push Krysty out of his way with his bony elbows—which turned out to be a big mistake.

Krysty turned on him, lifting her foot and scraping the side of the leather sole down the front of his shin as hard as she could, finishing by grinding her heel into his instep.

"Fuckin' bitch!" he moaned, only just avoiding slipping under water.

"I call that serious bad language from a man of God," Krysty said, doubling her fingers and jabbing Jarman with all her strength on the outside of the thigh muscle on the undamaged leg. The blow paralyzed it, so that he suddenly collapsed and slithered out of their sight, reappearing coughing and choking, hands flailing for a grip on the smooth walls of the kiva.

"Watch your tongue, Reverend," Ryan warned, "or you might not be able to come up for air next time."

A little later Dorina fainted and had to be supported until she came around again. Her eyes had rolled back in their sockets, and she was moaning and trembling uncontrollably.

Around ten o'clock a posse of guards came to unbolt the metal grille from the pit and order them out into the open. They were visibly on edge, pushing with their blasters and shouting inarticulate and incomprehensible commands.

"What do they want this late?" Helga asked. "Still, at least it means we can get out of this dreadful damp hole."

Ryan glanced at Krysty, whose hair was soaked and hung limply over her shoulders, and got a hurried shake of the head in response.

She felt the same as he did.

That what was about to go down wasn't going to be good news.

They were both right.

FOLSOM WAS STRIPPED completely naked, his pale body showing the livid bruises of the beating that the stickies' leader had interrupted. Blood was caked around his nose and mouth, trickling down over his chest, etched black in the dancing firelight.

His eyes were closed, though Ryan suspected that he was a good deal more conscious than he was letting on.

There was a gash across the top of his head, and his red hair was thickly matted. His hands had been tied behind him with thin wire, which had forced more blood to seep from under his now-purple fingernails.

"Stand the others over there and chain their ankles," Charlie ordered. "Let the norms see how we treat their kind."

There was no point in struggling against such overwhelming, armed force.

While the shackling took place, Folsom stood silent and still. Occasionally there would be a ripple of movement in the crowd of watching stickies, and words were called out. But Ryan couldn't make out what was being shouted.

Charlie turned to one of his lieutenants and said something. The mutie went immediately into the throng and was clearly handing out some sort of a warning.

There was no more shouting.

When every captive was safely in bondage, Charlie turned again to face them, holding a triumphant right fist in the air, like a victorious fighter.

"Now you shall see it!" he shouted. "Now we shall show you." There was a roar of pleasure, like animals scenting their evening meat.

At his side there stood a young woman, holding a rusty iron bowl.

"What's in that?" Bob asked.

Nobody answered him.

Nobody knew.

A NUMBER OF IRON BOLTS had been driven deep into the cliff at the distant end of the camp, beyond the last of the small houses. Folsom was drawn up against them, one hand fixed to a ring level with his head, the other strained out sideways, chained to another circular bolt. He stood there, skin fluttering across his stomach with cold and fear.

Charlie approached the naked man, the woman close at his elbow. He had drawn a short-bladed knife from his belt.

Helga called out in the quiet. "God go with you, Red Folsom."

But there was no response. The man's eyes stayed tight shut, his mouth an etched line.

When Charlie beckoned another of the young stickie women to join him, Ryan guessed. She was holding a small cooking ladle in one hand and a flaming torch in the other.

"Black powder," he whispered to Krysty.

Charlie was closer to Folsom, the knife dancing like a living flame in the reflected light of the camp fires.

"Why black powder?" Krysty asked, puzzled. "What's he going— Gaia!"

THE FIRST CUT WAS a slow, considered slice across the center of the chained man's stomach. The stickie was careful not to push the knife in too deep and cause any terminal wound. Just deep enough to peel back a flap of skin and muscle, five or six inches long. He pulled it wider with his fingers until it resembled the pouch of a kangaroo.

Harold Lord began to vomit copiously.

At an impatient gesture from Charlie, the girl tipped a ladleful of the fine, gritty powder into the oozing wound.

There was a buzz of excitement around the camp, almost loud enough to drown out Folsom's anguished moaning.

At a nod from Charlie the young stickie dipped the end of the torch toward the brimming gash in the man's stomach.

There was a roar of delight from the dozens of watching muties as first a fountain of sparks, then flame and smoke gushed out with a barely audible whooshing sound.

Folsom's scream rose way above the noise, harsh and high enough to shatter a crystal goblet.

Helga was weeping and the Very Reverend Joe-Bob Jarman was struggling to pray in a faltering, self-important voice.

Ryan was simply confirmed in his belief that Charlie, despite his undoubted skills and intellect, was just another vicious, maniac stickie underneath the polished veneer.

The next forty minutes were bloodily predictable and vile.

In the past Ryan had traveled through the deserts of the Southwest, and he'd witnessed firsthand the ingenious tortures of some of those peoples. What Charlie was doing to ensure the doomed Red Folsom an appalling and delayed passing was nothing new.

The stickie couldn't even contrive to carry out the protracted execution with any particular style or skill.

Folsom passed out at least four times and had to be recovered with water. The result of this was to make the incisions filled with black powder difficult to ignite.

And one cut, below the left knee, was so deep and held so much powder that the resulting explosion blew the lower part of the leg completely off, so that the wound had to be hastily cauterized with the torch and a clumsy tourniquet applied to prevent the trapper from dying off too quickly.

The blackened thing that hung against the blood-splashed cliff bore little resemblance to a human being.

Around the stickies' camp initial rippling pleasure had gone, to be replaced by boredom. Stickies had a very limited attention span. A few of the youngsters still greeted each puff of flame and smoke with a ragged cry, but the rest were quiet.

Charlie sensed that he was losing his audience and brought the proceeding to an abrupt ending.

Using the point of the knife he probed both eyes

from their sockets, where they dangled onto the mutilated cheeks.

Taking a wedge of wood, Charlie forced open Folsom's bloodied lips, jamming the jaws apart, grinning as he encouraged the girl to fill the mouth with black powder.

"Adios!" the stickie screamed, sheathing his knife and taking the smoldering torch from the woman.

He waved it around his head, the mane of golden hair dancing in the light. The flame roared into life and he pushed it toward Folsom's face.

The cheering from the expectant crowd dwarfed anything that had gone before, drowning out the sound of the explosive as it ripped the man's head off the top of his body, sending it a hundred feet into the night sky.

So it ended.

Chapter Twenty-Five

The next day was warmer, with a blue sky and a fine, drying wind blowing in from the north.

The corpse had vanished, leaving only dark smudges on the sheer face of the sandstone cliff where it had been chained.

Charlie was in a high good humor after the monstrous demonstration of his power.

"Loved it, didn't they?" he said to his prisoners, once they were outside and manacled again in the bright morning sunlight.

Ryan answered him. "Light a fire and you can be bastard certain to have every stickie in creation rolling on their backs, waving their legs in the air with pleasure."

The bitter verbal attack didn't faze Charlie. "You don't worry me, Ryan Cawdor. Talk's cheap. Only death counts. Sun's above. The stupe's body's probably around a hundred miles downstream by now. Let the little ones play some with it. Good for them to practice using their hands on norm flesh." He laughed delightedly. "Not that the poor son of a bitch had too much of that left."

THE DISTANCE JUDGMENT of the stickies' leader was badly flawed.

The mangled, bloodless remains of Red Folsom had finished up a lot closer to the Anasazi village than a hundred miles.

Dean had gone to relieve himself after breakfast that morning, picking his way along the narrow path, deep in congealed mud after the interminable rains of the previous twenty-four hours. The boy had found his father's disappearance extremely difficult to handle, and the knowledge that they'd now lost the trail, on account of the turbulent weather, had plunged him into the depths of misery.

He felt a strong disapproval from the limping Christina Lauren, almost as if she blamed him personally for what had happened. Jak had always been real friendly, but now the albino, only a few years older than Dean, seemed embarrassed to be seen with him, constantly glancing over his shoulder to see if his wife was watching him.

Doc and Mildred had been just as nice to him as ever.

But there was something seriously wrong about J.B. The Armorer was usually calm and taciturn, seeming like his mind kept focusing inward. But since Ryan had been taken, J.B. had been on edge, unable to sit still, looking around at the sound of a raindrop dripping from a high branch, hand fumbling for the butt of his Uzi. Every time they stopped he'd be taking off his glasses, polishing them on a piece of clean rag, just like he was trying to wear the lenses away.

J.B. had been at his worst when they realized that they'd totally lost the track.

He'd clenched his fist, knuckles as white as Jak's hair, his eyes staring blankly through the soaked trees, across the valley. His lips had been moving as though he were cursing under his breath. Dean had wondered whether he'd been praying, but that didn't seem too likely.

But now the sun was shining, and they were near a raging torrent.

It had only been a thin stream the day before, gurgling and chuckling its way over little green boulders.

Now it would be almost impossible to cross in safety, as it hurled a grat arc of rainbow spray high into the early-morning air.

Dean reached a bank of loganberries and wormed his way in among them, feeding himself as he lowered his pants, wiping himself with a handful of grass then making his way down onto the flattened turf at the river's edge. He kneeled and dipped his hands into the freezing water, washing them clean.

Then he stooped farther forward to wash his face and drink a cupped mouthful from a deep pool beneath him.

''Shit a brick!''

He jumped back so fast that he was fifteen feet away before he even realized that he'd moved. The turquoise hilt of his knife was gripped in his right fist, and his lips were peeled back in a feral snarl of terrified menace.

Then his brain started to reassure him about what it was that he'd seen floating in the bright water, shimmering like the forgotten ghost of some old yesterday.

Drowned man, he thought. Go tell the others.

THE DEAD BODY WAS LAID OUT on wet grass, the remains of its face turned toward the cloudless sky and the dazzling sun that filtered through the branches of pines.

They stood around it in a silent circle, looking at the horrors that had been performed upon what had once been a man.

Doc spoke first. "Hard time he had of it," he muttered.

Christina turned away, looking over the ceaseless river, her shoulders slumped. Jak put an arm around her, but she shrugged him off and walked slowly away, back toward the smoldering embers of their overnight camp fire.

Mildred had already given the corpse a cursory checkup. "No gunshot wounds. Don't think. Course, coming some ways down the river hasn't done a lot for the condition. Massive bruising. Some breaks that might have been premortem. Done by rocks. Damage from fishes here and there. But the rest..." She spread her hands to encompass the appalling injuries that disfigured the man's body.

Doc sighed. "What can possess a human being to commit such inhuman outrages upon another?" he asked. "I fear that we are dealing with dark forces here, are we not?"

J.B. took off his spectacles and polished them, not looking at anyone else, ignoring the slab of mottled torn flesh.

"Tortured with a knife and some kind of explosive detonated or ignited in the flesh. By the pockmarks and the scorches around the wounds, I'd guess they used plain old black powder. Typical stickies' game."

Jak rejoined them, his face tense and worried. "Saw first, thought was Ryan. Not much head left."

"Explosive in the mouth. Mebbe eyes as well." J.B. stooped. "Yeah. Looks like the eyes went before he was chilled."

Mildred bent and touched the cold flesh on the inside of the upper arm. "This what stickies do?" She pointed to where strips of skin had been ripped away, bringing sections of muscle with it. Near the gaping, white-lipped wounds she could see the clear marks of tiny circular scars.

"Yeah," J.B. replied. "That's the suckers on a stickie's hands. Bastards."

"We going to bury him?" Dean asked.

The Armorer shook his head. "Came out of the river, we'll put him back in there. Don't have the time nor the inclination to open up the ground for a stranger. Best get moving."

"Think they're the same lot that have Ryan and

Krysty?'' Mildred straightened, rubbing absently at damp patches on the knees of her reinforced military fatigues.

''Must be.'' J.B. looked around. ''River's in full spate. Might have carried the body a long way. But there's one thing for sure.''

''What?'' Dean asked eagerly.

''We follow it back upstream into the high country there, and we might just find your father.''

They stood around in silence, hearing a jay noisily defending its territory, somewhere close by in the forest.

None of them referred again to the hideous state of the dead stranger.

Not in front of Ryan's son.

SCANT MILES AWAY, up the steep and tortuous mountainside, the camp of the stickies had been enjoying a quiet day in the beautiful weather. Wet clothes were laid on warm rocks to dry, parties went out to seek kindling for the fires, and the hunters left in the middle of the morning.

For Ryan, Krysty and the other prisoners, the hours drifted by slowly.

None of them spoke much. There didn't seem anything worth saying.

Ryan was preoccupied with trying to come up with some sort of plan to save his life and Krysty's. And possibly some of the others as well.

If you could once break free and reach the far side

of the little bridge, then you had a fair chance of outrunning the stickies. But Charlie was more careful since Folsom's attempt to escape. Now there were patrols farther out, and guards posted on the high part of the ravine.

And the captives were never released as a group, except under the heaviest of armed guards.

Every route that Ryan examined in his mind seemed to end in the blank wall of recapture or death. But since being chilled was going to be the final scene in about thirty-six hours, there wasn't too much for any of them to lose.

"Come up with anything, lover?" Krysty asked quietly. "Can almost hear the gears grinding in your brain."

"Nothing. Well, almost nothing."

"Prefer *almost* to nothing at all."

He leaned toward her, his eye raking the camp to make sure none of the stickies was paying them any particular attention. "It's a last chance. Tomorrow morning, when they get us out. Only time we're not chained together. Just grab for blasters and then run."

Krysty half smiled. "That's it?"

"Yeah. I said it wasn't—"

"Grab their blasters and run. Now I know we're in deep shit, lover."

"You got a better plan?"

"Course not. But we have to do it all together, or it's down to a big nothing."

"Sure."

"We trust everyone?"

"I don't, but I don't know who we can rely on and who we can't. And we have to tell everyone. No other way."

"Guess not."

THE LONGER RYAN WAITED to mention his threadbare plan to the rest of the prisoners, the less chance of their being betrayed. His original intention had been to speak to Helga about it first, but the craggy, freckled woman was still distraught after witnessing the horrific butchering of Red Folsom.

As it happened, his scheme was altered during the middle of the afternoon.

One of the stickies who'd been out on a hunting patrol came running down the path and across the bridge, his bare feet flapping noisily on the planks. He was sweating hard, his shirt soaked and darkened under the arms and across his belly. The creature's stringy hair was flattened against his angular skull, and the eyes goggled even more than usual.

Charlie was close by the prisoners when his subordinate appeared, and he beckoned to him. "Come on, Josh! You look like you got a mutie grizzly on your heels."

The stickie glanced fearfully behind him at that thought.

"Not, is there?"

"No, no, no. There isn't. But what brought you back here?"

"Norms coming." A doubtful pause. "Sort of norms. Men and women. We seen them."

Ryan glanced at Krysty, his heart sinking.

Charlie smiled broadly, aiming his good cheer at the captives. "Company," he said. "We must get ready to give these visitors a hearty welcome."

Chapter Twenty-Six

J.B. called a halt.

"Not a breath of wind," he said, using his fedora to fan away some of the midges that had gathered hungrily about his head.

The river still thundered at their side, but its flow had been audibly slackening during the period after noon. The heavy rain that had fallen on the higher peaks above them had now mostly found its way down to lower levels. In another twenty-four hours or so, if the fine weather held, the river would have shrunk back to being a stream again.

"Think we're on the right trail, John?" Mildred asked, slumping down, panting, on a large fallen branch.

"Who knows? Corpse had been chilled by stickies. Stickies got Ryan and Krysty. River comes from this way. Been no other side watercourses coming in on either side."

Christina was suffering most of all on the arduous trek. The rain had turned what would normally have been a difficult climb into one that constantly verged on the impossible.

Again and again they had to negotiate fallen trees,

their roots washed away in the downpour. These had sometimes formed themselves into a malign tangle, twenty feet high or more, and completely blocked their access to higher ground. Each one took up to an hour to negotiate.

With her heavy surgical boot, the woman normally found that even a long hike on a broad flat trail tired her out.

Jak repeatedly urged her to go back to their base camp and wait for them.

"I'm not pretending I like this," she scolded her young husband, "but I'll go where you go. And that's that."

"I only..."

She pointed at him, with a hand that trembled with fatigue. "I will not give up all my hopes for our future and see them turned to ashes, Jak Lauren. I tell you I will not."

And she turned away to hide her tears.

Doc cleared his throat and coughed. "If I may so, Christina, I find you the most admirable and courageous woman that I have ever had the honor of meeting. Were I wearing a hat I would most certainly doff it to you."

"I'd second that," Mildred said. "We all got us a tough row to hoe. We stick together and we reach the end safe and unharmed."

"Hope you're right, Mildred. And thanks for the kind words, Doc. You're not so damned bad, yourself."

J.B. was prowling around like a caged puma, head back, scenting the air. Dean watched him, putting his own face to the wind, sniffing to try to see what was bothering the Armorer. But all he could smell was the familiar flavor of the sun on the pine trees. A rich, resinous scent.

"Don't like it," J.B. suddenly said.

"What?" Mildred asked.

"Just got that itching feeling, clear up my spine. I don't know what it is. Someone's watching us from hiding."

"Are you sure?" Doc queried.

"No. Never sure until the bullet hits you and you're down in the long grass, flat on your back, staring up at a china-blue sky. That's when you get to be certain about it."

"But you think—"

Jak interrupted. "Got same feeling. Could be stickies close."

"Could be," J.B. agreed. "Just have to be triple-red careful."

"Thought we already were," Christina said.

"You think it might be your friends coming?" Helga spoke quietly, not wanting to draw the attention of the cautious Charlie.

Ryan shook his head. "Could be. Normally in this kind of situation, they'd be on a triple-red careful patrol. But they reckon they're after ordinary stickies. Might not worry so much."

Krysty was next along the manacled line and she leaned in closer. "That storm would hold them up on tracking us."

"Yeah. Mebbe wash the trail out altogether."

"So, how will they find us? How will anyone find us?"

Ryan strained to look over the far side of the ravine, where the ambush was already laid. "It's not going to make much difference, anyways. Those fire-blasted stickies are ready and waiting for them. Whoever they are."

THEY HEARD THEM before they saw them.

Charlie was leaning against a tumbled wall, suckered tongue darting out to moisten his fleshless lips. His almond-shaped brown eyes were alight with private enjoyment.

He kept turning toward Ryan, who did everything he could to avoid meeting the malevolent grin.

Krysty had uncommonly keen hearing and she was first to hear the sound. "Listen," she said. "Listen."

Charlie straightened, the smile vanishing. "Yeah, Firetop. I can hear it, too. But what the blood smoke is it?"

Then Ryan caught the faint noise. "Yeah. I got it. But I don't—"

He shut his mouth abruptly, afraid that he might inadvertently let slip his own relief that the strangers weren't J.B. and the rescue party.

It was a kind of singing, chanting, arrhythmic, like a song sung by a staggering man.

And there was another odd sound that was riding along in the background, like someone clapping their hands together at irregular intervals.

Ryan looked at Krysty, who shrugged her shoulders and shook her head. "No idea, lover. Except I know for sure it's not—" she caught his warning glance, picked up on it and didn't miss a beat "—the local baron and his sec men riding in to rescue us."

Charlie had been listening. "You can stake your fiery scalp on that one," he said. The stickie was so delighted with the imminent success of his plan that he was actually hugging himself with his long, thin arms.

The singing was louder, nearer.

And the slapping noise was more clear. Ryan thought of Mex women turning dough on a large flat, sun-warmed stone.

Krysty remembered Harmony ville, and the sound of a large fresh salmon being thrown down onto a kitchen table by her uncle, Tyas McCann, come back flushed with success from a day's fishing.

It was the Very Reverend Joe-Bob Jarman who recognized it first.

"Fladgies," he said, his face contorting with contempt and disgust.

And then it all made sense.

Chapter Twenty-Seven

"Fladgies" was the common name for the small groups of religious extremists who traveled through Deathlands. Their particular milieu was in the areas of the desert Southwest, concentrating their activities in the wilder regions of what were once the states of Arizona, New Mexico, Utah, Colorado, Nevada, West Texas and Southern California.

The name was a diminutive of the word *flagellant*. Old predark dictionaries said that was someone who was preoccupied with the act of whipping, either as part of an extreme religious experience or as a way of heightening sexual and erotic pleasure.

The fladgies would go about punishing one another—and themselves—with a variety of whips, often tipped with glass or metal. The more the blood flowed, the more the fladgies felt they were worshiping their particular god.

In the past few years these grossly aberrant practices had virtually died out, often as a direct or indirect result of overenthusiasm on the part of the fladgies.

Ryan had, oddly, never actually seen a living fladgie. Once during a trip with the Trader they'd en-

countered a group of bounty hunters, who'd seen a
trio of the religious extremists a week earlier up on
the Brazos, and had come across their butchered
corpses a few days later.

The Trader had spoken about them. He had been
revolted by their self-mutilating excesses and had said
that he'd be happy to put a full-metal-jacket round
through the skull of any he saw. "Speed them on the
way to meet their Maker," he'd said, laughing.

And here they were, appearing on the brink of the
cliff across the valley, like a quintet of ragged scare-
crows.

The sunshine danced off the gold medallion around
Charlie's neck as he turned disbelievingly to his prisoners.

"What the fuck are they?" he asked nobody in
particular.

"God crazies," Harold replied, "bringing the word
of the Almighty to the heathen."

"Amen," muttered the traveling minister, closing
his eyes piously.

The chanting was louder, but it was still only possible to pick out an occasional few words, or the
windblown remains of a single line.

To Ryan, it sounded as though they were singing
about making someone's day, tonight. But that didn't
seem to carry a lot of sense.

Words like "God" and "salvation" seemed to oc-
cur quite often.

Now they could actually all see the whips, short

lashes, tipped with something that glinted as they were raised and then brought down, which explained the odd, slapping sounds that they'd been hearing.

The stickie guards that Charlie had been at such pains to conceal among the trees and brush along the valley above the shrunken river were a total waste of time.

The fladgies had obviously seen the camp fires from a distance and must have quickly suspected that they were coming into a stickie community, with all of the danger and risk that such a place always represented.

But they never checked their yelling, moaning and whipping.

The sentries appeared behind and around them, forming into a threatening escort. But the five tatterdemalion figures ignored them.

While Ryan and the others watched in silence, the bizarre tableau moved down the path, over the bridge and approached Charlie.

Four men and a woman.

Probably a woman, Ryan thought, though the stubbly white hair along the line of her jaw gave him pause for doubt.

All were long-haired, filthy, matted hair clotted with grease, sweat and blood. They were clothed in shreds of rags that dangled around their ankles. Every one of them was barefoot.

Each carried a short-thonged whip. The stock was hand-carved and covered in stained and torn leather, studded with brass pins. Each whip had several plaited lashes, and as they drew closer everyone could see what had been glinting in the sun: tiny splinters of broken glass and twisted wire, with splinters of razored steel at their ends.

"Sick bastards," Bob Leonard breathed. "Look at the blood on 'em."

The quintet stopped when they were a few steps away from Charlie, ignoring the crowd of stickies that was gathering around them.

Their leader was nearly as tall as Charlie, but his mane of wild hair made him somehow more impressive. His eyes were dark pits in the sunken caverns of discolored ivory. He had torn furrows down his cheeks with his own nails, and they brimmed with crusted pus and dried blood.

"We bring salvation!" he cried in a cracked, insane voice.

"We already have it," the stickie replied.

"This is the salvation of the blessed ones through suffering and pain."

"Yeah, we got that too."

Now it seemed to penetrate to the fladgie that he was in a situation that might be way beyond his control. His bugged eyes blinked, and he ran a blood-smeared hand across his forehead, smoothing back the hair.

"You a stickie?"

"You a norm?" The absurdity of the question amused Charlie, and he suddenly threw his head back and bellowed with laughter. "A norm!" He turned to his captives, hands spread in disbelief. "You hear that, Ryan Cawdor? I called this...this *thing* a norm. How about that, huh? They norms?"

The other crazies had dropped to a squatting position, their whips trailing in the dirt. None of them seemed very interested in what was going on around them, ignoring the crowd of stickies that were pressing closer to them.

"How come a stickie got houses like this? And who the bloodied savior are those?" He pointed with his lash at Ryan and the others.

"They are seekers after light," Charlie replied, casually unslinging the Uzi from his shoulder. "Little like you."

"We seek light through dark. Happiness through misery. Health through pain. Day through night."

It was obviously one of their ritual chants. The fladgie's voice rose higher, like a screech owl. The other four filtered erratically in like a demented chorus.

"Right through left. Riches through poverty. Wisdom through madness."

Charlie raised his voice to interrupt the seemingly endless threnody.

"How about life through death?"

"Amen to that. Oh, yes, amen to that. Life through death." The fladgie collapsed on the red rocks and rolled around in a delirious fit of ecstasy, legs kicking, his matted hair becoming coated in dust.

"Here it comes," Ryan said to Krysty.

"Life through death," Charlie shouted in his reedy voice, turning to his people. "They want life through death."

The sound of a mob is one of the most deadly and obscene noises in the world, a mixture of sullen anger and vicious anticipation, spiced with an eager taint of perverse, guilty lust. It swells as every member of the crowd gains power from the multiheaded monster.

Charlie pointed at the five fladgies with the muzzle of the Uzi. "They want to suffer. What are we goin' to do about that?"

Now the stickies were cheering, fists pumping the air, mouths sucking air.

The leader of the flagellants stopped rolling and moaning, sitting up, looking around in bewilderment. "No," he said.

"Yeah." Charlie grinned.

Chapter Twenty-Eight

The torture and execution of Red Folsom had been done with a vile skill, making the suffering last as long as possible to prolong the pleasure of the watching stickies.

The deaths of the flagellants were handled in a different way.

It only took a matter of minutes for five triangular whipping frames to be set up and for the fladgies to be stripped of their caked rags and bound to the frames by wrists and ankles.

Since Folsom's escape attempt, Abe had fallen into a strange, almost catatonic trance. He'd ignored Ryan's attempt to talk about any plans for getting away from the stickies, sitting with his head slumped on his chest, refusing to respond to any effort to make him stir.

Now, suddenly, he seemed reborn. He shook his head like a swimmer emerging from deep water, looking around him with eyes bright.

"Hey, I been real out of it, haven't I?" he said quietly. "Happens now and then. Saw a doc a year back. He said I was a narco or something like that. Been like it since I dropped some left-field jolt when

I was in my teens. Not often…like once a year or so. Big shock can bring it on.''

"You okay now, Abe?" Ryan asked. "We're going to have to take some triple-red action real soon and it'll need you."

"Sure, sure. I'm fine. Just sort of lost a day, that's all."

The activity at the center of the camp drew Ryan's attention away from Abe.

An incessant moaning came from the five new "visitors," a wailing that was being parodied and mocked by the whole camp of stickies.

Charlie strutted out to stand by the large fire at the center of the open space and held his hands up for silence.

"Thanks, brothers and sisters. Thank you. Just got something to say."

The fladgies' leader, his back already a ghastly mass of old scar tissue and fresh, weeping wounds, called out to Charlie.

"Spare me."

"Why?"

"Got some news for you."

"What?"

"Let me live."

"All of you?"

"Yeah."

"No."

"Then me. Just me."

"How about all these others? Your four fine friends? How about them?"

"Chill 'em." The word were flat and final.

Oddly none of the other flagellants seemed at all bothered by their leader's attempts to save his life by pawning theirs. They just hung where they were, occasionally moaning.

"Save you. Kill them." Charlie raised his voice. "That's a norm for you, friends."

"Has a point, doesn't he?" Helga said.

"I'll tell you about the big gang of lepers," the fladgie yelped.

Charlie's smile dropped like a stone off a cliff edge. "You say a leper gang?"

"Sure." His next words tumbled over one another in his panicked eagerness. "We seen them three nights ago. North over rim where there's a big fall before the rains came and trail goes like break-backed snake. We smelled smoke and kept clear. Seen a body a way back that made us know they was lepers with the hands, nose, and stumps and all."

"How many?" Charlie had glanced behind him, up to the far side of the wooded ravine, where every one of his guards had been pulled back into camp to watch the killings.

"Fifty. Hundred. Don't know numbers too good, mister."

"But a lot." Charlie pointed with the Uzi at a half dozen of the older men, ordering them immediately onto watch, snarling with a sudden rage as they hesitated. "Get the fuck up there, you stupes! And keep a good look out."

The flagellant had slumped. Now he straightened, trying to look around at the leader of the stickies.

"I told you. Now can I go free?"

"No."

"No?"

"No."

"But you said—"

"I didn't say word one, norm."

"I told you about the lepers. Saved you from a sneak attack!"

"Sure you did."

"You bastard!"

"That's right, norm. Accident of birth with me. What's your excuse?"

"We are the people of God."

"That don't mean shit." Charlie glanced toward the Very Reverend Joe-Bob Jarman. "Doesn't mean shit, does it, preacher?"

Jarman lowered his head and wouldn't meet the eyes of the stickie chieftain.

"Leave him," Danny muttered, not loud enough for Charlie to hear.

"You agree with me, preacher?" The stickie pressed him, but there was still no answer. Charlie laughed and did a little tap dance. "Well, you don't disagree with me."

The woman flagellant screamed out, startling everyone, her voice clear as a silver bell.

"Tonight I dine in the halls of Elysium, at the right hand of the Almighty power of celestial wonder! Ambrosia and wild honey shall be both meat and drink. White samite shall be my raiment and of chalcedony and onyx shall be my...plates and things. Through what some call death, I shall inherit what all call life eternal."

Charlie lost interest. "Whip the triple-crazie norm fuckers to death," he said. "Take it in turns and make it last."

Once again the line of prisoners had to sit as mute spectators to the stickies' acts of senseless cruelty and brutality.

The whole camp jostled and pushed to get at the fladgies' whips and have a turn at torturing the naked quintet.

Though Ryan would never have admitted it, even to Krysty, he appreciated that there was a certain grim irony in the punishment that Charlie had chosen to terminate the miserable lives of the five flagellants.

For a group who took such lunatic delight in flogging themselves to get nearer to their idea of the godhead, being whipped to death should have been close to paradise.

But it didn't seem that they appreciated the benevolent mercy of the stickies.

As the afternoon drifted toward evening, the cutting sound of whips on human skin grew muted by blood-sodden flesh.

Even the little children took turns at the flogging,

though some of them were unable to direct their blows higher than their victims's knees.

The stickie women were the best and most ingenious at using the multithonged whips.

One of the younger ones had gotten first go at the leader. Standing staring at his already lacerated back, she reached forward and touched him down between his spread thighs, very gently, with the butt of the whip. He screamed and tried to move, straining against the tight cords.

The woman turned to the chained prisoners, concentrating on Krysty, Helga and Dorina, and rubbed at the crotch of her own jeans with the whip in an unspeakable gesture. Then she spun and delivered a cruelly aimed blow at the helpless fladgie, the metal and glass tips slicing upward between the tops of his legs.

This time his scream was piercing and he fought against the knotted rawhide so hard that blood burst from the tips of his fingers.

The laughter of the watching stickies drowned out the cries of pain and plaints for mercy from the other four flagellants.

Everyone was allowed to strike about ten blows. Blood splashed on the ground and onto the clothes and faces of those doing the flogging. Ryan had witnessed ritual whippings, often administered by frontier barons' sec men. He wasn't that surprised to see how quickly the dark relief of unconsciousness came to the five crazies.

The fact that their victims were slumped against the makeshift flogging posts didn't deter the stickies from carrying on with their sport.

The woman died first, her bowels and bladder opening in the relaxation of death.

Three of the men followed soon after, but the leader clung to the last remnants of his agonized life for at least a quarter of an hour longer.

It was the same woman who'd discovered the success of whipping at his exposed genitals who finally pulled the plug on him.

She reached again between the blood-slick thighs, groping for a proper grip with the strong suckers on her fingers and palm, whooping in triumph as she found a hold.

"Oh, Gaia!" Krysty whispered, closing her eyes at the spectacle.

There was a moment of thrilled expectation from the crowd of stickies. In that stillness, the noise of the brutal castration was grotesquely loud, the sound of ripped flesh.

As the mutie woman flourished her limp, draggled prize, the last of the flagellants gave the loudest scream that Ryan had ever heard in his life. It seemed to flood out between his lips, carrying his soul with it. Out into the valley of the Anasazi and beyond.

Far beyond.

DOC SAT HEAVILY in a patch of luxuriant moss, close to the edge of the narrowing river. "Let us pray with all our hearts that the dreadful sound we have just heard did not emanate from either of our dear, lost friends.''

''Amen to that, Doc,'' Mildred said. ''Just remembering it makes my blood curdle.''

''You don't think that was Dad, do you?'' Dean looked around at the grown-ups. ''Or Krysty? It wasn't them, was it?''

Christina put a hand on the boy's arm and squeezed it gently. ''You think that sounded like either of them, son?''

''No. But it didn't sound like anyone...like anyone human.''

''Then it wasn't Ryan or Krysty.''

''But it was like someone dying in horrible pain, wasn't it?''

J.B. answered Dean. ''Yeah, I believe it was. Means we must be close to hear it that clearly. Human voice won't carry more than a couple of miles or so. Except at night, over water.''

Doc fanned flies away from his face, looking around at the gathering dusk. ''I recall something from my days of English history. Edward the Second, who was notoriously homosexual, was murdered by his barons. They inserted a white-hot iron poker into his...'' He looked at Dean and dropped his voice. ''His fundament. It was said that his dying screams were heard better than five miles away.''

Jak shook his head. ''Thanks for story, Doc. Just what we wanted.''

They all listened, but there were no further cries from higher up the valley. J.B. pointed out that evening was closing in and they'd better get moving on toward where they thought the stickie camp was situated.

Chapter Twenty-Nine

Dorina broke the silence after the prisoners had been herded back into the dark, damp kiva.

"We gotta fucking try."

Ryan sat quiet and waited to see what effect her pebble would have on the pool, how big the ripples might be and whether anyone else was ready to chuck in their own stone.

Helga was first. "She's right. All of you. They can't do more than chill us and we know, sure as God makes little chickens, that the bastards are going to do that."

"Not just kill us quick and easy." It was Abe. "We seen that they get real good at making it long, slow and hard. Rather take a bullet in the head and try and take a stickie with me on the last train west."

Danny clapped his hands softly. "Get me close enough, and I'll strangle one of the sons of bitches before they butcher me. That'll be better than biting their bullets."

Bob moved uneasily, the faint light that filtered through the grille gleaming off his bald head. "You got friends, Ryan. One who escaped and there's others."

"Yeah."

"Could be they're on their way to try to spring us."

Ryan was cautious. "I sure wouldn't want to try to stake my life on them getting here before tomorrow night. From what Charlie said, that's likely to be when we all get hit."

"You in or not?" Dorina did something that made Bob squeal.

"Hey, don't do—"

"Well, stop pussying and stand up like the man you aren't."

"I couldn't stop them when…"

"When they raped me sixty-seven times. Well, Bob Leonard, you could mebbe do something now."

"Sure, sure. If everyone wants to go for it, then I'll be right there."

His wife's little voice was tight with anger. "Sure. Right there at the back!"

"Keep your voices down," Ryan warned. "Last thing we need is some stickie going running to his boss with what we're going to do. Me and Krysty are going to go for it."

He'd already noticed that two of the other prisoners were keeping quiet—fat Harold Lord, the complaining candy salesman who looked like he'd spent too much of his life sampling his own wares and the traveling preacher, white-haired Joe-Bob Jarman.

"Nine of us," Ryan said. "Though I only heard

seven saying they were for fighting, not dying. Two didn't speak."

"I need time to think."

"Sure, Harold. You got thirty seconds. How about you, Reverend?"

A cough. Silence. Ryan was about to try again when Jarman answered. "It goes against my being a man of peace. A man of God."

"Stickies'll likely crucify you, Reverend. Painful way of passing the dark river."

"But, if it is the will of everyone to try to escape the wrath of the unbelievers…"

He didn't finish the sentence, but Ryan guessed that it was the best they'd get. "Thirty seconds are up, Harold."

"What if I don't want to agree to your plan?"

"You haven't heard it."

"Bet it's no good."

"Being burned alive or being fed your own cock with chili sauce isn't that good, Harold," Helga said, not even bothering to conceal her contempt.

"Guess not. But what if I don't like it?"

Ryan leaned forward in the darkness. "You're with us, Harold."

"Or?"

"Or you're against us. This isn't some kind of civilized debate on morality. This is all of us getting slaughtered in less than twenty-four hours, going down with a whimper. I prefer a bang, Harold."

The anger brimmed to the front of his voice giving

it a hard, lethally frightening edge. Ryan wasn't even aware of that.

Harold was. "All right, all right. Sure, I'm in."

HAROLD'S VOICE WAS a squeak of anguish. "Is that it?"

"Shut the fuck up," Bob snapped. "You heard what Ryan said."

"Sure, and what he said wasn't worth a spoonful of sugar in a vat of molasses. Not worth an ant's fart."

Ryan was suddenly angry, partly because he knew that the young man's reaction was justified.

His voice hissed across the circular pit, striking like the lash of a fladgie's whip. "You gutless little fuck! I'm going to grab you around your stinking neck until the eyes squeeze out of your skull, just like pips from an orange. You do the same as the rest of us, or I swear to God I'll chill you right here and now."

"But they all got blasters."

"Old muskets. Self-mades and patch-ups." Abe laughed. "Do better with a good bow and arrow. Believe me, Harold, I know."

"Yeah, but, but… They take us out, and we jump them and grab blasters and run for it." He couldn't hide his terror and disbelief. "Danny's a crip. Three women. Me and the preacher aren't combat sec men, Ryan. You gotta see sense. There's only truly three of you who can fight."

He was nearly crying.

Krysty shuffled to be near him. "Harold, listen to me."

"I'm listening. I am really."

Ryan had seen every aspect of his beloved's character. So he thought.

But now she was the older, wiser sister, comforting and encouraging, teasing a little, wiping away the sudden flood of tears that rolled over the unseen, plump cheeks, praising Harold for his courage in the face of ghastly adversity, cheering him along.

"If we're to die, Harold, isn't it better to go out fighting? On your feet, not cringing on your belly? Isn't it?"

In the end, Krysty was so successful that Harold had to be dissuaded from a new plan, which had them all breaking out in the middle of the night.

THREE MILES AWAY, down the meandering valley, J.B. was on solitary watch. He had chosen to take the patrol from midnight until four in the morning, the longest four hours known to man.

The others were all sleeping quietly, wrapped in blankets, blasters ready to hand. Doc was on his back, snoring in a regular, muffled beat.

J.B. sat with his back against a Sitka spruce. The wind had veered northerly, and he could taste the threat of rain on his tongue. The Smith & Wesson M-4000 12-gauge rested across his lap, its eight fléchette rounds ready for use.

The night was quiet, with the occasional howl of a distant coyote, way down on the desert.

The Armorer thought of Ryan, trying to guess what might be happening. He'd already thought through the strong possibility that his oldest, closest friend was two days dead. Stickies weren't known for keeping their norm prisoners alive for very long.

If Ryan and Krysty had been snuffed out, then what was left was revenge.

Total, absolute revenge.

Just as dark came down, he'd spotted a narrow trail, high up on the far side of the ravine, looking like it had been established by goats, clinging to the edge of the sharp cliff. It had occurred to J.B. that it might be worth trying to cross the river and reach the trail. The path they had been laboring along had been ravaged by the rains, and any farther deterioration in the weather could make it utterly impassable.

Clouds came sailing across the moon, darkening the forest. J.B. automatically slid his finger onto the trigger of the M-4000, straining his eyes into the blackness. Wind rustled the trees, and the sound of the tumbling water seemed to have become suddenly louder.

But there was something else.

Like smoke coiling from a fire, the slightly built Armorer stood up, melting into the blackness around him.

Something moved.

He corrected that as he heard the faint mutter of voices. *Someone* moved.

J.B. glanced over his shoulder, his keen night vision enabling him to pick out the lumpy shapes of his sleeping friends. There was a grave risk of one of them waking and calling out to him, bringing the strangers down like a pack of hunting wolves. But the alternative risk of trying to ease them all silently from sleep was infinitely higher.

J.B. stood still and waited and watched, trying to work out how many were moving north, toward the higher ground.

And who they were.

The clouds thwarted him in the former while the insistent river remained just loud enough to blur any speech.

But there was enough sound to tell him that the group moving through the night was a large one. J.B. didn't much care for guessing, but when there was no choice... He figured there was fifty or more in the party.

Once they'd all passed, he kept perfectly still and counted a thousand heartbeats, waiting in case they'd posted a rearguard. But the night remained quiet.

RYAN WOKE WITH A START, feeling his heart jump. He opened his eye and saw only the faint glow of the big camp fire peeking through the cover of their prison.

For a moment he couldn't work out what jerked

him from sleep. Then he realized that the weighted silk scarf was missing from around his neck.

On the far side of the kiva he caught the whisper of movement and harsh, strained breathing.

"Krysty?"

"Yeah?" Her voice barely audible.

"What are…"

"Just chilled us a traitor," she replied.

Chapter Thirty

Within seconds everyone in the kiva was awake, asking urgent, whispered questions.

Krysty explained in short, shocked sentences. "Woke when I felt movement. Was trying to tap on the grille above to attract the attention of the stickie guard. Heard what he was saying. He wanted to tell Charlie about an escape. All that I heard."

"What did you do?" Dorina asked. "You got a knife hidden, Krysty?"

"No. Ryan's scarf is white silk. Really strong." She paused. "Strong enough."

"Strangle him?" Bob Leonard's distorted voice reflected all of their shock.

"Had the scarf in both hands, looped in the middle. Had it around his throat before he knew what I was doing."

Abe coughed. "Nothing like a good garotte for a quick, quiet chilling." His admiration was obvious. "You did him without disturbing me, five feet away, Krysty. Real good."

"Yeah, Abe. Throttling a man is real good, isn't it?"

"Had it coming," Ryan said. "We all know you did the right thing and did it well."

The Very Reverend Joe-Bob Jarman didn't share that opinion at all. "Oh, terrific. Now we got us a strangled corpse in here with us. How in the name of the Savior do we explain that one, Ryan?"

"Won't have to. We stick to our plan and leave him down here. By the time we make the rush on them, it'll be way too late for anyone to notice one dead man more or less."

"Never have thought it," Helga whispered. "Would have expected that someone else..." The words faded into silence.

"You mean you thought that if we had a traitor it'd be me, didn't you? Ugly old bitch!"

"Shut the fuck up, Harold!" Ryan reached out and grabbed a handful of sleeve. "One more word and I'll break your whining neck."

"Yeah, then you got two chills in here," he retorted defiantly. "And Danny shit himself when he died. We got to put up with that all night."

Ryan let go of the fat young man and laughed quietly. "I never met anyone who complained as much as you, Harold. You got it to a real art, boy. If Krysty hadn't choked Danny for us, then that faint glimmer of light would've been plucked right away. You never think of that, Harold?"

"Guess I didn't. I'm real sorry, Krysty. Got a loose mouth."

"Why'd he do it?"

Krysty, recovering from the midnight shock of committing a hands-on murder, answered Helga herself. "He sounded like he was desperate. Lost his mind, almost. I think it was probably the pain of his broken ankle turned his brain."

The older woman sounded relieved at having an explanation that she could cling to, something that might eventually help her to come to terms with her ramrod's betrayal.

"Guess that'd make sense. Danny never coped too well with suffering. Remember the time he was way south in Mex country after mustangs. Picked up some of them pokies."

There was a collective shudder through the kiva. Joe-Bob Jarman made a sound of utter disgust. "Had one once. In my right ear. Where did he get...did they get him?"

Pokies were small beetles that were found both north and south of the big Grandee. They had black iridescent bodies, about an inch long and a third of an inch across. Their legs were tipped with barbed spikes that hooked themselves onto anything convenient.

They also had hugely disproportionate jaws, like miniature scythes.

Their name came from their ceaseless desire to poke into the warm, moist places of the human body. Once there they would hook on to the living flesh and start eating, dining in comfort on fresh meat. There was no orifice known to man or woman that a pokie wouldn't try for.

Sleeping on the ground often meant tying lengths of whipcord around the bottoms of your pant legs to try to keep them out. But then there were ears, noses and mouths. Ryan had even heard ghastly tales of pokies insinuating themselves into the tear ducts at the corner of a sleeping man's eyes, working their way deeper and deeper.

But the folklore on pokies concentrated far more on their affinity for the lower regions of the human body.

Ryan recalled a scrawled warning he'd once seen on the tarred wall of an outhouse: No Good Standing on the Seat. The Pokies Here Can Jump Six Feet.

He'd never personally witnessed anyone who'd been attacked by the burrowing insects, but Death-lands lore was full of tales: a man who'd been squatting to relieve himself had been penetrated; a woman who'd been bathing in a shallow lake on the Keys. Best known, and probably apocryphal, was the wretched man taking his pleasure in a gaudy, with a breed whore. He didn't know she was infested with pokies. The carnivorous little creatures traveled from her to him during intercourse.

Rumor was he'd finally gone insane and poured gasoline over his cock.

And lighted it.

Jarman's question had made Helga hesitate. "Where did they..."

"Doesn't matter. But how did Danny..."

She regained the thread of her thoughts. "He had them up his nose. Three of them, I got 'em out with salt, but he sure made a fuss. Pain was—hell, there's no use. Boy's dead and that's the end of it."

"Someone coming," Krysty warned.

"Changing sentries," Harold guessed.

Wrong.

"One-eye?"

It was a woman's voice. Ryan ignored it. But it was repeated.

"One-eye? Know you're in there."

"Might as well answer, lover. Or she'll call the sentries and they'll be on the alert. Find Danny's corpse."

"And goodbye'll be all she wrote," Abe whispered. "Better see what she wants."

"Yeah?" Ryan called.

"Knew you was in there."

"What do you want?"

"You out here."

"Why?"

"Me to know and you to fucking find out. Just get out here, One-eye."

Ryan stood, hands fumbling to keep his balance as he picked his way between the others. He looked up, able to see only a dim shape through the bars of the grille.

"I'm here."

"Rest of you stay real still. Got plenty of blasters up top. Just One-eye comes out."

One of the stickie guards said something, and there was a burst of soft, obscene giggling.

Bolts grated and the grille was hauled off to one side, sliding across the bare rock. Ryan smelled the familiar scent of burning torch oil, and the orange flames danced around him. Coming from the blackness of the kiva, it was difficult to make out how many of the stickies were around him, but his eye caught light off musket barrels.

"Get his hands tied good behind him," said the unseen woman. "Want to do what I want to the norm with no trouble."

"How about his feet, Marcie?" asked one of the guards, sniggering.

"Best tie his feet to the bottom her bed. Or he'll get sucked out of sight," called another of the stickies. "Charlie'll never see him again, and he wouldn't like that."

Ryan stood still. Behind him, he caught an urgent whisper from Krysty. "Control, lover. Think control."

It was good advice.

But it didn't do Ryan much good.

Chapter Thirty-One

Ryan had tried the old trick of flexing his muscles when they began to bind his wrists behind him, so that he might win a little play in the narrow length of whipcord.

The stickies might have been stupe in a lot of ways, but they knew about tying norms up so that they stayed tied.

As soon as they spotted what Ryan was trying to do, one of them punched him in the stomach, winding him, making him relax so that the cords could be pulled brutally, efficiently tight.

"Don't hurt the norm or I'll cut your balls off, Jack," the woman warned.

"I'll leave the hurtin' to you, Marcie" was the response, bringing yet more laughter from the ring of sentries.

Ryan heard the grille slid back and bolted into place again.

A loop of coarse hemp rope was slipped over his head and pulled until it closed around his throat. The mutie woman held the other end in her right hand and she jerked hard at it, making Ryan go stumbling after her.

"Make sure you got him back before dawn, Marcie," a sentry called.

"Yeah. What's left of him."

THE WOMAN'S TUMBLED HOUSE was at the far end of the camp, nearest to the ravine and the muttering stream. It was back under the lee of the massive cliff's overhang, the smoke-crusted stone soaring into the darkness above it.

She pulled him through the doorway, which was hung with a length of dusty sacking. A single torch was jammed into a hole in the ancient brickwork, showing a three-legged table propped in a corner. A stout-framed bed with a yellow blanket crumpled on top of it occupied a large area of the room.

Ryan had time to notice a faded picture pinned above the head of the bed. It seemed to show two naked men, one kneeling in front of the other. The shadows concealed what they were doing, but it didn't take a giant leap of the imagination to guess.

The stickie turned to face him, confirming Ryan's suspicion that it was the same woman who'd "accidentally" spilled the stew on him. And used it as an excuse to feel him up.

"Well, ain't this fucking cozy, One-eye? They call you Ryan, don't they?" When he didn't answer immediately she reached out and laid her suckered left hand against his cheek, the tip of the index finger just touching his good right eye. "Want to lose this baby-blue glim as well?'' she said, grinning at him with a soft, insistent menace.

''No.''

Her breath was like the firefight stench of punctured guts, the protruding eyes as cold and dead as a basking shark.

''So? Ryan?''

''Yeah.''

''And I'm Marcie. Now we know each other's name we can get to it.''

The hand moved from his face.

Lower.

IT WAS THE WORST of times. Ryan lost track of how long the woman had kept him in her stinking hovel. He consciously tried to use techniques that Krysty had attempted to teach him: ways of controlling the mind, and through the mind the body; ways of moving out of the horrors of the immediate present; ways that failed him utterly under the manipulations of the stickie woman.

MARCIE WOULDN'T take any chances, so Ryan's hands stayed tied behind his back. But that didn't stop her from stripping him naked below the waist, pulling his pants off over the combat boots. Ryan considered trying to kick her unconscious, but she was too careful.

She was also extremely strong, her naked body rippling with ridges of muscle. He figured her at close to six feet, with a fighting weight of about one-eighty pounds.

Apart from the rings of bristles around her thick nipples, Marcie had a nest of pubic hair that curled up to her navel and seeped onto the tops of her powerful thighs.

She took the rope around his neck and knotted the loose end to the top of the bed. "Move and you strangle yourself, Ryan." She grinned. "I'll do all the moving for both of us."

Despite all his efforts, he rose to her. The fingers, with their hundreds of tiny lips, were surprisingly delicate, touching and fondling him, pressing with insistent lust between his legs. Ryan made the serious mistake of trying to close his thighs against her. Marcie simply sat up and dealt him three contemptuous, open-handed slaps across the face, which made his ears ring.

"Do that again and I use my hands on your chest. Peel little round circles of skin off of you like acid, One-eye. Best be nice and give me your best shot. Do that, and you might get back alive to the firehead norm bitch."

The mutie's orgasms were like wrestling with a puma in a typhoon.

But she kept her mouth snapped shut, saliva seeping between her own lips from the intensity that surged through her. Marcie rode him like a vaquero spurring an unbroken stallion, her heels digging into his thighs, rising and falling faster and faster. Her head was thrown back, eyes closed, breath rasping like a turbine in overdrive.

After the second one she lay flat against him, her sweat running down both sides of his chest, her face against his stubbled chin, fingers groping across his stomach, to keep him ready.

With an enormous effort, Ryan had managed to tread the tightrope between losing his erection through a sickly disgust, and risking Marcie's violent displeasure by coming himself.

During the third time around, she had leaned over him and jammed fingers into the corner of his mouth to force it open, deliberately dribbling a thread of frothy saliva between his parted lips. She grinned at his struggle not to throw up.

"You puke, and the fourth time is with your tongue up me, norm," she growled, eyes narrowing with a vicious delight at the idea, sensing his gut-deep repugnance. "In fact, we'll make that one into a real nice promise, Ryan."

THE STICKIE WENT to a ramshackle cupboard in the corner of the little room, reached in and withdrew an earthenware jug. She brought it to her lips and took a long, noisy swig.

"Pulque," she explained, licking her lips. "Mebbe I ought to give you some. Keep that pecker of yours up. Though this time it won't be your pecker that sends me to the top and back, will it?"

Marcie carried the jug back to the bed and straddled Ryan, her knees spread wide to show him the glistening, moist lips of her sex. She nearly drained the jug of fiery liquor and kept smiling at him, leaning down and kissing him on the cheeks and mouth, nipping him with her needle-sharp teeth, pushing her tongue into his mouth.

Now she had a knife in her hand.

The weapon had a wooden shaft, the blade set in at a clumsy angle, and was bound around with frayed cord. The point had been broken and badly resharpened, but the edge looked to be well honed.

Marcie reached behind her and touched the cold steel against Ryan's groin, giggling at the way his scrotum shrank against the contact.

He closed his eye and took a slow, long breath, managing, just, to keep control over himself. She shuffled a little higher, toward his head, giving him a coy smile. ''No peeking at a lady, One-eye. Not if you want to keep the family jewels.''

The rope around Ryan's neck was taut, keeping his head immobile. Marcie edged a little farther up his body, her breasts quivering with barely contained excitement, nipples standing out like desiccated cherries.

He felt bile rising from the depths of his stomach, swelling toward his chest and throat. If the repulsive stickie carried out her threat and forced him to pleasure her with his tongue, Ryan was suddenly certain that he would vomit. Uncontrollably and violently.

And then Marcie would use her knife on him and he'd be dead.

At that second, Ryan didn't find that option too appalling.

"Now," she breathed, lifting herself for a moment, ready to plunge down onto his face.

Under the curve of her buttocks Ryan glimpsed the sacking over the doorway, saw it move as though there had been a violent gust of wind.

Then it was obscured and he was suffocating, about to puke.

He wriggled his head to try to breathe and felt the woman's body jerk in response.

Marcie's thighs clamped tight over the sides of his head, shutting out any sound. She convulsed again, her full weight on his face.

Ryan felt consciousness slipping away, with the last thought of what a stupid and undignified way it was to die.

Chapter Thirty-Two

Air.

Noisome, stinking, smoky air, but it squeezed its way into Ryan's lungs. And light, from the guttering torch on the orange wall.

The powerful stickie woman above him rose half-way up, the big muscles along the inside of her thighs fluttering, then came down, sideways toppling off him. The knife fell to the floor with a fragile, tinkling sound.

Ryan blinked, seeing Marcie down on hands and knees, her face only a hand's span from his. She coughed and blood gouted from her open mouth, splattering on the floor.

"Not fuckin' fair," she gasped, then slid forward onto her stomach, bare feet drumming for a few seconds on the stones.

Ryan glanced from the bullet wound in the center of her naked back, up to the murderous figure that stood poised in the doorway, holding the sacking curtain to one side.

There was a filthy M-16 in the right hand, pointing toward Ryan. The man wore a shapeless coat over torn and muddied pants. His right hand was missing a couple of fingers, and the left hand seemed to have no fingers at all. Just raw stumps. His face was blank, lacking any expression. His mouth had slipped sideways, as though something had eaten a part of it away. The nose was missing, revealing a cavernous, snuffling, snot-crusted hole.

Ryan had encountered groups of lepers before. Mostly they had the reputation of being untrustworthy and violent outlanders.

"Sorry to spoil your fucking fun," the apparition said, steadying the carbine with the stubby left hand.

"Not a stickie," Ryan gasped. "You saved me..." But he realized that the leper wasn't listening to him. He had decided to chill Ryan and that was that. Nothing would stop him.

Nothing except the musket ball that smashed into the back of his narrow skull.

It hit at a slightly upward angle, penetrating to the left, splintering the cranial bone, then distorting and tumbling down through the brain. It exited near the top of the nose in a spray of pink, gray and crimson, bringing half of the leper's diseased face with it.

The corpse dropped to the floor, alongside Marcie, twitched for a moment and then lay still.

Ryan waited, shifting his position so that the rope around his neck was less painful.

But no one else appeared.

Outside there was shouting and a fusillade of firing, sounding like it came from a variety of weapons.

Ryan took a few moments to steady his breathing,

hardly able to believe that his life had been saved twice in less than ten seconds.

"So it goes," he muttered, concentrating his energy on getting free.

If Marcie had decided to tie his ankles to the bed, he'd have been utterly helpless. As it was, he could wriggle on his back, careful with the noose around his throat, slide his legs over the edge of the straw mattress and fumble with his toes for the dropped knife.

The stickie's hand was on top of it, but again luck rode with Ryan.

The suckered fingers hadn't closed on the hilt with the immovable spasm of rigor mortis. He was able to kick Marcie's wrist out of the way and pick up the clumsy blade.

Then it was some struggling contortions to bring it onto the bed and lay it where his tied hands could reach it.

Ryan was deathly aware of the noise outside, indicating that a large force of lepers was attacking the sleeping camp—and that at any moment one might choose to burst into the lighted room and shoot him down.

The steel cut through the thongs. Ryan could feel a trickle of warm blood over his wrist, but he was nearly free.

It only took a moment, then, to slice the hemp apart and tug the loop from his neck.

As he swung his legs to the floor and reached for

the M-16, Ryan trod full on the naked buttocks of the
dead woman, producing an eructation of trapped gas.

"Sorry," he said, grinning mirthlessly.

First thing was to take the torch and bring it against
the bloodied stone floor, bringing a measure of safety
with the swooping darkness.

Ryan hesitated before pulling on his pants, aware
of the cloying stickiness around his groin. He grabbed
the stickie's shirt and quickly wiped himself with it.

Ten seconds later he was fully dressed, the carbine
in his hands. Ready to go.

A sudden burst of flame somewhere to his left illuminated the whole area, and he saw a number of
struggling figures, scurrying like disturbed ants. He
also spotted a number of bodies draped around the
central part of the encampment.

Ryan licked his lips, grimacing with disgust as he
realized that he could still taste Marcie on his tongue.

He turned back from the doorway and picked up
the cool earthenware jug of pulque. Taking a mouthful, he swilled it around his mouth and spit it onto
the two tangled corpses. Then the one-eyed man took
a swallow on the powerful liquor, feeling it ice its
way down his gullet, then turn to flame as it reached
his stomach.

"Fireblast! That hit the spot," he said.

He pushed the sacking drapery aside and stepped
cautiously into the vicious maelstrom of close fighting.

Keeping in the shadows that lay deepest under the

overhang of dark rock, Ryan picked his way along
the narrow alleys between the old ruined houses. The
blaster he'd taken from the dead leper was in appalling condition, looking as though it had been used to
hew coal and then to stir fish stew in a filthy caldron.

He'd also stuck Marcie's knife into his belt, as
backup.

Hearing someone running toward him, he'd backed
into a storeroom filled with crates of dried fruit. The
footfalls darted past with the familiar flapping sound
that told him it had been a stickie.

From a tiny rectangular window, Ryan was able to
look out over the main part of the ancient Anasazi
mesa township.

The lepers seemed to have gained a hold on the
side of the camp nearest to the river, doubtless infil-
trating down the flank of the ravine, then gathering
for a concerted attack, sweeping out of the early-
morning blackness.

The stickies were fighting back in scattered pockets, but there didn't seem to be much pattern to their
efforts.

There was no sign of Charlie.

Ryan peered through the smoky gloom to where
the rest of the prisoners were being held. Several kivas were aligned through one side of the main plaza
area of the site, but Krysty and the others were in the
most distant. From where Ryan was hiding, it was
impossible to see whether the sentries were still there.

''See a chance, take a chance.'' The Trader's old saying was rarely wrong.

Either the lepers would overwhelm the defending stickies and take over the camp, or the muties would hold them off and drive them back into the surrounding wilderness.

Whatever way it went, Krysty, Abe, Dorina, Helga, Harold, Bob and Joe-Bob all faced a severely restricted future.

As RYAN DODGED CLOSER to the row of kivas, a figure loomed at him from a narrow entrance, brandishing a long cleaver. The M-16 kicked against his hip as he pulled the trigger, the bullet kicking the shadow backward.

It was all over so quickly that Ryan never even had time to decide whether it had been a stickie or a leper.

Not that it made any difference.

The metal grille was totally unguarded. Ryan paused, glancing around, watching for any movement among the ruins. But everyone seemed completely involved in the fighting.

Away behind him he caught the high, thin sound of Charlie's voice, shouting orders, and there was a triple salvo of explosions that he figured for some sort of fragmentation grens, the bangs followed by the weird noise of stickies cheering.

It began to seem as if the defenders might be winning.

A ball whined off the cliff a yard above Ryan,

showering him in fine dust. There was no way of knowing whether it had just been a stray round, or whether someone was trying to get him fixed in the cross hairs of his musket.

He dropped to a crouch and jinked to the kiva, kneeling and calling through the bars.

"Everyone okay?"

A babble of voices responded, with the sonorous boom of the preacher soaring above them all. "The saints bless you, Ryan!"

"What's going on, lover!"

"Lepers attacking. Big firefight. I'll get you out now."

The bolts had been greased with what smelled like rancid cooking oil, but they slid back easily enough and Ryan was able to heave the heavy iron cover out of the way.

Helga climbed out, hefted up by Abe. The rest jostling after her.

Krysty was last, taking Ryan's hand, giving him a quick kiss on the cheek. "Thought you were gone."

"Me, too."

"Could we get us some blasters?" Abe asked, his eyes darting hungrily in the direction of the heavy gunfire.

"Want to try and get the ones we had when they took us. Krysty had a Smith & Wesson 640. I had a SIG-Sauer handgun and a bolt-action Steyr rifle. Plus some knives."

"They'll be where Charlie lives," Bob said. "Took all blasters there."

"Where?"

Dorina answered. "Same place they took me for their funning. Follow me."

They picked their way back toward the center of the action.

Ryan was second, following the skinny young woman, his carbine ready, the others trailing along behind them.

Thick smoke drifted across the camp, making visibility difficult. And it had begun to rain again.

The first burst of fire from Charlie's Uzi cut down Helga and Bob.

Chapter Thirty-Three

The woman fell, four bullets stitched across her chest and stomach. She rolled sideways, thrashing, knocking Abe into the dirt with her, screaming in a deep, hoarse voice.

Bob started to duck away, one arm half raised in a useless gesture to try to hold off the stream of 9 mm bullets. The first two severed his arm at the wrist, the hand dropping, fingers curling as the tendons were hacked through. The next two rounds pulped the side of his head, tearing most of his face away, teeth splintering against the wall of rock beyond him.

Ryan half turned, seeing instantly that both of them were down and done for.

He spotted Charlie, crouched on a pinnacle of crumbling red rock, his yellow hair streaked with dirt and matted with what looked like somebody's blood. His eyes were stretched wide, and his mouth was tugged open in a soundless scream of triumph and hatred.

The first round that Ryan snapped off from the M-16 kicked a handful of dirt, inches from the stickie's feet. The second tug on the trigger produced the dry click of an empty mag.

"Fireblast!" He was furiously angry that he'd omitted to check how many rounds remained in the leper's carbine.

"You fuckers are all dead!" Charlie howled, steadying the Uzi.

Little Dorina saved them.

Stooping and picking up a jagged rock the size of a small apple, she whipped back her wrist and sent the missile hissing toward the stickie.

It hit Charlie on the right forearm with an audible crack. He nearly dropped the blaster, snatching at it with his left hand as it began to fall. The sudden movement unbalanced him, and he slid backward, vanishing from sight with an almost comical expression of dismay on his sweat-stained face.

"Come on!" Ryan yelled, dropping the useless blaster and sprinting toward the shelter of another group of semiruined adobe houses.

"What about Helga?" Harold shouted. "You can't leave her."

The woman was rolling from side to side, a string of intestine trailing from the gaping stomach wounds. She'd stopped crying out, her face unrecognizably contorted with shock.

"She's dying." Krysty grabbed Harold by the arm and steered him with her.

The half-dozen survivors reached a moment of safety, crouching together in pitch darkness.

"Nice throw, Dorina," Ryan said, fighting to slow his breathing.

"Used to knock possum out of trees. Yellow-headed fucker was easier."

"It was the best throw I ever saw, my child," the preacher boomed.

"Worst," she replied. "I was aiming at his nose."

Abe had twisted his ankle and was massaging it. "Hurts like a bastard," he said, whistling softly between his teeth. "Always happens. Trader used to say he'd take me out back and put a bullet through my head. Like an old hound dog who got too old."

"Can you run?"

"We get out and those lepers and stickies start in after us, Ryan, then you better get clear or I'll run over the top of you."

OUTSIDE THE COVER of the towering cliff above them, the rain was sheeting down again.

"How far to Charlie's place?"

Dorina turned to Ryan, her face only a pale blur. "Close."

Ryan thought about it for a moment. "Fewer of us moving around the better. Dorina'll show me and Krysty where the blasters are hidden. You three stay in here. Safe as it gets."

"Sure. Two hundred lepers and stickies murdering one another about ten paces away." Abe laughed. "I like what you call safe, Ryan."

The trio moved away from the others.

As soon as the young woman had pointed out which of the old dwellings was occupied by Charlie,

Ryan sent her scurrying back to rejoin the others in hiding.

"I could come with you."

"No."

"Want to chill some stickies. Make up for everything that—"

Ryan hushed her. "We know. Before we get clear of this place you'll probably get your chance. Now do like I say."

She nodded and turned, vanishing out of sight.

Krysty bit her lip. "She doesn't even seem to realize her husband's been gunned down."

"Only five rounds in the chamber, that one." Ryan tapped his forehead.

"Do you blame her, lover?"

"What she's been through? Course not."

Ahead of them they saw a leper and a stickie rolling over and over in the slippery mud that was already covering the camp. Both had knives, struggling to hack at each other. But the leper was missing fingers from both his hands, putting him at a terminal disadvantage. The stickie had his free hand clamped to his enemy's face, sucking off strips of skin. Both of the combatants were dappled with blood, streaming pink in the rain.

At a gesture from Ryan, Krysty backed off with him behind a low wall, crouching to watch the outcome of the mortal combat.

Because of their various physical disabilities, lepers

were never rated too highly when it came down to hand-to-hand.

By the time the stickie had given its whooping shriek of victory, the leper's head had been reduced to a hairless, skinless, blood-slick skull, eyeless and featureless.

The mutie stood up unsteadily, facing away from Ryan and Krysty.

"Could get you his knife, lover," Ryan said.

"Get it myself."

She walked out, the noise of the storm drowning the clicking of her boot heels. The rain immediately soaked her hair, dulling its bright glow, pasting it to her neck and shoulders. It only took her eight strides to reach the exulting stickie.

Krysty wasted no time, chopping the man across the back of the neck with the edge of her right hand, chilling the mutie with an ease that was almost contemptuous.

She stooped, picked the knife from the trembling fingers and rejoined Ryan.

"Like taking honey from a hive of dead bees," she said.

"Weren't you ever stung by a dead bee?" Ryan asked her.

"No. Not that I remember."

They waited for the moment to cross an open space, by the hissing remains of the biggest of the stickies' camp fires.

The doorway to Charlie's house was pitch-black, with no sign of life within.

A woman ran past Ryan and Krysty, holding her severed left hand in her right hand, blood jetting in spurts from the raw wound.

A musket cracked to the left of the valley and someone cried out with shock and anger.

Ryan glanced at Krysty. "Now," he said.

Just as they reached the entrance, a tall stickie came out, holding the butt of a musket. The barrel was missing.

He looked up, recognizing Ryan in the gloom. "You the One-eye went with good old Marcie." A puzzled look clouded the mutie's eyes. "Hey, how come you..."

Ryan and Krysty stabbed him at precisely the same moment, almost as though they'd been rehearsing the move for weeks.

The man went down like a sack of coal, dropping stone dead without a sound at their feet.

They slipped out of sight into Charlie's home, finding a small brass oil lamp still burning.

All their weapons were there, lying on the top of an old oak chest at the foot of a double bed.

Less than a half minute later they rejoined the others.

Chapter Thirty-Four

"Which way we going to get out?"

The Very Reverend Joe-Bob Jarman was the biggest block of shadow in the building, and his voice was the loudest.

"Next time you shout like that, I'll cut your damned throat, preacher," Ryan snarled, peeking around the corner of one of the windows to watch what was happening out in the teeming night.

It seemed as though the stickies still had the edge. The downpour made it hard to see, the rain mingling with the smoke from the fires and the muskets.

But there seemed to be a lot less shooting and screaming.

Ryan gave his rifle to Abe, keeping the SIG-Sauer for his own use. Krysty held on to her 5-shot Smith & Wesson. After some thought Ryan gave Jak's big .357 Magnum to Harold, keeping the teenager's precious throwing knives for himself.

The captured blades went to Dorina and to Joe-Bob Jarman, who complained in an endless monotone. "Leaving a man of God without a weapon against them that threaten me. I need more than a fucking rod and staff to comfort me with lepers and stickies and

Christ knows what else is running around in this valley of the fucking shadow of death. You give the blasters to women and to a fat kid.''

''Don't call me 'kid,' Reverend,'' Harold warned, a new note of confidence in his voice.

''Cut it out.''

''Which way we going to go?'' Dorina was trembling with excitement at the thought that they might actually escape from the stickies.

''Shortest route isn't always the best one to take. This rain'll swell the stream in an hour or so. Charlie'll expect us to go back down the valley. Quickest way out. So, we go up.''

''Up?''

Ryan tightened his knuckles on the butt of the blaster. ''Yeah, Harold. Try listening so I don't have to keep saying the same thing. We go across the bridge and then move up the farther side of the valley. All right?''

''Sure, Ryan, sure.''

THE SUDDEN ERUPTION of gunfire out of the black night had awakened Mildred, Dean, Jak and Christina. As usual, Doc was locked into a long-ago dream of an endless summer yesterday and proved harder to wake.

''Upon my soul, are we under attack from some nameless entity?''

''No. Guns up the mountain.''

"Might it be Dad breaking out from the stickies' camp?" Dean asked.

Jak shook his head. "Shooting isn't moving around like they chasing anyone."

Mildred looked at J.B. "You make out what it is, John?"

The Armorer stood still, eyes closed, head on one side. "There's some muskets and some carbines. An M-16 and I think I heard an Uzi. No. Figure that somebody's attacking the stickies." And he thought of the group he'd heard moving quietly north earlier in the night.

"Who?" Christina asked. "Apache? Navaho? Mexes? Or just the usual renegade bastards?"

"Can't tell. Seems like…dark night! Now it's starting to rain again."

"We going up there?"

J.B. looked at the boy. "Sure we are, Dean. Fast as we can."

FOR A FEW MINUTES the storm seemed to have passed by.

Someone threw gasoline on one of the dying fires, bringing it back to a brilliant, roaring life. The sight obviously cheered the stickies and took more of the heart out of the attacking lepers.

It also made it more risky for Ryan and the others to leave their hiding place and break across the camp for the relative safety of the higher ground farther up the valley.

They watched as scenes from the tableaux of life and death—mainly death—were played out around them.

They saw Charlie twice, and Abe leveled the Steyr at the stalking, hunting figure, his finger moving to settle on the trigger.

But Ryan laid a hand across the sights. "No. Not when we're so close to making it clean away from here."

Abe nodded, but he still followed the stickies' chief, keeping the blaster trained on the shock of yellow hair.

It looked like Charlie was searching for someone, and they all knew who that was.

After he'd gone, they saw a skirmish line of a dozen or so lepers picking their way haltingly along the line of buildings, opening fire at anything that moved. Or looked like it had moved.

"Boy! It's as though they've opened the gates on every crip's home in Deathlands," Harold commented. "Had one up in Castle Rock and you'd see them all slobbering and hobbling and being triple odd. Mostly double wrinklies, of course."

"Like to be around and see you when you get old, Harold," Krysty said coldly.

"Hope I die before that," he replied, grinning amiably.

Ryan couldn't help thinking that Harold's comment wasn't entirely unjustified. Apart from demonstrating that they shared with the stickies a virulent hatred of anyone normal, the lepers were just amazingly stupid, which made Charlie such a double freak. But lepers had the major problem that they were all rotting away—maybe only the end of a finger here and there, or the tip of a nose. Or just one ear.

But the lepers in Deathlands didn't ever get any better.

Once they'd had that telltale numbness in the extremities and began to lose a sense of what was hot and cold, it was downhill.

The group that stumbled by were typical. The classic, almost leonine heads, and the obvious lack of toes and fingers.

Most had blasters, with the traditional M-16 carbines predominating. But some had small hideaway handblasters, while others had only spears and long knives. A couple had bows and arrows, though Ryan suspected that these weren't likely to be great weapons if you didn't have a full set of fingers on each hand.

One went down right in front of the hidden watchers, a musket ball striking it through the side of the neck. The others ignored its death throes, moving toward the end of the camp where the overhang was steepest. And where most of the stickies lived.

The fire seemed to be burning even more brightly, illuminating the room where they were hiding. Joe-Bob Jarman glanced behind him and gagged in revulsion, drawing the attention of the others to what he'd just seen.

Two stickie children lay on a truckle bed. They had been stripped naked. The little girl showed the visible stigmata of having been the victim of rape. The boy had been castrated. Both had been strangled.

"Gaia!" Krysty looked at Ryan. "These sick bastards sure deserve each other."

Dorina spit on the floor. "Mebbe they'll wipe each other out, right down the line. Make for a cleaner world!"

"Rain's come back heavier still." Abe was leaning on the crumbling wood of the windowsill.

"Might still be stickies out in the woods," Ryan warned. "Anyone we see's an enemy. So shoot first and we can worry about corpses afterward."

J.B. GATHERED them around, hunching his shoulders against the downpour. "When we get close to the camp, there could be sentries. Stickie guards. Don't hesitate. Pull down on them before they do it to you. All right? Then let's go get Ryan."

Chapter Thirty-Five

The explosion in the small building that held the stickies' supplies of cooking and lighting oil was devastating. It turned the wet and windy night into the brightest day.

The falling rain resembled a great wall of red and orange flames, spitting into the lake of mud. The liquid from the ruptured containers streamed everywhere, pouring into the kivas, where it also ignited, making the circular ceremonial pits look more like blazing oil wells.

The deep, echoing boom bounced around the camp, seeming to become amplified beneath the cliff. It was welcomed with wild cheers and whoops from the triumphant stickies, giving them extra courage to surge across and finally begin to drive out the surviving lepers.

"We have to go now," Ryan told his companions. "If we don't, then we could get stranded in here. Won't take Charlie long to get himself reorganized and sweep the place to find us. Think he might even bring our execution time forward for us. Just try and keep close."

"But the fire makes it easy for anyone to spot us.

Perhaps we should be better advised to try and remain
hidden.''

Ryan closed his eye for a moment, drawing a slow
breath to control his anger. "Fine, Reverend. You
stay here and wait to be crucified by the stickies.
Mebbe you could really enjoy that. Give you a deep
and meaningless experience.''

"But the rest of us is going." Abe grinned. "Here
and now.''

A DEAD LEPER LAY SPRAWLED half off the wooden
bridge, one abbreviated hand trailing in the foaming
water. It worried Ryan, as it looked like the man had
been chilled while trying to escape the camp, rather
than gunned down during the attack. It could mean
that some of the lepers were already out ahead of
them, hiding somewhere in the dank woods.

The center of the firelight was clearly away at the
far end of the encampment, where the remainder of
the lepers were trapped under the overhang, forced
into a bloody and savage last stand. The gunfire was
slowing, as victims were picked off one by one.

Ryan glanced behind them once more, making sure
his little group was still together after the dash down
the slope.

"Get on," Jarman shouted, "before the mutie curs
see us.''

The rain was sheeting down in swirling banks of
water, pitting the mud and turning the puddles into
frothing orange lace. Ryan picked his way up the slip-

pery steps on the other side of the ravine, marveling at their good fortune in managing to get away without any of the stickies spotting them.

"Lose some, win some," he said over his shoulder to Abe, who was next in line.

But the skinny man was on his knees, the hunting rifle lying in the dirt. His face was contorted with pain and his hands were pressed to his stomach, low on the right side.

"Lose some," he said, making a brief try for a brave grin and failing by a distance.

"Bad?"

"Like being kicked in the kidneys by a fucking mule. Oh, jeez..."

The scream of rage from behind them was chillingly recognizable as Charlie, being told that his choice captives were off and running.

Jarman pushed by Krysty, knocking the wounded man to one side of the path. "Stand away!" he bellowed at Ryan.

If he hadn't been concentrating on how best to play Abe's injury, Ryan would have killed the preacher without hesitation.

The tall white-haired figure bounced away from them, quickly vanishing into the wet darkness near the old Visitor Center.

"Get going, Ryan," Abe said, his voice surprisingly calm and gentle.

"Shut it."

"Bad hit. Had 'em before. Tell you it's a bad one. Leave me."

"We can carry him between us," Harold offered, lifting himself up a couple more notches in Ryan's estimation.

"Won't make it very far," Krysty said.

"Yeah," Abe agreed.

A couple of bullets hissed through the night and kicked up plumes of spray behind the small group.

"Give me the rifle," Dorina suggested. "I'll keep the bastards' heads down."

"Do it," Ryan ordered.

"Leave me here, Ryan. You four can make it."

"No."

"Rain covers tracks. Go and—ohhh, hurts. Put one between my eyes, Ryan. Old times' sake. Be a friend, won't you?"

Abe was doubled right over, one foot tapping uncontrollably in the slime. He was moaning now on every indrawn breath.

Dorina leveled the Steyr and fired off three spaced rounds.

"Get any?" Harold asked.

"Difficult to see. Think one went down. Light's near impossible."

"Don't waste ammo," Ryan warned.

"Come on, man. Do it for me. I'm going to get you all chilled. Time's ticking fast."

"Cover us, Dorina. Harold, give me the Magnum.

Get Abe on your back. Just as far as the top. Then I'll come and help. Can you?''

"Sure." He handed over the borrowed blaster. "Upsadaisy, Abe."

"I said—''

"Shut the fuck up, Abe," Ryan said. "Krysty, go with him. Watch for lepers up top. Or any stickies. Just watch for anyone."

Dorina fired again, this time slapping her hand delightedly on the muddied stock of the rifle. "Got one, clean through the head. Only way to take out a stickie for sure."

Harold was gone, feet splashing in the pools of water. Krysty was at his heels, her Smith & Wesson 640 ready in her right hand.

They could still hear Abe moaning, some way above them.

But now Ryan was able to focus all of his attention across the bridge, where he figured Charlie would already be trying to rally his people.

"You okay?" he asked Dorina.

"Never better. Pay back the rapists. Only way they know. Dead man rapes nobody."

They were both as wet as you can get, staring toward the Anasazi houses. The camp fire was extinguished by the storm, but the oil still blazed in a haze of yellow light and black smoke.

"Them lepers gone?"

The voice came from a stickie, who'd emerged from the thick brush at the side of the path where he must have been hiding, terrified, oblivious to the group of norms making their escapes right by him.

"Nearly squirted my shorts when I saw them. Ugly bastards!"

He was short and chubby, his sunken eyes and dark skin marking him for a breed, the product of a stickie mother and a norm father. It wasn't very often the other way around.

"Hey, I asked if—"

The penny still hadn't dropped when Ryan shot him through the bridge of the nose with the SIG-Sauer P-226. The 9 mm round exited the back of the head, taking with it a piece of bone the size of a small dinner plate. The contents of the skull were sucked out by the misshapen bullet in a great gout of brains and pale blood.

Quite literally mindless, the stickie staggered a few steps on automatic pilot, then vanished off the path, crashing back into the undergrowth where he'd been hiding.

The baffle silencer on the blaster still functioned fairly efficiently, and Dorina blinked at the muted cough, seeing the devastating effect of the single shot.

"Way to go, Ryan," she giggled.

IT WAS a contained, organized withdrawal.

Under fire from the rifle, Charlie had enough combat sense to realize that he wouldn't chance a frontal attack. As the rain continued to pour down, the river was once more a raging, impossible torrent, meaning that the narrow, exposed bridge had become the stickies' only option.

Ryan waited until he felt that Krysty, Harold and Abe had been given enough time to reach the top of the steep incline, then he tapped Dorina on her shoulder and jerked a thumb upward. She put one last round in among the shadows below them and joined him, scampering agilely up the streaming steps.

There was no return fire.

Abe was laid on his back on a carpet of pine needles, under the spread branches of an enormous tree. Rain dripped around him, but he was relatively dry. The first fumbling fingers of dawn were appearing in the eastern sky. In their pallid light, the wounded man's face seemed a sickly gray.

He looked up as Ryan and Dorina came jogging into view.

"Chill me some, lady?" he asked.

"One or two," she replied. Dorina was streaked with great gobbets of crimson mud, making her look as though she'd been on the losing end of a brawl in a slaughterhouse.

"Good on you."

Harold was leaning against the trunk of another big piñon, fighting for breath and trying to look casual about it.

Krysty grinned at Ryan. "We made it, lover. If we take turns with Abe we can still do some reasonable time. Find some place to hole up. Rain takes out the tracks."

"Any sign of the Reverend Jarman?"

She shook her head. "No. Long gone." She sucked in a great breath of the cool morning air. "Being free beats all, lover."

"We want to stay that way we'd better get moving again. Charlie won't wait forever before he sets his hounds after us."

Dorina looked around them in the widening light. "There's some tough peaks upstream. Why not go down and have the easy running?"

It was Harold who answered her question. "Ryan's right, sweet thing. Stickies goin' to figure we took the soft road. Me and Ryan can manage old Abe here for a good few hours yet."

Ryan managed to conceal his grin at the soft boy's new confidence. Wouldn't be right to tease him about it, but he knew in his heart they were setting themselves a triple-tough row to hoe by climbing north.

"What about J.B. and the others?" Krysty asked as she helped Abe painfully to his feet.

"Could be anywhere from Portland, Maine, to Portland, Oregon," he replied, using one of Doc's favorite sayings.

IN FACT, J.B. and the others were less than a mile away, on a converging trail. All of them had blasters ready, fingers on triggers.

Minutes later it was Mildred who fired a single shot.

With a fatal result.

Chapter Thirty-Six

Before Mildred Wyeth had gone into hospital for minor abdominal surgery, just after Christmas in the year 2000, she'd been one of the United States' leading authorities in cryo surgery, which was ironic when precisely those medical skills were used to freeze her after the operation went tragically awry. Mildred was to stay clinically frozen for close to one hundred years.

Apart from being a highly respected doctor, she was also a fine shot with a pistol, winning the individual silver medal in the Olympic Games of 1996 in Atlanta—the last ever Olympic Games.

Now, in Deathlands, her expertise with a good blaster hadn't deserted her.

Mildred had been briefly in the lead, taking over the point position from J.B. while he paused to try to wipe his glasses clear of the interminable rain. She held the butt of her revolver steady, index finger tucked in close to the trigger.

Dean had moved in second, right on her heels, with Doc helping Christina over the rougher parts of the mud-slick trail. J.B. was next to last, with Jak bringing up the rear.

The stocky black woman was momentarily happy. She relished the kind of high-adrenaline excitement of going out at the front of a patrol, through dark forest, with the certain knowledge that there were some seriously evil people close by.

The hideously mutilated corpse that they'd found after it had drifted down the pike—worse than anything she'd even seen during her brief flirtation with forensic pathology—had warned Mildred what might be waiting for all of them when they finally emerged above the head of the valley.

Her experience of Deathlands was still very limited, but she'd already seen and heard sufficient to be ready for the deepest pits of human suffering.

Now they were closing on where J.B. had guessed the camp of the stickies must be. There'd been the shooting and screams, the familiar stink of burning oil.

Now the ceaseless rain.

As she picked her way carefully upward, Mildred pondered on the changes in the weather. In predark times there'd been spring, summer, fall and winter. You had good days in winter and even more often there were miserable ones in the best of summers.

But not like in Deathlands.

There were still the seasons, but now there might be a sweltering day in January in the northern plains, with snow by evening; thunder before midnight and rain by dawn; fog in the morning and then more snow, followed by baking sun.

A whole year's weather in a single day.

She guessed it must be something to do with the searing radiation that had ravaged the entire world and still lingered in certain hot spots. J.B. had told her about the acid rain, now less common than fifteen years ago, which could strip a man to bare bones in a couple of hours.

Mildred made a mental note to ask John about the great gales that he said he'd heard about from old-timers, winds that would scour paint off trucks and bark off trees.

Ahead of her, the trail was almost invisible. Dawn was in the air, and she'd already heard the beginnings of the birds' chorus. The rain was depressing, and it numbed all the senses.

You couldn't see so well, and there was a tendency to keep your head lowered, so that the icy drizzle didn't blind you. It also blurred the hearing.

Mildred didn't see or hear the running, sliding figure until it was almost on top of her. She heard the gasp from someone behind her, and the beginnings of a warning yell from Jak.

Then it was only a heartbeat away from being too late.

A massive shape appeared, black against the blackness, clothes glittering with rain, water tumbling off shoulders and off the halo of lighter hair. A knife was gripped in the right hand, raised like a terminal benediction for her.

The man's mouth opened as he saw her, only ten

paces away from him, and a strangled scream of terror and rage burst from his throat.

Mildred's survival reflex took over.

Her right arm straightened like a lunging sword, her left hand coming up to grip the other wrist. Both her eyes stared straight along the steel barrel, the foresight aligned with the back, drilling at the indistinct shape of the attacker's face.

There was time for only one bullet.

At the exact second that Mildred squeezed the trigger, the figure lurched, feet going out from under it in the wash of mud and rain that lay heavy on the trail. But the .38 round did its job.

Instead of punching a steel-jacket hole through the middle of the man's face, smack between the eyes, it hit a half inch above the left eye and drove up at a slight angle, the heavy frontal bone of the skull distorting it so that the bullet started to tumble. It shredded nearly a quarter of the man's brain before slamming against the upper part of the head, lifting a splintered chunk of the skull like a saucer, the scalp and sodden hair still attached.

Before Mildred could snap off a second round, she was sent flying by the man's flailing legs. His heavy body whacked into her, knocking the breath from her lungs and making her drop the revolver.

She slid down into the next person in line, who was Dean. He whooped in shock and cannoned into Doc and Christina, both of whom went over in a shower of slimy mud.

Jak and J.B. had a second's warning and they stepped neatly off the trail, clinging to some overhanging branches to help keep their balance.

Mildred saw a knife blade in front of her eyes and she grabbed at an arm, trying to fend it off, conscious that she was part of a cascading procession of uncontrolled bodies.

They'd been very close to the level of the stickies' camp, maybe even a little above it. With the rain and the dark it was close to impossible to be certain.

Now, they might have fallen fifty feet or five hundred feet.

Someone was screaming, a horrific, strangled, gurgling cry, like an elderly woman being forcibly drowned. Mildred wondered, amid the confusion, whether the voice might belong to her.

With a jerk that rattled her teeth, the downward momentum stopped. Mildred opened her eyes, wiping a coating of mud from her face, and saw that they'd been halted by the rotting, moss-covered stump of an old tree at the edge of a small clearing. The first light from the eastern sky was breaking through, over the tops of the high mountains, making it possible to see what was happening.

Dean was a few yards away, already scrambling to his hands and knees, spitting dirt and cursing. Doc was just below her and a little to one side, still hanging on bravely to Christina with one hand and his silver-topped cane with the other. The woman was half on top of him, face buried in his coat, kicking at something that had trapped her legs.

It was the figure that had triggered the chaotic panic.

Mildred blinked at the dead man lying sprawled at her feet, most of his face blown away. All she could tell in that first stunned moment was that he was tall, with hair so sodden with mud and blood it was hard to tell it might once have been white. He wore the ragged remains of a dark suit.

Above her she could hear J.B. and Jak picking their way down the greasy path.

"You all right?" the Armorer called, keeping his voice low.

"Sure. Think so. Few bruises and a lot of mud." She paused. "And a corpse."

"You got him?" There was delight in J.B.'s voice.

Jak arrived on the edge of the clearing, steadying himself, his white hair flaring like a dazzling burst of fresh snow. "Never saw him. Just shot. No time. You did good."

Mildred sniffed, pleased to get praise from the teenager. "Yeah. But I don't know who he is. Had a knife, I think."

Doc was on his feet, helping Christina to rise. "By the three Kennedys! I have not had such a thrilling adventure since I last rode Colossus at the mountain of magic."

J.B. was stooping over the body. "Not a stickie."

Mildred joined him. "Oh, God! You don't think he's a friend of Ryan, escaping from up there?"

The voice came from the fringe of trees. "Don't worry, Mildred. His name's Joe-Bob, and he's no friend of mine. No loss to anyone."

Mildred joined him. "Oh, God. You don't think he's a threat of that, escaping from the dirers—"

The words came from the group of friets. "Doc, I

Chapter Thirty-Seven

"Clean in and out. Neat hole in and not much bigger going out."

"Musket ball," Ryan said, kneeling beside the black woman. "Low velocity. Tends not to fragment or distort. What did it hit?"

Abe was flat on his back at a turn in the winding path. His face was deathly gray in the watery morning sunlight, and he kept trying to reach down and hold himself.

"Didn't hit my balls, Ryan. Tell you that for nothing."

"Shame. One thing you never use."

Mildred patted Abe on the shoulder. "Knew a patient once. Lawyer. Most evil, corrupt and unpleasant man I ever saw. Found he had a growth on the colon. When we operated and took it out we found it was benign. Not cancerous. We told his wife—they were just starting a messy divorce—and she shook her head. 'Typical,' she said. 'You find the one part of the bastard that isn't malignant and you remove it.' Get it?"

Abe nodded. "Yeah. When I hear a doc making jokes I figure it's to cover the bad news up."

"No. Might have chipped the crest of the ilium—that's your hipbone—on the way through. But I don't think it did. Some muscle damage to the transversus abdominis. That'll heal quickly. Not like tendons." She hesitated.

"Here it comes." The wounded man sighed, biting his lip at a sudden spasm of pain.

"No. Only question is what it might have done on the inside."

"Like what?"

"Shouldn't have harmed the central nervous system. Not that far to the side. You got no trouble with moving arms or legs or anything, have you, Abe?"

"Don't know about anything, Doc."

"I'm Mildred. He's Doc." She gestured with her elbow toward Doc Tanner.

"Sorry, Doc. Both Doc and Doc."

She was pressing on his naked stomach, watching his face for a reaction, and touching him gently around the dark hole that was now only leaking a small amount of bright blood.

"Not too painful?"

"Had worse."

"Near as I can guess, it might just have nicked the ascending colon. Part of your guts, Abe. Don't worry too much about it. I think there'd be some evidence if the bullet had struck you there. Close to your appendix."

"That bad?"

"Take out your appendix with a musket ball? Drastic method of surgery, I suppose. Not likely to lead to any problems.''

''No?''

''Apart from an extra belly button.''

WITH SO MANY of them to help, it proved much easier to carry Abe along. They made something that was a cross between a stretcher and a travois, dragging the wounded man on the smoother sections of trail and taking turns to carry him when the going became more difficult. By noon they'd reached a wider trail, with the ruined remains of buildings that indicated the area had once been some sort of park. There were rotting benches perched near what must have been a spectacular scenic observation post.

The rain had been blown away, and it was a glorious morning. Above them they could see the trail leading toward a notch between two of the peaks, a place that Christina said was called Bear Claw Ridge.

''Pa used to hunt over that way. Plenty of goats, years ago. Small kind of township up there. All ruined. Snowed up most of the winter.''

Now that the two parties were once again reunited, the disabled woman seemed much happier. But she kept very close to Jak, and her whole body language demonstrated the depths of her hostility toward Ryan.

As they traveled steadily along, Ryan and Krysty were able to fill in the others on what had been happening, learning themselves of the discovery of the mutilated corpse in the river and of J.B. hearing the group of lepers on their way toward the stickies' camp.

Harold and Dorina kept more to themselves, as though they were shy at suddenly finding themselves among this group of combatwise travelers.

They kept turning and looking behind them, more often than the others. Harold realized that Ryan had noticed, and grinned sheepishly. "Guess it's like having a fly on your neck you can never swat. Worried about the stickies."

"We all are."

Very soon after dawn, when they had just gotten back together, the sky to the south had been smeared with a huge black, oil cloud, rising like a finger of doom from the ravine where the old Anasazi settlement was hidden. Gradually the freshening breeze tore at its tip, shredding it, dissolving the dark pillar of thick smoke, spreading it far away, toward the distant east.

It was after noon before they spotted any sign of pursuit.

Krysty had been standing at another of the places where a dented metal marker indicated there had been a scenic observation post, this time with an added informative, period flavor.

Doc read it out in his orotund voice. "It is a historical marker, placed here by the good auspices of the New Mexico Historical Society, financed by a gift from Jim and Carla Wright of Albuquerque on July 4, 1990. It recalls the site where Elder Marcus Howell of the eighteenth Episcopalian conference saw a vision of the golden city of Halcia. As a consequence, an attempt was made immediately to build the city but this sadly failed after only six weeks due to lack of water.'' He turned and grinned at his listeners. ''Upon my soul, dearly beloved brothers and sisters, but I *love* historical markers.''

Amid the laughter, Krysty moved forward and placed one dark blue Western boot on the metal marker. She shaded her green eyes with a hand and posed as if staring into a biblical wilderness. ''I see no city of Halcia.''

''What do you see?'' Ryan asked.

She smiled at him, looking back down into the valley. The smile disappeared. ''I see a bunch of bastard stickies coming after us, Strawhead Charlie leading them.''

They all crowded to the edge of the drop, staring back among the tall stands of timber where Krysty's finger pointed.

Jak's sight was never that good in bright sunlight and he blinked, turning to his wife. ''You see?''

''Sure. I make about fifteen.''

J.B. nodded his agreement. ''Same here. They're way back.''

''And we're way slow,'' she snapped, face crumpling, near tears. ''Don't forget you got a sick, gut-shot man to carry, as well as a crip like me to slow everyone down.''

J.B. stared at her, the sun reflecting off his glasses,

making it hard to see the expression in his eyes. "For an intelligent woman, Christina, you sometimes talk a load of crap. From where they are now it'll take close on two hours to reach this spot. We got the firepower to think about holding them off. But that could bring some other kind of threat down on us. So, we move on. All of us. Not just some of us. But all of us."

RYAN AND J.B. DISCUSSED the possibility of one of them staying behind to hide among the trees with the Steyr rifle and pick off two or three of their pursuers, dishearten them. But there was a serious risk that a lone sniper might get himself isolated and surrounded in the forest.

If not by the stickies, maybe by some of the fleeing lepers that might still be around.

So they moved higher, toward the beckoning haven of Bear Claw Ridge.

They stopped at regular intervals so that all of the men took a spell on the travois. Once it collapsed as the bindings fell apart, spilling Abe onto the narrow trail.

He hardly moaned as they helped him back on, and Mildred knelt quickly by him, laying her palm on his forehead.

"Hot," she said. "Getting feverish. Could be bad." She looked up at Ryan.

"Be at the top in less than an hour. Put out a rifle to cover the trail and take a rest."

"He might have to take more than just a few minutes. Lot of time until dark. I think he's going to need a break well before then."

"Leave me," Abe said, licking his lips.

"Shut it."

The comment drew a ghost of a smile. "Fuck you, too, Ryan. Give me a drink of water and leave me with a blaster. I can keep them off awhile."

Ryan considered it. If he'd thought Abe was critically wounded he wouldn't have hesitated to take him up on the offer. But there still seemed a chance of him pulling through.

"No."

"You done it before."

"That was then and this is now."

"I made it then, Ryan."

"Just shut the fuck up, will you?"

Christina moved to crouch over Abe, carefully tilting her canteen to enable him to sip from it.

"Thanks, lady."

Chapter Thirty-Eight

Ryan's guesstimate of how long it would take them to reach the crest and Bear Claw Ridge didn't take the lepers into account.

There were six of them.

Ryan had taken up point himself, with Krysty at his elbow. She had stopped him with a hand on his arm.

"Something ahead, lover."

"What?"

"Not good."

"Close?"

"Yeah."

Ryan held up his hand, stopping the straggling line behind him. He heard a sigh of relief from Harold as he laid down his end of the stretcher, and a muffled moan from Abe as he was jolted back to earth.

"Krysty feels something up ahead," he said quietly. "Near."

"Bad?" J.B. asked, the Uzi machine pistol cradled under his arm.

She shook her head. "Odd. Can't tell. There's a kind of feeling of a threat, but it's like, far off. No. Don't know."

"Come on." Ryan beckoned to J. B. Dix, and, automatically, to Jak Lauren, catching the glance from Christina and cursing himself under his breath.

"Back soon," the albino teenager said, but his wife turned away from him.

THE PATH WIDENED and became less distinct at the same time, opening onto the remains of an old two-lane blacktop. A century of frost and sun had combined with weeds and bushes to break it up, but its course was still clear.

Off to the left, they could still hear the stream that had been their constant companion for the past few days.

This high it hadn't gathered the momentum from runoff water to turn it into a roaring brown torrent. Here it was just a narrow, shallow stream of ice-cold, milky water that surged over rounded boulders and tumbled across eroded ledges of granite and sandstone.

The blacktop was spotted with animal droppings. J.B. identified one recent pile as being almost certainly grizzly.

"Think that was what Krysty saw?" Jak asked, glancing around.

"Not usually animals," Ryan replied, "but you just never know, kid."

Jak turned and glared at him, then grinned. "Have own kid soon."

"Sure. I'm real pleased." Ryan stopped, halting

the others. "I know Christina is pissed at me, Jak. And I understand. Really."

"Had bad times, Ryan. Now good times come. Doesn't want to lose that."

"Yeah. She sees me as some kind of snaggle-toothed ghost come beckoning to you from the grave. Once this is over, we'll be gone."

"How about rebuilding the spread?" J.B. said. "Lot of work."

Ryan looked at the teenager. Jak sighed and ran his hand through the unruly mop of pure white hair. "Use help. Think Christina would be okay. Once danger's gone. Talk to her. I will."

J.B. was sniffing the air. "Smell something," he said, bringing up the Uzi.

"What? Smoke?"

"No. Just like...something sort of rotting. Like bodies, but not quite the same."

"Now *that* could be something that Krysty was seeing." Ryan hesitated a moment. "Jak left, and J.B. right. Skirmish line and I'll take the middle. Triple-red alert."

THE HIGHWAY DIPPED and swept left in a gentle curve, revealing a huddled cluster of buildings in the distance. Close by was the ruins of a gas station, the Exxon sign broken off in a jagged stump eight feet from the ground.

There was a small group of people sitting close

together by the stained concrete base of the derelict heap of rubble.

"Lepers," J.B. said.

They all stopped, looking at them. Ryan counted six. At a distance of a hundred feet or so it wasn't possible to make out any details of sex or age.

"Take them out from here?" the Armorer suggested. "Burst from the blaster'll chill most of them. Pick off the rest with the Steyr."

A couple of the lepers stood, the ragged hoods drawn over their stooped heads. One was holding what looked like an M-16, but it was at the trail. There didn't seem any sense of threat or defiance. Just a slumped, hopeless defeat.

The Trader's rule had been steel hard. "Take them out. Dead man hurts nobody."

Ryan had survived in Deathlands long enough to recognize the validity of that inflexible commandment. Common sense said chill the little gang of lepers. He assumed that they were the miserable bunch of survivors from their failed attack on the stickies who'd picked their way up the steep trail and had now collapsed from exhaustion or hunger.

"Hold fire," he said. "Cover me."

"No," J.B. argued. "You know Trader's way. Safe way."

"They look a threat to you? Fireblast, J.B., we can't chill everyone we meet!"

"They're lepers, Ryan. Bad news." Jak had retrieved his Magnum and held it drawn and cocked.

"Wait here." Ryan stepped forward, the heels of his combat boots ringing out bravely on the surface of the blacktop.

One of the other lepers held up his right hand in what might have been a gesture of friendliness. Or of warning. Only half of the middle finger remained on the hand.

"You got food?" came the croaking voice.

"Enough for us. Nothing to give."

"We're starving."

"We give you our food and we starve. That's the way it is."

"Help us."

"Can't."

Now he was a scant thirty feet from them. Close enough to make out the details.

One of the lepers lying down had the slack, discarded, unmistakable appearance of a corpse. Another seemed to be unconscious, with a massive stain on the front of his coat that was obviously a mixture of old and fresh blood. A third was squatting, back to Ryan, trying to knot some rags around a gaping knife wound to the face.

The three standing and looking at him were all male. The other leper, who had remained sitting, seemed to be female, but she was ignoring him, hands wrapped about herself as though she was trying to combat a deep and bitter cold.

"We got no place to go."

The voice was thick and difficult to understand.

Ryan looked hard at the speaker. "Then stay right here."

"We got stickies after us."

"Why?" Ryan asked, pretending he didn't know about their attack on the encampment.

"They figure we harmed them. Some shitting load of stickie lies."

Ryan nodded sympathetically. "Know how it is."

"Just the three of you?"

"No. Another half dozen back in the trees, waiting for me to call them on."

"They got food?"

Ryan moved a few steps closer. "I told you. We got no food."

"But we—"

"Tell you a second thing. We know how you sneaked up on the stickies' place and tried to massacre them all. Not our business. But we know."

The leper threw back his hood, revealing a face that had been hideously ravaged by the disease. His nose and ears were gone, as was most of his upper lip and part of his cheeks.

"You see what God's done to us, mister. Can you blame us for trying—"

"Keep getting told the ways of God are strange," Ryan replied. "And I don't blame you for anything you did."

"Then why..."

He held up a hand. "One other thing you should know. Those same stickies are coming after us like goose shit off a shovel. Be here in a couple of hours or so. If I was you, I'd move my ass before they get here. Stickies aren't known for their forgiving nature.''

The woman seemed to explode from the ground in a bundle of tattered rags and flying dust.

Ryan glimpsed a hairless, misshapen skull, and a face with a weeping raw hole at its center.

He also saw the sunlight glinting off the broad-bladed knife she gripped clumsily in her right hand.

Though he'd been ready for an attack as he'd walked down the narrow highway toward the old gas station, Ryan had been lulled into a false sense of security by the apathetic and defeated air of the little group of survivors.

But the leper woman stumbled, catching her foot in the cloak of the man with the slashed face. The quarter-second delay was enough for Ryan.

The SIG-Sauer coughed once, and his attacker flew backward, feet flying in the air, hitting the dirt with her shoulders. Most of the rear part of her skull had been blown away by the 9 mm round.

The knife was hurled into the air, whirling with a strange slowness, before it came tinkling back to earth again.

''Stupid,'' Ryan said through gritted teeth. ''That was stupid.''

''Gabrielle was always real stupid,'' said one of the other lepers, looking sorrowfully down at the twitching corpse.

"Ryan?" The shout came from J.B., farther up the blacktop.

A wave of the hand to reassure him and Jak that everything was under control. Though Ryan knew in his heart that he'd been a lot luckier than he'd truly deserved.

"You going to chill us all?"

"No."

"Do us a favor."

"I'm not in the business of doing fucking favors!" Ryan knew as he shouted that his anger was mainly directed at himself.

"We got two dead. One gut-shot and floating into the big dark. What kind of stinking chance the four of us got?"

"Chance to take some long steps out of here. Move now and you'll mebbe find a place to hole up for dark. Could be the stickies might miss you."

"How about him?" one of the hooded figures asked, pointing to the leper with the caked blood across his coat.

"Dying."

"Give him a bullet, mister. Least you can do for us."

"You got a carbine. You do it. Your friend, not mine."

"Empty."

Ryan was tired of wasting time. He stepped in and kneeled, his eye watching for another piece of treachery, placed the four-and-a-half-inch barrel of the handgun behind the dying man's ear and squeezed the trigger. The head bounced and a splatter of blood and brains appeared on the dirt.

"There. Now get out of here."

Still trying to wind the crimson strips of rag around his face, the other wounded leper rose to his feet. And all four of them began to move wearily off along the road, toward the cluster of buildings.

"Don't even think about stopping in that township," Ryan warned. "We'll be there, and we'll chill anyone in the way. Just walk on."

The spokesman turned. "You said stickies was coming. That a lie?"

"No. Truth. But we're goin' to be ready for them. So long."

"But you—"

Ryan pointed the gun at the man's chest. "So long," he repeated.

Slowly, looking to be in the last stages of exhaustion, the four lepers trudged away, following the blacktop, leaving the corpses of their colleagues where they lay.

Ryan watched them until he was sure they weren't going to dodge into the buildings and try to hide. Then he lifted the SIG-Sauer and waved J.B. and Jak toward him.

"Bring the others!" he shouted. "Let's get ready for the stickies."

Chapter Thirty-Nine

"Do like I want."

"No."

"Want me to beg?"

"No."

"So, I'll beg you, Ryan."

"Still no."

"Please. Just leave me here with some water and a handful of jerky. Blaster and enough ammo so I can spare one for myself at the ending. You know that's what makes sense for everyone."

Abe was hovering on the edge of delirium, drifting in and out of madness. When he was sane he would argue logically that Ryan and the others should go on while they had a chance and leave him behind. When his fever soared he would shout at them to get out and abandon him. Like he'd do to them if he only could get a lucky break.

Mildred had finally had to control him physically by binding his wrists and ankles to keep him still on the stretcher.

Ryan left her with Dean, Christina, Jak, Harold and Dorina while he went with Doc, Krysty and J.B. to explore what remained of the tiny township of Bear Claw Ridge.

SEVERAL OF THE constituent parts of the township had already collapsed. The offices and restaurant of the Overlook Resort Motel had tumbled into ruins, showing the scorched signs of an ancient fire. The nearby vacation cottages had also long gone, absorbed into the wilderness. Some of them had been ranged along a cliff to the northwest, doubtless with wonderful views of the setting sun. But the earth tremors during the long winters had felled tens of thousands of tons of rock into the abyss below, taking many of the cottages with it.

All that remained was a squat, single-story shack of rotting wood, its sign still proclaiming that it had been called Verne's Place. Doors and windows were gone, and the shingle roof had fallen in. A rattler glided away from under the old porch as they approached.

Part of the SkyHi Mall still stood. It had been two floors, divided into a number of small boutiques, but it looked as though one of the quakes had rocked it off its foundations. It leaned like an elderly dowager, complaining that it was old, ill, terrified and drunk.

And there was the Beacon Multiplex Cinema.

Rectangular and sturdy, its wind-washed concrete shell was the only place in the tiny settlement that had kept itself together.

The outer glass doors were long gone, shattered

into a million shards of bright crystal. But the inner doors had been armored, layered with protective wire. They'd been cracked and splintered, and they showed the signs of some serious attacks, but they still stood against the elements.

The Beacon was where Ryan had helped to carry the wounded Abe.

"We could separate and scatter through the shopping mall," J.B. said thoughtfully. "Wait and pick them off."

Ryan shook his head. "Building's double dangerous. You move a hand, and you got the roof girders in on top of you."

Doc was shaking his head in amazement. "This takes me back, my dear friends. Oh, so far back, to such happy times with my dearest Emily."

"You came up here?" J.B. asked.

"Not here, John Barrymore, but to places like it. In far Montana and in the snowy fastness of Colorado. The hotels then were not gimcrack little tinplate boxes. They were grand. Giant trees ranged around the lobby and balconies in serried rows. Magnificent. Did I tell you of the barge wherein she sat, with..." His voice trailed away as he was swallowed up by his own bewilderment.

Ryan took the silence. "Abe's worse. Mildred reckons he has to rest."

"It's down to numbers." J.B. looked around. "They come at us in the dark, then they can do us some serious damage."

"You mean that they might kill some of us," Doc said. "I have always been fascinated at the euphemisms employed by dealers in death. High body count. Necessary removal. Large-item discounting. Successful site clearance. When all that is meant is the deliberate destruction of other human beings. Now you calmly stand there and say that there could be 'serious damage' to us."

The Armorer listened to the old man's outburst. "Comes down to the same thing, Doc. Flat on your back and rain in your open eyes. We all know about that, don't we?"

Doc sniffed and wiped his nose on his sleeve. "Yes, yes, of course, my dear fellow. But we all know that talk is cheap, while the price of action is utterly colossal."

Ryan looked around once more, trying to visualize the appearance of the stickies, and worked out in his mind how dark it might be before they reached the crest of the trail and looked down the blacktop into Bear Claw Ridge.

"Time's running through our fingers," he said finally. "Let's go talk to the others."

ABE WAS UNCONSCIOUS.

Mildred had reported that this wasn't necessarily terminally bad news.

"Partly delayed clinical shock. The bullet went in, through and out, and I still don't think it did Abe any life-threatening injury. But there could be some internal hemorrhage. No bowel motions, so I can't be that certain. So, Abe could come out of the shock syndrome in around twenty-four hours.''

"Or?" The monosyllabic question came from Ryan.

"Or he'll be dead sometime tomorrow morning. Before noon is the likely prognosis.''

"And if Abe's moved?" This came from Christina.

Mildred looked at her in the gloom of the old cinema. "I believe it would mean his death. The shaking would do it.''

Ryan coughed. "In any case, all of us moving with Abe isn't really a viable combat option. Slow us down too much. Did a recce the far side of the ville. Trail goes back down someplace. Very steep and narrow. Stickies would take us easily by first light. If not before.''

Christina spoke again. "That's a path that comes eventually to Brightwater Canyon. Get back toward the desert floor that way. Comes out between our spread and Helga's place.''

"You know the way?"

"Sure, Ryan. Born and raised.''

Her answer decided him on what he knew they should do for the greatest good for the greatest number of them.

"All right, everyone. This is the way it'll be. Don't waste time arguing about it. I'm staying here with Abe.''

There was a moment of silence in the vault of the

multiplex, which was broken by J.B. "Tough on your own. I'll stay with you."

Harold broke in, the familiar worried, whining tone back in his voice. "You mean we go on and hope the stickies follow us?"

Dorina slapped him on the wrist. "Don't be a stupe, Harold."

"Why?"

"Carrying Abe, they'll be on us anytime now. We can move real fast without him."

"And Christina knows the country. If we play it right, then the stickies won't bother looking around the ville here. You get clear. They give up. We come out safe." Ryan looked at Krysty, knowing what he'd see in her eyes.

"I'll stay with you," she said.

"I'll remain with you," Doc offered.

"You and me, Ryan." J.B. glanced at the others. "Got to be me."

Ryan stood and stamped his feet, the steel tips on his boots striking sparks off the stone floor. "Charlie isn't your usual stickie. Too many drop out, and he might read it on the trail. Take the stretcher and drag it with you. Could help fool him. J.B., you have to go. Need a top gun with the group."

"Why can't I stay?" Krysty asked.

Ryan sighed and closed his eye, fighting anger. "Because I don't want to risk you getting chilled. This is some seriously dangerous shit."

"That's why I offered, lover."

"Dean'll need you, if anything happens to me in here."

"I need you, you triple-stupe bastard!"

She spun on her heel and ran out.

Christina broke the uncomfortable stillness. "Only really one person who can stay with you here, isn't there, Ryan?" Her voice rose. "Isn't there, Ryan?"

Chapter Forty

Partings were swift and painful.

Jak had already slipped away, returning with the report that Charlie and the stickies were still a fair distance down the trail. But they seemed to be moving faster as the sun dipped behind the snow-tipped western peaks.

"How long?" Ryan asked.

The red-orange sky had tinted the teenager's white hair a fiery crimson, almost the same color as Krysty's. His eyes glittered like rubies in a furnace.

"Hour. To trail head. Mebbe longer to here. Mebbe not."

"You look to see if the lepers have gone?" J.B asked.

"Yeah. No sign. But track's twisting and lots trees. Double red."

"Better go," Krysty said. "We stay too long, and all this is for nothing."

There was a depth of cold in her voice that Ryan had hardly ever heard before. It crossed his mind that she could see some sort of disaster striking them and wasn't telling him. But he dismissed that. If there had been some unknown threat, Krysty would have told him.

She kissed him on the cheek, once, like the brush of a moth's wing.

"You better come through this safe, lover," she said with something that might almost have been a half smile.

Almost.

Christina was bright and brittle, seeming like she was holding on to the last shreds of self-control by a single ragged fingernail. She smiled a lot and kept hugging Jak, patted Ryan on the shoulder and urged him to look after her man. She mentioned her pregnancy several times, looking around the dank building with eyes that brimmed with unshed tears.

Dean offered his hand for Ryan to shake, keeping his lips from trembling as he said goodbye.

"All goes well, son, and I'll be back with you in a day. Two at the outside."

Mildred embraced Ryan and Jak, kneeling to check the pulse of the unconscious Abe.

"He could let go the hold anytime," she warned. "Best keep a good watch."

Ryan nodded. "Yeah. You take care, too." He turned to J.B. "Later," he said.

"Right."

Harold and Dorina were standing near the door, holding hands and looking like a couple of orphans of the storm.

"Good luck," Harold said. "If you want, I'll stay with you."

"Thanks. But you go."

"Pay off some more of the debt for me, Ryan." Huddled in a man's coat, Dorina looked, absurdly, even younger. If he hadn't known, Ryan would probably have taken her for eight years old.

"Yeah," he said. "Even up the score if I can for you."

There was no point in telling her that he hoped he wouldn't even have to pull a trigger on the stickies. That wasn't the idea of the plan at all.

FINALLY THEY WERE all gone.

Abe was still sunk deep into a blank coma, eyes closed, a thin line of saliva dribbling from the corner of his mouth. His respiration was way down, and his pulse had dropped so far it was difficult to register it at the pressure point in his wrist.

Jak and Ryan had stood in the main entrance of the multiplex, watching the line of shadows move away into the setting sun, watching them until the last one had waved and vanished.

The albino teenager turned away, looking at the squat building behind them. "Best check out all around," he said.

Ryan took a deep breath, savoring the delicious scents of piñon and sagebrush that floated across the plateau of Bear Claw Ridge. The light was fading fast.

"Wish we could meet them out here."

Jak grinned. "Like old times, Ryan."

"Sure. You and me, head-to-head, eye to eye. But we got to go inside and hide in the dark. Watch over Abe. And hope those stickie sons of bitches walk on by."

BEAR CLAW RIDGE had never been a winter settlement. No, never at all.

The blacktop generally became difficult in September, with four-wheels able to pick a cautious way through. By October the red barrier came down and the route up was closed off.

A few cross-country jocks would try to ski and climb up to the notch, but everything was shut and everyone had gone. Gradually it became a ghost town from autumn right through to late April or May.

The thick walls of the Beacon Multiplex Cinema were well insulated, and a powerful generator kept it heated until the caretaker came in the spring to open up again. Like Telluride, not that far to the north, Bear Claw Ridge had its own film festival, specializing in cult classics from the previous century and forgotten directors.

But it was a long drive, and the motel was archaic and uncomfortable. The planetary holocaust of January, 2001, only completed the process of the little township's slow death.

There was a ragged, brittle poster still clinging to a wall in the old lobby, high up in a corner. The last double bill of Beacon, at its largest screen in Septem-

ber of the year 2000: *Attack of the Fifty Foot Woman,*
playing in tandem with Dario Argento's early mas-
terpiece, *L'ucello dalle piume di cristallo.*

In a dusty corner was a collection of discarded
ticket stubs from the last day's performance, rustling
like dried leaves in a graveyard. The interior was surprisingly undamaged, partly due to the extreme iso-
lation of the place. Only the occasional hunter had
passed by the ville during the drifting decades, while
the sturdy construction of the cinema had kept it tight
and solid.

The smell of damp and urine permeated the interior, as it did in any similar building anywhere in
Deathlands. But many of the seats remained in the
three auditoriums and the tattered silver rags of one
of the screens still hung in place. The maroon flock
paper dangled in baroque peeling strips, and a carving
of a pair of peacocks glowered down from above the
projection box.

Ryan had seen pictures of movie houses in old
books and magazines, had even seen flickering
glimpses of them on the rare old vid. But this was the
best-preserved one he'd ever seen.

"Shame we don't have popcorn and grape sodas,"
he said to Jak, who looked at him as though he'd
suggested some delicacy from the planet Mercury.

Abe was sleeping in the largest of the viewing
rooms, beneath a tilted sign that proclaimed it as
Screen One.

"Catch us here and chilled," Jak said, glancing

around the windowless box, with its single entrance and exit doors. Outside, the light was failing fast, and its filtered rays were barely penetrating the auditorium.

Ryan had to agree. "Have to move Abe out of here. There's a broken display counter in the main lobby. Get him behind that. I'll take that projection box. Got a trap out onto the roof. I checked it before everyone left."

"Me?" Jak asked.

"Where do you want to be?"

The red eyes darted around the dimly lighted room. "Could be one stays Abe?"

"Yeah, I'll go with that." Ryan bit at his lip, considering the teenager's idea. "Look, Abe's my friend. My problem. My responsibility. You take that little room up there, Jak. And I'll stick down in the lobby with Abe."

ABE DIDN'T MOVE a muscle as he was carried up the shallow stairs and out through the broken swing doors into the main access area of the multiplex cinema.

Ryan lifted up the broken plastic counter and made a shelter with it, covering Abe and leaving himself enough room to slide in beside him. It was a good fire position with a fine range across the entrance to the main doors. He could see anyone coming into the Beacon either from outside or from the SkyHi Mall along the way.

Jak vanished into the dark, through a concealed

door and up a narrow flight of stairs into the little projection box, with its rusting and broken comp control equipment that had run the vid films for all three of the theaters in the complex.

Ryan stood a moment, trying to guess what it must have been like to visit a picture palace in the old, prenuke days. He knew that movies had once been the great family attraction in the United States, but he wasn't altogether clear about when that had been. He thought it could have covered the last quarter of the twentieth century, but it might have been fifty years earlier than that. Information about social life before the blurring effect of the long winters was incredibly hard to come by.

Doc was sometimes helpful, but his own sense of any time scale was so confused and erratic that he had once sworn to Ryan that he had actually seen the Apache war chief, Geronimo, driving in a gleaming Cadillac automobile.

And Ryan *knew* that was ridiculous.

He checked out Abe, but there didn't seem much change. If anything his breathing seemed to be a little more steady and his pulse was just a tad stronger. But he was still deeply unconscious, occasionally moaning and muttering something inaudible.

On an impulse Ryan decided to go outside.

He eased open the small door, calling out a warning. ''Me, Jak.''

''Okay.''

''Going out.''

"They coming?"

"Don't know. Going to take a look and see if I can spot them."

"Careful."

"Sure." He pushed the door closed again, feeling it fit snugly into the padded wall.

The main door moved at a touch, and he was out into the New Mexico night. The temperature had fallen sharply in the past half hour, and Ryan could see his own breath as it plumed around him. Unless it was bitterly cold, you could prevent that by blowing hard and taking shallow breaths in and out.

There was a slice of moon sailing calmly behind banks of raggedy cloud. It reflected off the acres of broken glass along the frontage of the SkyHi Mall, making it seem to glow like a magical fortress.

There was no sign of life, though Ryan caught the far-off sound of a pack of coyotes hunting its prey through the late evening.

There was a narrow soft shoulder at the edge of the blacktop, and he walked there, feeling his boots sinking silently into the dirt, keeping the belt of conifers close to his left side. He had the rifle across his back, the SIG-Sauer drawn and ready in his right hand.

Twice he stopped and crouched, squinting toward the point where the trail opened onto the overgrown highway. But there was no movement. Nothing broke the plane of the horizon.

Halfway toward it, Ryan stopped, dropping to his knees.

Something *was* there, keeping low, on the opposite side of the blacktop, about three hundred yards away from him. For several long minutes there wasn't a flicker of movement. But Ryan knew his instinct was right.

There was a hunting owl behind him, passing overhead like a vengeful spirit, its fawn wing feathers tipped with silver. It floated toward the far side of the road, suddenly cutting up and away as it neared where Ryan had seen someone hide.

It was enough.

The stickies had arrived, and it was time to go back to the multiplex and hide.

And wait.

Chapter Forty-One

It was so easy to get back into the Beacon Cinema without alarming any of the stickies. The screen of the trees gave a perfect backdrop, and the soft shoulder swallowed up any sounds.

Ryan paused for a moment by the doors, staring back into the gloom, trying the traditional hunter's trick of looking a little to the side of what you actually want to see.

But there was nothing moving out there.

He'd carried out a full recce of the complex of ruined buildings, finding that there were a couple of back ways into the multiplex movie house—an emergency fire exit around the back that had probably doubled as a staff entrance, and a narrow broken window at the side away from the mall, in what had once been the rest rooms.

There was a security bar inside the door, and Ryan had managed to jam it into place to keep it closed. A serious attack would easily shift the bar, but it would also make a terrific clatter and give plenty of warning.

Ryan took a last look through the smeared armaglass, pausing as he thought he detected movement in the watery moonlight. But it didn't much matter now.

The stickies were on their way and would reach Bear Claw Ridge in a matter of minutes.

The one-eyed man opened the hidden door a couple of inches. "Coming, Jak," he whispered.

"Ready."

He crossed the lobby, knelt and wriggled under the makeshift barricade, alongside the motionless figure of Abe, who stirred for a moment. "Recon the LMG action, Trader," he said in a clear voice.

Ryan clenched his fist, ready to punch Abe out if he showed any signs of making further noise. But the man had slipped back deep into his own personal darkness.

TIME PASSED.

Every nerve strained, Ryan could almost hear time passing.

As the night grew colder, the building began to shrink around him. Contractions of the tiniest fractions of inches in the concrete and the underpinning steel girders made faint sounds like a raw fingertip rubbing on the inside of a long-buried lead coffin.

Every noise tugged at Ryan's attention. Each time it happened he listened harder, wondering if it could be a stickie trying to crawl in through the broken window at the side of the building.

He glanced down at his luminous wrist chron.

It was just after eight o'clock.

The wind was rising, and Ryan's keen hearing

could catch the shuffling sound of dried leaves being whisked against the broken outer doors.

Ten more minutes crept by.

He wondered what was going through Charlie's mind, out there in the chill night.

THE LEADER OF the stickies was less than a hundred paces away, crouched in the darkness at the edge of the forest, listening to the breeze as it stirred the branches above his head. His force was stretched out behind him, waiting for his next order.

Charlie's mind was clear and calm, and he was humming a dissonant tune to himself. He reviewed his options and thought back over the past twenty-four hours.

"Good and bad," he whispered. "Bad and good. Bad times. Good times. Bood and gad. Tad bimes and—" His face suddenly shifted and contorted into a mask of malevolent anger. "Fucking Ryan Cawdor!"

The man behind him caught the words and leaned closer. "What, Charlie?"

"Nothing, Tony, nothing. Go back to sleep, will you?"

"Not sleeping, Charlie." There was a note of panic in the stickie's voice, as though his heart had leaped for cover behind his ribs.

"Sure, sure."

From what Charlie had been able to piece together,

it looked as though that triple-slut Marcie had been up to her old tricks again.

At least she'd paid the final price.

Charlie felt a passing tightness around his groin as he recalled some sweating, shuddering moments with Marcie.

It must have been the woman who'd liberated Ryan from the kiva at the very time that the lepers had attacked. Charlie's first gut reaction had been that it had been a crowd of norms storming in on a rescue mission.

It had been a brief time of relief when he'd realized that it was nothing more threatening than a mob of stump-fingered lepers.

But they'd been lucky, timing their strike for the middle of the night, when stickies were never at their best.

Charlie grinned toothlessly in the darkness. Stickies were *never* at their best.

Then there had been the fires and the explosions, beginning among the stores of black powder and lamp oil.

The flames and thunderous booms had delighted the stickies, sending them capering wilding into the gunfire of the lepers. For a time it had been in the balance, and only Charlie and his Uzi had tipped the scale in his favor.

But the encampment had been destroyed, many of the ancient buildings finally reduced to blackened heaps of shattered red brick.

Charlie had ordered a few of the older men to stay with the surviving women and children, telling them to get everything ready to move to a new site while he took the rest of the stickie men with him on the vengeance trail.

"Clever fuckhead, Cawdor," he whispered, eyes raking the shapes of the small ville ahead of him.

And he'd fallen for it, his mind clouded by the gibbering antics of his followers, letting them go surging down the steep side of the valley where the river pounded and raged, watching them slide and fall. Only when one of the older stickies slipped into the torrent and was whirled screaming to his death did Charlie finally come to his senses.

"No. They've gone up!" he yelled. "Gone higher up."

The trail of the travois was the clue, the deep furrows along the damp mud, sometimes vanishing where Ryan and his companions had lifted their wounded man with them. Or wounded woman. Charlie didn't know which, and didn't care, either.

Then it had been a question of plodding uphill. Stickies weren't great hikers, and Charlie had to keep on chivying them, kicking and cursing the stragglers. At times he'd only had a half dozen with him, then they all had to stop and wait for the rest to catch up. He knew he couldn't risk going up against the well-armed Ryan and his group unless he had all his power with him.

Which meant around twenty in total.

Now darkness had overtaken them all and he was stuck in the wilderness by the old blacktop, wondering where Ryan had gone. His guess was that he'd probably be hiding among the buildings of the little ville, ready for an ambush.

Or had he gone through, hoping to fool Charlie again? Was he even now making a cautious, slow escape down the trail on the far side? Charlie knew the region well, and he was aware of the escape route off the plateau. It was utterly hopeless in adverse weather, but walkable the rest of the year.

Walkable, with care, even in the semidarkness of the night.

"What we doin', Charlie?"

"Shut your mouth, Tony. I'm thinking about it, aren't I?"

He heard the man pass this information back down the line.

"Boss Charlie's thinkin' about it."

"Charlie's thinkin'."

"Think."

Running his fingers through the mane of bright yellow hair, Charlie suddenly stood.

"Come on," he said. "Let's go and take us a good look."

FROM HIS HIDING PLACE, Ryan could just see out through the doors, but the armored glass was so dirty and cracked that it was almost impossible to make out any details.

However, he saw the arrival of the stickies.

A darting white figure, close by the doors, almost brushed against it with his shoulder. There and gone in a second.

Ryan steadied the SIG-Sauer and eased back farther into the shelter.

He heard feet moving inside the outer doors, then saw a suckered hand, deathly white in the moonlight, reaching around the edge of the inner doors ready to push them open.

Ryan's finger tightened on the trigger.

And Abe started to cry.

Chapter Forty-Two

J.B. was walking second, almost on the heels of Christina.

Despite her disability, and the built-up surgical boot on her left foot, the woman was making a good pace. She limped along so fast that Doc and Harold, near the back of the group, had to keep on asking her to slow down.

"You have some passing familiarity with this terrain, madam," the old man complained. "But it is utterly alien to us. And the silver beams of the night's huntress are somewhat nugatory for our purposes."

"What the fuck's he on about?" Dorina asked, still clinging to Harold's chubby arm.

Krysty answered her. "Doc means that there isn't much moonlight."

"Why don't he say so? And when we goin' to take us a break?"

J.B. held up a hand. "Everyone quiet. Krysty, you hear anything?"

"Nothing. How long since we left Ryan?"

The Armorer glanced at his wrist chron. "Just gone half-past eight."

"More than an hour," Mildred said. "Surely something must've happened by now."

J.B. nodded. "Figure the stickies must be around the ville by now."

The black woman bent and rubbed at the muscles along the front of her thighs. "Funny how going downhill's sometimes worse than going up." She straightened. "Wonder if Abe's still alive."

Krysty was staring back up along the trail, toward its invisible crest.

"I can't tell," she said, her voice carrying a bitter, ragged note of desperation. "Mildred, I just can't tell."

THE DOOR OPENED and a cold draft came crawling over the lobby floor, bringing dried leaves with it. They rustled up against Ryan's chest, sticking in Abe's hair.

But they didn't disturb Abe.

Ryan had put his old friend into a deeper level of unconsciousness than before by the simple expedient of rapping the butt of the blaster hard against his head, just behind the left ear.

The trickle of moans that threatened both of their lives stopped abruptly.

The stickie appeared like a night wraith, the suckered fingers making faint kissing sounds as he released the armaglass.

He was carrying an M-16 that Ryan guessed had been liberated from one of the dead lepers. The sheet of moonlight was further blocked when a second figure appeared in the doorway.

"Anything?"

"Too black."

Charlie's voice was thin and piercing from the street outside. "Anything?"

"Too dark. We got no lights fucking to see? Not no lights for fucking seeing?"

Charlie spoke again, unable to conceal his irritation. "No, we don't have any torches."

"Why?"

"Because I fucking well forgot to— It doesn't matter, Tony."

"Too dark," repeated the stickie who had his head and shoulders inside the lobby of the Beacon Multiplex Cinema. Ryan had a perfect bead at less than twenty feet range and was ready to blow the mutie's skull apart like a watermelon rolled under a speeding semi.

The indecision in Charlie's voice was loud and unmistakable. Without lights it was madness for him to risk sending any of his party into the derelict building.

But if he hung around and waited until dawn, then Ryan and the others could be long gone, way out of his reach.

"What we doin', Charlie?"

"You can't see anything in there?"

"Darker'n the back end of Marcie's—"

"Yeah, yeah," his leader interrupted.

Ryan suddenly felt that wonderful sensation when you know you've got it right.

Life-and-death combat situations were, as the Trader often remarked, just like playing a good game of poker. Sometimes you had to bluff on an eight-high hand, but mostly it was knowing odds, drawing to an inside straight or filling a flush.

Or tricking a gang of stickies into thinking you'd all gone down the side of a mountain.

"Come on out," Charlie shouted.

"You mean us?"

"He mean us?"

"Just get the fuck out here. Likely they kept moving. We'll follow on and pick up the trail at first light." His voice was fading as the door swung slowly shut. "Then we'll..."

And that was all that Ryan heard.

He waited until the tiny digital numbers on his wrist chron clicked around, showing double-two, double-zero.

At his side, Abe's breathing was slow and steady, with a regular catch to it, as though he were dozing and was just going to jerk awake and ask for breakfast.

Ryan checked on his pulse, which was slow and strong, also feeling the lump on the head. A little thread of drying blood had matted the hair and congealed on the floor.

"Sorry about that, buddy," he whispered, sliding silently out from under his precarious barricade. He stood and stretched, making sure his muscles hadn't tightened too much.

There was a little more moonlight filtering in, making the lobby seem like some vast, sinister undersea cavern.

He catfooted across to the hidden door and opened it an inch, putting his lips to the crack. "It's Ryan, Jak."

"They gone?"

"Think so. Wouldn't take chances though. Not with a stickie like Charlie."

"Coming up or me down?"

"I'd like a look up on the roof. You come down and watch over Abe."

"Sure."

Ryan was right by the stairs, ears honed for any sound. But Jak still made him jump, materializing out of the Stygian darkness.

"Fireblast!"

A quiet chuckle. "Christina says I move real silent for skinny kid."

"She call you that?"

"Kid? Sure." Again that quiet, contented chuckle. "Not same from her, Ryan."

"Guess not."

"How's Abe?"

"Had to coldcock him with the blaster. Started to make some noise just when one of the stickies was nosing in."

"But is…"

"Good, as far as I can tell. Go keep an eye on him, Jak. Don't stick your head out the doors until I come back down."

"Okay."

On the stairwell the light had almost totally vanished. Ryan was conscious only of the dimmest glow, which he assumed was coming from the open trap onto the flat roof.

He felt his way along, his fingers encountering something small and slippery that writhed away from his fingers. It fell from the wall with a faintly disgusting plopping sound.

Halfway up there was a landing with a door that was either locked or jammed, then another flight of steps, this time of echoing iron.

The projection control suite was right at the top, with its door missing. The room was about twenty feet square with wrecked equipment scattered everywhere. Now the light was better, and Ryan's eye had adjusted to it, seeing to pick his way across to the rectangular window of thick glass that looked down over the main auditorium.

There was a folding steel ladder against the wall, which was hooked on to the bottom of the trapdoor. Before climbing it, Ryan moved over to the projectionist's window and peered through, trying to imagine what it had been like when the ragged seats below were filled with laughing, excited people.

From what he knew, Ryan guessed that something like ninety-five percent of that last-ever crowd in the

Beacon would have been chilled within less than six months.

The breath of sound from behind and above him warned Ryan what was happening.

And he started to spin around, lifting the SIG-Sauer, knowing he was way too late.

Chapter Forty-Three

Krysty stopped dead, her hand going to her mouth. She half turned on the trail, nearly stumbling, and swallowed hard. Looking back again, her eyes locked on to Christina's face.

Both women had gone corpse white.

"You felt it?" Christina breathed accusingly. "Didn't you?"

"Yes. Oh, Gaia help me! Yes, I did."

A FLAILING NAKED FOOT kicked the blaster out of Ryan's hand, jarring his wrist. He tried to push the stickie away from him, but the creature was on top of him, its falling weight knocking him helplessly to the floor.

There wasn't time to call out to Jak.

Not even time to draw a breath.

Charlie had obviously been sharper than Ryan or Jak had suspected, leaving a man behind to watch the buildings and to creepy-crawl around in the dark to see what he could find out.

The mutie must have spotted the open trap in the roof and climbed up, seen Ryan in the darkness and simply dropped in on him.

Now it was a desperate battle, with the stickie having the initial advantage. His suckered hands were groping for Ryan's face, ripping at his coat.

After the first heart-stopping shock, Ryan's first realization was that his attacker wasn't carrying any sort of weapon. No blaster threatened him, not even a knife.

But there were sharp teeth scratching the skin on his throat, jaws snapping in his face, the rank stench of rotting fish flooding his nostrils, a bony knee jabbing between his thighs and trying to crush his genitals.

And a slobbering moan of bitter hatred filling his ears.

Ryan was used to direct physical confrontation, able to make a fast decision on what kind of person was fighting him.

The stickie was close to six feet, but much skinnier than he was. And from hanging on to his assailant's wrists to try to control him, Ryan was very aware of the brutish strength that resisted him.

One hand brushed against the side of his head and jerked out a clump of hair, bringing a section of bloodied scalp with it.

"Bastard!" Ryan hissed, digging his fingers into the stickie's upper arm, exerting all of his own power to try to separate the muscle from the bone.

There was a strangled scream from the mutie, who tried to roll and kick himself away from the agonizing pain.

The moon veiled herself behind some tatters of high cloud, throwing the projection room into total blackness. Ryan let go of the stickie, crawling toward the observation window at the front, cursing as he felt and heard tiny splinters of glass crackling under his knees.

"Charlie was right. Said you might stayed. Told us to look an' hide."

Even in the heightened tension of a battle for his life, Ryan was able to notice the significant use of the word "us."

There were others around Bear Claw Ridge.

He had to warn Jak as quickly as possible.

"You hurt my arm, norm. Real bad."

The voice was like Harold's had been, a nagging, whining sound that seemed to grate at the inside of Ryan's skull.

He crouched and waited. On the off chance, he brushed cautiously with his fingers in a sweeping circle, in case the blaster had dropped within reach. But there was nothing except dirt, glass and broken pieces of the old projection machinery.

"Where are you, norm? Frightening of chilled?"

Ryan's hand crept to the hilt of the eighteen-inch panga, tightened and drew it from the soft leather sheath.

The voice moved, closer to the stairs from the lobby of the multiplex.

"Go see how many norms lived in these place. Charlie thinking some lot."

To try to use the panga totally blind was to court disaster. It might crack against the wall or just strike the stickie a glancing, wounding blow. Either way there was a real risk that Ryan would lose his hold on it.

He had to get close enough to be sure of a firm blow against the enemy.

"Stay there, norm, when going to see what's down here."

Ryan tried to shuffle after the mutie, but he was noisier in the heavy boots. Aware of this, he stopped and remained perfectly still.

Above him there was a very faint increase in the light as the moon began to shrug off the insistent clouds.

It was enough for him to make out the wispy hair of the stickie, disappearing out of view, down the narrow stairs.

Ryan considered throwing the panga, but it was a clumsy weapon and the odds favored a miss. Better to stalk after the man and hope to trap him between himself and the teenager.

"Down and down I going and arounds, arounds. Maked my head to be spinning, norm."

The voice was becoming hollow, with an echo. Ryan finally moved across the room, glancing up at the open trapdoor in case there were any more stickies waiting to jump him. But the rectangle of silver light was unbroken.

The mutie was out of sight, but Ryan could hear

its sliding, insistent voice, babbling away to itself as it drew nearer the bottom.

"Door closed, closed and shut as well it is." A rattle as the stickie grabbed the handle and tried to force it open. Ryan heard the squealing of hinges, but the door held. "Seen another down here. Try that one too."

Now there was enough light coming into the cramped little room to enable Ryan to make out where the SIG-Sauer had landed. He stooped and picked it up, holding it in his left hand, keeping the panga in his right. If, as now seemed likely, there were other stickies prowling the night, it was as well to be triple ready.

Ryan paused at the top of the dark stairwell, unable to see anything. He concentrated his hearing, catching the tiny click of the latch opening.

Below him, moments later, there was the whisper of a door being closed.

The stickie might be waiting for him in the midnight velvet stillness.

If it had been Charlie himself down there, Ryan would have hesitated for a long time before risking the descent.

But this was an ordinary stickie with the usual intelligence level of a broken fence post.

Ryan went down after him, feeling carefully for the rail.

The access to the lobby was closed.

Here the light was almost gone. Ryan reached out

with the hand holding the pistol and pushed very gently at the door. It moved an inch or so then stopped, as if someone were standing with their foot jammed against it.

Ryan let his breath slowly out and counted off sixty seconds, pushing the door again. This time he felt the same resistance and heard the smallest scuffling sound, as though a baby rat was caught inside a large bureau.

There was a ghostly light in the lobby that showed along the crack every time Ryan pushed at the door. It would mean that he would be completely exposed to anyone who might be waiting there.

The other option was to go back into the projection box and climb out through the trap, over the roof and down into the street at the side of the SkyHi Mall. Then come all the way around and approach the Beacon Cinema from the front.

Which didn't seem a great idea, either.

He set his shoulder against the door and gave it a great heave, powering himself through the gap, rolling over onto one shoulder and coming up with the SIG-Sauer raking the gloom around him.

"Bang, you dead!" said a quiet voice, coming from the shadows where Abe was hidden.

"Thanks, Jak."

"Welcome, Ryan."

"Nearly crapped my pants."

A soft laugh. Now Ryan could see the white smudge of the teenager's hair, low down. Behind him, by the closed door, there was another pale blur, lying stretched on the floor—the body that had been blocking the exit from the stairs.

"Took the stickie," Jak said.

"Didn't hear the..." Ryan began, shaking his head at his own foolishness. "Course. Not the blaster. Throwing knives."

"Yeah. Just one. Wasn't sure how things might be with you. Figured I'd wait."

"Think there's more stickies around. He slipped by me in the dark. But he talked of 'us' being left by Charlie."

Jak was standing, coming toward him like a Halloween wraith.

"Better go look for them?"

"Leave Abe on his own?"

"They come find us he could die anyways, Ryan."

"True."

He thought about their options. The idea of hiding was now undermined. Having killed one of the stickies, it would bring any others searching around. Chill them and Charlie might come back in the dawning to see what was happening to his missing patrol. Either way, it was going to mean taking a serious risk.

"How is Abe?"

"No change."

"Then we'll go do some hunting."

THERE WERE TWO MORE of the murderous muties loose around Bear Claw Ridge. Ryan and Jak separated outside the movie house.

One of them trailed and chilled his prey successfully.

One of them didn't.

Chapter Forty-Four

J.B. stopped and beckoned Krysty to his side.

"See the terrain here?"

"Yeah."

"What do you think?"

"What for? Oh, I see. Could be."

"Put the guns on both sides, but the rising slope means there's no risk of pouring lead into one another. Be firing downhill a little, which isn't so good for accuracy. Still…"

The Armorer's glasses glinted silver in the moonlight. He licked his lips in the eager anticipation of a good ambush.

The others joined them, quickly understanding what he planned.

Dorina punched one hand into the other. "Give 'em some shit," she hissed.

Harold nodded reluctantly. "Could be a good place to catch them, 'specially if they're moving fast and careless."

"Never heard of a stickie that wasn't always careless," Christina said. "Excepting for that Charlie, of course."

"Mebbe I could sort of lure them," Dean offered,

"pretend I got a bad ankle or something. Limp back there so they see me. Then they'll be thinking about me and start chasing me, and you can easy take them."

"No," J.B. replied flatly.

"It'd work."

"And then I get to tell your father that some stickie got a lucky shot and blew half your head away? Dark night!"

Doc cleared his throat. "Forgive my interruption, John Barrymore."

"What?"

"I am a famous dullard when it comes to subtle variations in the fine art of warfare. But it does seem to me that the little rascal has come up with a potentially game-winning suggestion."

The forest closed around them. The trail ran straight for about one hundred and fifty paces. On each side the hills rose away, with excellent cover for hidden shootists.

J.B. sighed, looking at the others. "I'm the one in charge. I don't like the risk."

Doc pressed him. "A perfect ambuscade. We can annihilate the enemy, then return safely to liberate Bear Claw Ridge and all who sail in it." He coughed again. "And do business in great waters, for they— I'm sorry, I appear to have momentarily lost the thread of my discourse."

Mildred broke the silence. "I say let him do it. It's a real good plan."

"Dad would let me if he was here."

J.B. wasn't the sort of man to waste time once he'd finally made up his mind.

"Let's do it," he said. "Then go make sure everyone's safe up the hill."

STORAGE UNITS had been ripped off one of the walls of the mall, leaving brackets scattered all over the floor. Trying to move quietly through the concrete maze of small units and gaping doorways, Ryan slipped and turned his ankle, falling heavily.

Fortunately if there were any stickies nearby, none of them seemed to have been attracted by the clatter.

All around him, the retail catacomb was still and silent.

He lay there for a moment, cursing beneath his breath, then pulled himself up, gingerly testing the injury. He put his weight on it and winced at a feeling like a white-hot needle lancing through the bone. Ryan had broken his ankle about ten years earlier and could still remember the extraordinary pain that had seeped in after about fifteen minutes. This time it had hurt immediately, which gave him some hope that it might only be a bad sprain.

He rolled his ankle, gritting his teeth, trying again to stand on it. This time it was markedly easier and he limped up and down a few times, eye scanning the main part of the mall for any sign of movement. But it was still deserted.

JAK TURNED A BLIND CORNER to find his target—an unusually stout stickie—leaning casually against a tumbled wall, head back, taking a great gulp from his flask.

The teenager didn't want to use his .357 Magnum, which would bring every mutie for ten miles around.

Just for a moment he hesitated. A year earlier his automatic reflex would have taken over and carried him through. He would have taken the step in and crushed the barrel of the weighty blaster against the side of the stickie's skull and put him down, stooped and opened up his throat with a single slicing cut from one of his many knives.

But Jak Lauren had been a married man for many months now. Running a homestead in the wilderness of New Mexico wasn't an easy ride.

Nor was it quite the same as roaming through Deathlands at the shoulder of Ryan Cawdor.

The stickie was so startled at the sudden appearance of the supernatural demon, with the hair of white fire and the eyes like living flames, that he gobbed out the mouthful of liquor, which sprayed into Jak's face.

The alcohol was home-distilled, close to one hundred proof, and it blinded the albino teenager.

"You triple-stupe fucker!" he staggered backward, pulling the pistol's trigger three times, totally unable to see where the bullets had gone.

One went into the side of a dirt wall three hundred paces away to the south. A second one was still rising when it disappeared into the dark forest, well over a quarter mile away, having missed the drunken stickie by less than three feet. The third full-metal jacket struck the chubby mutie high on the inside of the left thigh, neatly opening up the femoral artery on the way in and removing much of the quadriceps muscle and the hamstring on the way out.

Blood began to pour from the gaping wound, jetting into the sand near Jak's face. The stickie was blown backward onto the ground and immediately became preoccupied with the puzzling affair of his own death.

The teenager heard the unmistakable wet, solid noise of a heavy caliber bullet striking flesh. He wiped at his eyes with the back of his hand, blinking through a sea of tears, and saw the dying man writhing on the floor.

Jak turned and was immediately knifed in the chest by Charlie's third scout.

DOWN THE STEEP TRAIL, on the farther side of the plateau, everyone heard the echoing sound of the three shots.

Dean hesitated and stumbled, nearly falling. He recovered his balance and carried on.

Charlie had dropped behind his raggle-taggle army of stickies, urging them on. The disorderly gang was whooping as they saw the slim figure of the boy so close ahead of them. But Charlie had also heard and recognized the sound of the shooting. He knew that none of the three men he'd secretly left behind carried large-caliber blasters, which meant they'd flushed at least one of their prey out of hiding.

Amid the cheering, the rest of the stickies hardly noticed the distant peal of thunder. They charged on down the straight section of the track.

Charlie stopped, considering calling them back. He saw the boy turn around and peer over his shoulder. As though he was looking for...

"What?" Charlie said.

Realization came moments too late.

J.B. had also heard the noise of Jak's big blaster and, like Ryan, knew that it might mean some seriously bad news. But for the present, the Armorer had to concentrate his attention on the ambush.

The time was now.

"Stop!" Charlie screamed, his voice cracking into the darkness.

"Now!" J.B. yelled, spraying the muties with a sustained burst from the Uzi.

The night exploded into a bedlam of shooting and tumbled death.

THE MOON HUNG in a cloudless sky. There was a hint of frost in the air, and the mountains around were sharp and clear.

Ryan's combat boots rang on the blacktop as he sprinted toward the sound of the shots. It was so calm and still that he caught the sharp odor of gunsmoke before he reached the scene.

He came in from the other side, seeing the dead stickie and a great lake of blood seeping black and glossy around the corpse's shattered leg.

"Fireblast!" Ryan put his head slowly around the corner, seeing the second sprawled body lying still in another patch of leaking blood, this time from what looked like a stab wound in the chest.

"Oh, Christ, Jak," he said. "No!"

Chapter Forty-Five

J.B. had gone around with the hot blaster, putting a single 9 mm bullet into the forehead of each of the stickies that had survived the swath of cutting fire. Every one of them had gone down without being able to return a solitary shot against their unseen attackers.

The bodies lay wherever the dance master of death had discarded them, tangled and sprawled, totally without dignity.

"Got 'em all," J.B. said, reloading the Uzi.

Krysty shook her head. "No, we didn't."

"Dark night! Course. That yellowhead you talked about isn't here. Must have been him screamed a warning, just too late. He's gone free."

"Which way?" Christina asked.

"Think he's gone up the trail after Dad?" Dean was out of breath, trembling, standing with Mildred's arm around him.

J.B. looked at him. "Mebbe, boy." He paused. "We'll go up right now."

"Sure."

"And Dean?"

"Yeah?"

"You did really good. Ryan'll be proud of you when we tell him all about it."

Christina was deathly pale. "That was Jak's blaster that we heard, wasn't it?"

J.B. nodded. "Yeah. Means there were stickies back up at the ridge."

"I'll never ever forgive that one-eyed bastard if anything's happened to Jak! I swear it."

"He'll be fine," Krysty said reassuringly. But her heart felt as though it had suddenly been injected with a lethal surge of Sierra meltwater.

THE KNOWLEDGE that Jak's attacker was still close by filled Ryan with a more violent chilling lust than he'd felt in many years.

As he knelt by the still figure, brushing a streak of matted white hair off the hooded eyes, Ryan was closer to the berserk killing madness than he'd ever been.

During the time that they'd ridden together, he'd come to love Jak, seeing him as the son that he thought he'd never had. The unexpected arrival of Dean hadn't really done anything to change his feelings for the albino boy at all.

Glancing around for a sight of the stickie, or stickies, that had done for Jak, Ryan peered at the wound, placed the index finger of his left hand on the side of the teenager's throat and felt for a pulse.

It was there, faint and fluttering.

The wound was obviously made by a knife, with a

reasonably narrow blade, driven straight in and out at speed. At a first glance, in the cold moonlight, it looked to Ryan as though it hadn't been done by an expert. There was no sign of the jagged tear that a savage twist of the wrist would have given to the dagger, causing infinitely greater harm to living tissue.

But an amateur could stab you to death just as well as a professional.

The blood was still seeping out, and Ryan carefully opened up the boy's jacket, easing away the sodden shirt from the wound.

It was a clean cut, barely an inch wide, black-lipped, that had penetrated from the front, slightly upward, to the right side of the sternum, sliding between the ribs. It obviously hadn't touched the heart, but there was a faint frothing of the blood as it oozed slowly from Jak's chest.

"Lung," Ryan said.

Critical and often fatal. But not always.

Ryan draped his coat over the wounded boy, trying to keep him as warm as possible. As he was tucking it around Jak's throat, the ruby eyes blinked open, staring blankly up at the star-sprinkled heavens above him. They didn't seem to focus, then became aware of Ryan's presence.

"Stupe," he whispered, his voice barely disturbing the cold air.

"How many?" Getting no reply, Ryan held up one

finger and the boy nodded. "Just one?" Jak managed a feeble movement of the head.

Ryan straightened, looking around the deserted ville, wondering if the stickie would have tried to hide or run.

"Ryan."

He bent again, hand on the boy's shoulder. "What is it, Jak? Don't talk. Keep quiet and we can get help. Mildred's not that far away."

"Got him."

"What?"

"Knife. Me down. Threw. Hit. Not chill but won't get…" Then the dark wave swept up the silent beach of the boy's consciousness, and he passed out again.

THEY'D AGREED immediately that they wouldn't stick together. The main thing was for some of them to get back up to Bear Claw Ridge as fast as possible. It was Christina, slowest of them, who'd insisted that everyone should make their own best speed.

J.B. had set off at a steady jog, leaning forward, arms pumping to carry him back up the jagged trail. Dean was at his shoulder, occasionally spurting ahead, his power-weight ratio helping him on the grinding ascent. But the Armorer ordered him to slow down and keep with him.

Krysty was a close third with Mildred fourth. Harold and Dorina started together, with Doc and Christina sharing last spot.

"I vow that climbing a mountain at full speed is

very far from my idea of excellent sport," the old man panted.

Harold also began to labor, Dorina letting go of his hand to run easily ahead. She quickly passed Mildred and Krysty, then overtook both Dean and J.B., vanishing into the shimmering moonlight way out in front of everyone.

"Hey, wait up!" the Armorer called, but the slim figure was gone.

RYAN TRACKED DOWN the last of the stickies in the abandoned ville, finding small spots of blood that glistened on the side of the blacktop.

Jak had been right.

His thrown knife *had* done damage.

The trail led Ryan on, stalking through the shadows of Bear Claw Ridge, back toward the multiplex movie house.

Near the rusted stump of a Parking sign, Ryan saw the silver gleam of the leaf-bladed knife, the steel smeared with fresh blood. The stickie had obviously managed to pluck it from his body.

"Oh, too shit hurts!"

The voice was so close that Ryan stopped in his tracks, leveling the blaster into the shadows at the corner of the SkyHi Mall.

"Come on out, with your hands up and showing," he called.

"Fuck off, norm."

There was movement in the darkness. Ryan edged

to one side, trying to avoid turning himself into an easy target.

"One chance, then I hand you the ticket to stickie paradise."

"What?"

"Come out now or I chill you!"

"Me got I a blaster."

"So, use it."

Time was passing. Ryan wanted to get back to Jak and carry the boy into shelter and check on how Abe was doing, not stand in the freezing street and argue with a wounded stickie.

"Not chill I?"

"Throw out your gun, stupe. And come after it. I won't chill you. I swear it on Charlie's life."

"Charlie's here?"

"No. Now, move."

There was a rattle as a musket came wheeling out of the shadows, landing on the highway, the stock splitting like a piece of dry kindling.

"Here I am."

The stickie stepped out slowly, both hands up, the moonlight showing the murderous suckers on the palms and along to the tips of the fingers. It also showed a dark stain near the shoulder of the torn coat that must have been the result of Jak's uncanny accuracy with a knife.

"Hurt I am," he repeated, face crumpling into an almost believable replica of normal grief.

"Chilled you are," Ryan said, pressing the trigger of the SIG-Sauer.

The bullet hit the stickie precisely where it had been aimed, plumb through the center of the right knee. It pulped the delicate joint so that it instantly disintegrated into bone, tendon, muscle and flesh. And blood.

Before the stickie could even manage to topple over, Ryan shot him again, this time through the left knee.

Two more carefully placed rounds pulverized the joints at both elbows, leaving the arms to flap helplessly.

The stickie didn't have time to start screaming. His mouth opened and closed like a gaffed salmon, eyes protruding so far that Ryan wondered for a passing moment whether they might burst messily from their sockets.

"You murderous freak bastard!" Ryan snarled, his fiery rage now cooled to an icy calm.

"Noooo...." The word stretched until it was simply a meaningless noise.

He pumped four more rounds into the writhing creature's belly, seeing the body jerk at the impact of each 9 mm bullet.

The stickie was the embodiment of pure agony, rolling from side to side, the smashed limbs flopping behind him. Blood poured from elbows and knees, flooding from the exit holes that had been ripped out close to the spine.

Ryan smiled and slowly reloaded the blaster, turned on his heel and walked away from the dying stickie. He stopped and hesitated.

The noise Jak's assailant was making might bring Charlie and some of its fellows, and it might just live long enough to tell them that Ryan was effectively alone.

He walked back and stared at the dying mutie, spit into his upturned face and put a final bullet between his goggling eyes.

The skull bounced once and the screaming stopped, letting the silence return.

Chapter Forty-Six

Ryan carefully carried Jak, wrapped in the long coat with the fur collar, along the deserted street and into the lobby of the cinema. He placed the deeply unconscious teenager on the floor, close to the motionless figure of Abe.

He put his hand onto the man's forehead, feeling that it was burning hot. Abe's eyes opened for a moment, and when he spoke he sounded amazingly lucid, though his voice was weak and hoarse.

"What gives, Ryan? Been ill, haven't I? Looks like J.B.'s dark night out there."

"Been some fighting. Jak's been stabbed in the chest. Cut his lung. The breathing's bad. How do you feel, Abe?"

"Been better. Been worse." He coughed. "Cold in here."

"Sure is."

"I can feel my legs. Times I couldn't. Think I could manage to stand awhile."

Ryan shook his head. "Don't try it."

"If there's fighting—"

"Most done. Charlie left three stickies here to try

and sneak on us. It was one of them that took out Jak.''

Abe started a slow, wheezing breath. "Any still talkie-walking around the ville?''

"All crow meat.''

"That's good. Still think I'd like to stand up. Where's everyone else? Do I know that and I've gone and forgot it? Or don't I know it? Fucked if I know which.''

"They're away safe. Probably be five or six miles off the top of the ridge by now, heading back down toward the open desert and the site of the old homestead. Unless...''

"What, Ryan?''

"Jak fired off three rounds.''

"From that big Magnum? Must've brought folks running.''

"Don't know. I don't know how far off the rest of the stickies were. Or J.B. and the others. If any of them heard shooting, they might try to get back here. Depends on the wind. I thought I heard a lot of shooting a few minutes back, but I was kind of busy at the time.''

Abe sighed. "Want to go out and look around, Ryan? Give me a blaster and I'll watch over the kid.''

"Don't call him 'kid.' Not unless you want to be walking on stumps. Jak really doesn't care for that name.''

Abe grinned, looking for a moment more like his old self. "Sure.'' He started to wriggle out from the cover of the leaning countertop, stopping as he encountered the long splinters of broken glass that covered the floor.

"Watch yourself," Ryan warned.

"Now you tell me. Some of these could take your fuckin' head off."

"Stay there, Abe. I'm going to look if anyone's moving out there."

"Who?"

"Friend. Or not."

A FLURRY OF WIND picked up a handful of dried leaves and hustled them along the deserted blacktop, past the blank-eyed ruins of the SkyHi Mall.

The sound was like the skeletal feet of the long-dead as they rise from the graves and sepulchres on the Eve of Allhallows.

Or it might not have been the rustling leaves. It might have been someone running as fast and as silently as he could toward the low buildings of the small ville.

It was so soft and so distant that Ryan didn't hear it.

He pushed open the inner doors, looking out across the moonlit ville. It was stark and still, with no sight or sound of life.

Outside, his breath gathered in the air in front of his mouth, hanging like ectoplasm seeping from the lips of a medium.

If someone came up off the northern trail, it was

just possible that he might try to circle around the rim of the plateau and creep up behind the multiplex, use another entrance to sneak in and try to coldcock him.

Ryan walked to his left, past some faded graffiti boasting that rock and roll would never die.

He eased up to the corner, squinting around it.

All he could see was the dark, swaying curtain of the forest. It might have been hiding ten thousand stickies for all he knew.

Keeping his left hand against the tomb-cold wall of the old movie house, Ryan picked his way carefully along the overgrown path.

When he reached the next corner he stopped, looked around it and saw the rusting remains of the fire escape that gave dangerous access to the flat roof.

Nobody.

Ryan suddenly straightened, feeling the short hairs at his nape beginning to prickle.

Someone was close somewhere behind him, in the darkness of the night.

He spun around, finger only a bare ounce of pressure from firing the blaster. The feeling of menace was as strong and imminent as anything he'd ever known.

"Charlie," he whispered, not even aware that his lips had formed the name.

J.B. HAD FINALLY REACHED the brim of the trail, fighting against a painful muscle cramp in his stomach. He was deeply out of breath, bending over, hands on knees as he fought for control. Behind him he was aware of Krysty closing with him.

Ahead he thought he had caught a glimpse of a tiny, elfin figure, darting from silver light to velvet shadow, but he couldn't be certain. What he was certain of, with a gut-wrenching knowledge, was that he was going to be too late to help out in whatever was going down.

RYAN'S COMBAT INSTINCT was so powerful that he didn't hesitate for a second. He raced back toward the front of the Beacon Multiplex, out onto the main drag of Bear Claw Ridge—to be met at close range by a fountaining arc of bullets from Charlie's Uzi.

The stickie was standing right in the entrance to the movie house, less than fifty feet away. If Ryan had been any closer, the burst would have simply torn him apart. If he'd been any further off, then Charlie would easily have been able to blow him away at his leisure.

But there was just time for the razor-honed reflexes to save Ryan.

He saw the dark figure before the Uzi exploded, threw himself down and to the side, the stream of high-velocity lead slicing inches above his head, ricocheting off the wall in a shower of vivid orange and silver sparks.

Ryan snapped off two shots as he rolled in the dirt, hearing the smashing of glass as one of them hit the main entrance doors.

But the stickie had vanished inside the building, and the blacktop was deserted.

"Fireblast!"

Inside the multiplex Jak Lauren was quite possibly already dead, and Abe, lying partly under cover, still desperately frail from his wound.

If Ryan tried to get in through the front entrance, the Uzi would wipe him away. He turned and sprinted toward the rear of the building and the decrepit fire escape.

THE CORRODED LADDER squeaked under Ryan's weight, but it held safe as he scrambled up onto the roof, where he picked his way between the various heating and ventilation stacks to find the open trapdoor into the projection box.

He dropped through, ignoring the clatter of his boots.

A quick glance through the projection window showed the empty auditorium. Ryan paused for a moment to gather himself, then moved quickly down the iron stairs toward the lobby.

KRYSTY STOOD by J.B., staring toward the buildings. "See anything?"

"Think someone went inside the old movie place, just after firing the Uzi. Think I heard two silenced rounds that must've been Ryan's SIG-Sauer. Nothing since then."

She glanced up at the sky. There was a heavy bank

of low cloud moving steadily across from the east, threatening the moon.

"Going to be real dark in about three or four minutes," she said.

"Could be all over by then." They both turned as they heard Dean panting up the trail with Christina, amazingly, right on his heels. There was still no sign of Mildred, Harold or Doc.

IN THE PITCH-DARK WELL at the base of the narrow staircase, Ryan paused again. He pressed his ear against the concealed door that opened into the lobby, but it was insulated and he couldn't hear a thing.

He dropped to his knees and pushed it open a knife-blade crack.

There was a splinter of a second to glimpse the lobby before another burst from the machine pistol tore through the door chest-high, showering him with splinters of wood.

Charlie was crouched near the main doors, which stood wide open behind him. Jak's body lay completely still, where Ryan had last seen him. Abe was invisible under the tumbled display top.

"Come on, you fucking one-eyed bastard! Come see me finish this white-haired little shit right in front of you."

Charlie's voice had the thin, fragile sound of insanity, but that didn't mean he wasn't holding all of the cards.

Ryan, flattened against the bottom of the stairs, couldn't move up or out without being blown away.

Abe was out of it and Jak was done for. Krysty and the rest of the group could be anywhere.

It wasn't even a stand-off. To try to get at Charlie, Ryan had to put his own life into jeopardy. Go out through the door and hope he shot the stickie before being ripped apart himself.

"Come on, norm!" Charlie screeched. "I take out this little... Looks like he's already chilled anyway. Couple rounds should make..."

Ryan braced himself, deciding to come out fast and low, going straight into a slide, hoping to put one in the stickie before the Uzi sent him off on the last train to the coast.

"This is it!"

Ryan kicked the door open and tumbled into the lobby.

Everything happened at a grotesque and unbelievable speed.

And there was pain.

Chapter Forty-Seven

Charlie's lips were clawed back in a snarl of utter delight. The Uzi spit flame, but the bullets sprayed in a great arc over the ceiling as the blaster fell from the stickie's hands.

A round stone rolled across the floor, after it had smashed into Charlie's elbow.

Out of the corner of his eye Ryan could see a slight figure, capering in the street, ragged clothes flying about its androgynous body, stooping to pick up and hurl another stone at Charlie.

But the stickie was recovering, bending to grab up the Uzi with his other hand.

Ryan realized that Dorina's accuracy might simply have postponed his death, rather than averted it.

"Bastards!" Charlie growled as he straightened.

Face shining white, staggering like the living dead in an old horror vid, Abe lurched toward Charlie with a jagged knife of glass in both hands. He loomed up behind the mutie and lunged at him with the make-shift dagger.

The stickie turned at the last second and pushed at Abe, knocking him off balance. But the thrust struck home, the glass splintering as it drove into Charlie's stomach.

Ryan steadied the blaster, ready for another shot at the stickie, but the moon finally vanished behind the clouds and the old cinema became instantly pitchy dark.

There was the patter of naked feet and a yell from outside, and Charlie was gone into the night.

And none of them saw or heard anything of the yellow-haired stickie from that moment on.

RYAN SAT ON THE PORCH, reminiscing as he sipped a glass of buttermilk.

It had been an odd time.

Mildred had been able to help get Abe back properly onto his feet within a couple of days. Now the two of them were down by the stream, working on fixing the earth dam. J.B. was with them, stripped off to the waist, his body pale in the bright sunlight.

Doc and Dean were helping each other replace a damaged blade on the windmill. From where he sat, Ryan could hear an occasional snatch of conversation, the young boy's light voice overlaid by Doc's resonant tones.

Krysty had felt a little sick after a large lunch and was sleeping it off in their bedroom at the west side of the new homestead. Harold and Dorina Lord had been over in a buckboard to visit and see the baby. Dorina couldn't wait to tell everyone that she, too, was pregnant.

The couple had taken over the neighboring spread that had once belonged to Helga.

Now they'd headed off into the afternoon sunshine, the trail of dust from their rig following them across the open land.

Christina was out back, hanging up some washing. Little baby Jenny was in a crib on the rear porch. Every now and again Ryan heard the tiny gurgling voice and the soft reassurance of her mother.

Christina hadn't forgiven Ryan for what had happened to Jak two months earlier, and he knew that she never would. Which was why it was time to move on.

"Think we'll leave tomorrow morning," he announced.

Lying on the swing seat across from him, the white-haired teenager started awake.

"Broke dream," he said. "Thought was back in bayous. Fishing."

For forty-eight hours after the dramatic climax on the ridge, Mildred had believed that she was going to lose her patient. The knife wound had penetrated one of Jak's lungs, and he had suffered an internal hemorrhage that had left him on the brink of the black river.

But he'd pulled through.

Mildred reckoned that he'd never be quite as fit as before, and would always tend to suffer from breathing problems in cold, wet weather. But he was alive.

"I said that I thought we'd go tomorrow. Stayed long enough. Mebbe too long."

Jak stretched. "Know what you mean. Christina thinks you came and—"

"Yeah, I know. Look, Jak, you know I understand. Her feeling the way she does." He put down the glass, holding his finger and thumb a quarter inch apart. "You came that close to buying the farm. She'd have been a widow and Jenny would never have known her father. Course she wants me to go."

"Be always welcome here, Ryan."

"Sure."

He could hear Christina talking to the baby in a calm, gentle voice.

"Wish Dean would have stayed while with us."

"His decision. I wanted him to stay. Mebbe a year or so."

Part of him was aware that someone else was talking at the back of the house very quietly, having a measured conversation with Christina.

Jak sighed. "Way of kids, Ryan. Like I said. All of you always welcome."

Ryan started to stand, very slowly, concentrating on what he was almost hearing.

The voice was oddly familiar, but he couldn't quite hear it clearly enough.

"Who is…" he began.

Jak opened his mouth, hands gripping the arms of the seat.

Doc laughed, far off across the meadow, sounding in another world.

Ryan and Jak heard a strange sound from behind the building, like a butcher's cleaver hacking into a hanging carcass.

Then Christina's voice called, "Jak, Ryan, could you come here a minute, please?"

Still as calm and unhurried as ever.

Ryan had his hand on the butt of the SIG-Sauer as he and the teenager stepped onto the back porch. As soon as he saw what was out there, he let go of the blaster.

It wasn't necessary.

Christina was standing facing them, holding the swaddled, gurgling bundle that was her daughter, Jenny. There were speckles of fresh blood on the woman's dress and on her hands.

The corpse lay at her feet.

It was stretched out as though it had decided to take advantage of the fine weather and snatch itself half an hour's sleep. The clothes were ragged and torn, showing pale skin through the holes.

The head was covered in blood, from two gashes in the side of the skull. The weapon, a long-handled ax, was buried in the back of the neck, almost decapitating the man.

Despite all of the blood and the leaking puddle of brains, the matted yellow hair was unmistakable. As were the suckered hands, now relaxing in death. A slim skinning knife lay in the dirt of the yard, by the right hand.

Ryan tucked a foot under a shoulder and rolled the body over, making sure who it was.

"Charlie?" Jak asked.

"Yeah."

His eyes were glazing and the mouth sagged open. The dozens of tiny suckers on the protruding tongue were all slowly closing, like delicate pink flowers in the evening.

"Said he was starving." Christina was shushing the baby by letting it suck at her little finger. "I knew who he was from the hair. I just told him to go away."

"Why not call us?" Ryan asked. "We'd have taken him out."

"I know, Ryan. I know what you do. He was starving." She repeated it as though she were dealing with an obtuse child. "But he drew the knife to threaten Jenny. So I took the ax to him."

"We'll bury him out the other side of the stream," Ryan said.

"Sure."

"We've been talking, Christina. Think we'll be moving on at first light."

She looked at him with her steady blue eyes. "That's good, Ryan," she said. "Yeah, that's good."

Chapter Forty-Eight

The walls of armaglass were already beginning to glow, and a faint miasma of gray mist was appearing at the level of the gray ceiling of the gateway chamber.

Everyone was sitting in a circle, backs against the wall, facing inward.

Mildred was close to J.B., holding his hand in hers.

Doc had his knees drawn up, the swallow's-eye neckerchief already in his hand, ready to staunch the nosebleed he so often suffered from at the end of a jump.

He caught Dean looking across at him and smiled at the boy, showing his oddly perfect teeth. "Make sure to keep your dreams as clean as silver, my dear young man," he said.

Krysty leaned her head against Ryan's shoulder as the mist thickened and the disks in the floor began to shimmer and blur.

"Abe looks like he's ready to have kittens," she said.

"I'll be there before you, lady." The lean man grinned, but his voice betrayed his tension at what might be about to happen to him.

Ryan could feel the insides of his brain starting to scramble. The last thing he heard was Krysty, whispering gently to him, her breath soft against his cheek.

"Good time the past few weeks, lover. I envy Christina what she's got. Husband and baby. Nice home. Be good..." The words started to fragment. "One day... You and... Real good...us...lover."

The rest vanished into the blackness.

RYAN OPENED HIS EYE, realizing something had gone appallingly, hideously wrong.

Desperate times call for desperate measures. Don't miss out on the action in these titles!

#61910	FLASHBACK	$5.50 U.S. ☐
		$6.50 CAN. ☐
#61911	ASIAN STORM	$5.50 U.S. ☐
		$6.50 CAN. ☐
#61912	BLOOD STAR	$5.50 U.S. ☐
		$6.50 CAN. ☐
#61913	EYE OF THE RUBY	$5.50 U.S. ☐
		$6.50 CAN. ☐
#61914	VIRTUAL PERIL	$5.50 U.S. ☐
		$6.50 CAN. ☐

(limited quantities available on certain titles)

TOTAL AMOUNT	$	
POSTAGE & HANDLING	$	
($1.00 for one book, 50¢ for each additional)		
APPLICABLE TAXES*	$	_____
TOTAL PAYABLE	$	_____
(check or money order—please do not send cash)		

To order, complete this form and send it, along with a check or money order for the total above, payable to Gold Eagle Books, to: **In the U.S.:** 3010 Walden Avenue, P.O. Box 9077, Buffalo, NY 14269-9077; **In Canada:** P.O. Box 636, Fort Erie, Ontario, L2A 5X3.

Name: _____

Address: _____ City: _____

State/Prov.: _____ Zip/Postal Code: _____

*New York residents remit applicable sales taxes.
Canadian residents remit applicable GST and provincial taxes.

GOLD EAGLE®

GSMBACK1

Take
2 explosive books
plus a
mystery bonus
FREE

Follow Remo and Chiun on more of their extraordinary adventures....

Shadow THE EXECUTIONER®
as he battles evil for 352 pages of
heart-stopping action!

SuperBolan®

#61452	DAY OF THE VULTURE	$5.50 U.S. ☐
		$6.50 CAN. ☐
#61453	FLAMES OF WRATH	$5.50 U.S. ☐
		$6.50 CAN. ☐
#61454	HIGH AGGRESSION	$5.50 U.S. ☐
		$6.50 CAN. ☐
#61455	CODE OF BUSHIDO	$5.50 U.S. ☐
		$6.50 CAN. ☐
#61456	TERROR SPIN	$5.50 U.S. ☐
		$6.50 CAN. ☐

(limited quantities available on certain titles)

TOTAL AMOUNT	$
POSTAGE & HANDLING	$
($1.00 for one book, 50¢ for each additional)	
APPLICABLE TAXES*	$ _____
TOTAL PAYABLE	$ _____
(check or money order—please do not send cash)	

To order, complete this form and send it, along with a check or money order for the total above, payable to Gold Eagle Books, to: **In the U.S.:** 3010 Walden Avenue, P.O. Box 9077, Buffalo, NY 14269-9077; **In Canada:** P.O. Box 636, Fort Erie, Ontario, L2A 5X3.

Name: _____

Address: _____ City: _____

State/Prov.: _____ Zip/Postal Code: _____

*New York residents remit applicable sales taxes.
 Canadian residents remit applicable GST and provincial taxes.

GSBBACK1

Countdown to Armageddon...

DON PENDLETON's

MACK BOLAN®

Termination POINT

After destroying the cult's sinister laboratory, Bolan learns the maniacal cult has set its sights on a target that will set off a global cataclysm—the Russian president.

It's now or never as Bolan prepares for a final confrontation with the doomsday organization in this sizzling conclusion to the 3-part miniseries!

Book #3 in The Four Horsemen Trilogy, three books that chronicle Mack Bolan's efforts to thwart the plans of a radical doomsday cult to bring about a real-life Armageddon....

<u>Available in June 1999 at your favorite retail outlet.</u>